When Heaven and Earth Kiss

MARIAN DAVENPORT

Scriptures taken from the New Spirit-Filled Life Bible Copyright 2002 by Thomas Nelson, Inc. unless indicated.

Publisher: Royal Scribes Publishing

Categories: Christian, Fiction, Novel

Cover created by Katherine Schumm

Facebook: Marian Davenport, Author

Email: writethevisions@gmail.com

DEDICATION

This book is dedicated to God, who continually surprises me with His amazing ways, and to all the people who shared their God stories with me which are woven into the pages of this book. Also, to the Wannabe Writers who critiqued this work, and Darla Porter for her help and loving encouragement.

Chapter 1

The Great and Glorious day of the Lord is at hand. *For the earth will be filled with the knowledge of the glory of the Lord, as the waters cover the sea.* **Habakkuk 2:14**

Heaven rumbled with excitement. The Father's host of angels have waited to be released to their assignments ever since He spoke the words *Let there be light.*[1] Now, Almighty God, Creator of the Universe, is ready to say, "Go forth to the nations."[2]

Darkness covers the earth. Not physically, as in the night, but spiritually through the power of lies and deception. It came subtly so mankind hardly noticed the pressing oppression. Everything just seemed harder. Fear griped nations with wars and rumors of wars. Random murders of innocent people became common in cities around the world. Powerful security, created to make everyone safe, felt more like being imprisoned than protected. Government officials declared the problems impossible to solve.

But, God in heaven, the Father of all mankind, watched. The prayer bowls were full from the cries of his people. He determined the time had come to answer their prayers asking him to let his kingdom come, and his will to be done on earth as it is in heaven.[3]

***

Cassius's excitement could hardly be contained. "We're going. We're finally going. Oh, this is great. I wonder who I'll unite with." As if mail was instantly delivered, a message dropped into his thoughts. *Randal Wright, Millbrook Community Church,*

Millbrook, United States of America, Earth. "Wow! Earth. United States. Where's my unit?" He zoomed forth to join the others.

***

Michael and Gabriel stood before the multitude of angels. Worship music permeated the atmosphere where no sound system was needed because the royal attendants hear with their hearts.

The great archangel, Michael[4] spoke, "Glory to our Great and Mighty God."

A roar of praise and excitement erupted from the crowd.

Michael held up his hands to quiet the glorious audience. "His Majesty's reality will now manifest on earth. We will help his people pluck out every stumbling block. Heaven's kingdom will unite with those he deeply loves."

Another great outburst of delight filled the atmosphere.

"We will partner with our fellow servants who are already on earth assisting the human race." He turned to acknowledge his companion. "Gabriel will lead the Messenger and Harvest angels as you go to your assigned people to help them fulfill their destiny."

Gabriel nodded in agreement.

Cassius was so excited he lifted above the others. *That's me. That's me. I'm a messenger. I follow Gabriel.* The glorious one next to him tugged Cassius' robe to bring him back down.

Michael continued, "Many people on earth do not believe we exist. Those who know we're real still lack enough faith to see clearly into our realm."

The heavenly host looked puzzled by his words.

"Some of you are assigned to key people our Father has chosen to lead the nations. Many of you will come alongside those who prayed for his kingdom to come to earth. They will experience the answer to their prayers."

Michael looked across the white-robed multitudes with a

6

glowing aura all around them. Concerned, he continued. "The people may not accept you at first. We will be aliens in a foreign land. When you introduce yourselves, they might not want you around. Don't be impatient."

He paused to reflect on his past experiences. "Some people know God's love but they have become set in their ways. Give them time, and some space, to accept your presence. Each encounter with you will remove their blindness to our universe a little more."

A confused look covered Cassius and the other holy faces as Michael continued. "Earth isn't an environment of love like it is here. Even the most loving humans there have barely experienced the love our Father offers them."

Michael turned his head and looked across the masses of kingdom warriors who were clothed in light, carrying large swords that sizzled with electrifying power. "I will lead our armies."

In unison the glorious soldiers came to attention and saluted their General. Great compassion filled his next gentle words. "Omnipotent God has declared liberty to the captives.[5] The enemy will not be allowed to torment and destroy the lives of the Father's children any longer. We will go forth and unite with the people in their righteous fight against our foe, and destroy the works of the oppressor."

Cheers exploded with uncontrollable joy.

"Most of you have not experienced battles with our enemy, but you are prepared. Fight valiantly. Always remember." He pauses for effect. "We win."[6]

Shouts of excitement rang out again as God's supernatural army prepared to deploy.

Cassius looked across the enormous span of heaven's best. *What a privilege to be part of God's great and glorious plans.*

***

Michael stood before the Almighty. "God of All, your troops are prepared to descend."

"Well done, Michael. The prayer bowls overflow with the prayers of the saints[7] asking for my kingdom to come to Earth. I will answer."

Tension held the warrior as he lowered his head reverently.

"Michael, I feel your concern."

"Yes, Lord, two worlds are about to intersect. They are so different from one another. Our warriors have never known the darkness and evil they will fight. Some have no battle experience, but the earth is trembling under the devastation of mankind's wrong choices."

"I know, son, but you have prepared them well. The time has come to push out evil so my precious ones can live and love fully. I allowed the people to be tried and tested to see if their hearts would still choose to follow me. Satan's arrogance has pushed him past the boundaries I allowed. Now people are crying out. We will come to their aid."

"Thank you, Father, for allowing me the privilege of leading them."

"You have been a faithful servant, most valiant Michael. Release heaven's best to unite this kingdom with my precious ones on earth."

The soldier bowed low, his wings touched the floor. He rose, turned and walked out of the throne room to stand before the holy ones again.

As he stepped forward he paused and scanned the beautiful crowd. He stretched tall and breathed deep. "Mighty warriors, I loose you to the nations of earth."

Cassius joined the exuberant celebration cheers as each took their assigned spot. Father of All leaned back on his throne to watch the magnificent procession. Jesus, who sat next to his Father, smiled. Soon, he would unite with his bride.

Angels, who waited a long time to fulfill their destiny, began to descend. In awe, the beautiful angelic host moved forward on what appeared to be an invisible circular highway. If seen, we would think the Milky Way, with its billions of shining stars, was spiraling toward our planet.

The earth groaned as the warriors' swords clashed like lightning in the second heaven. They valiantly pushed through the enemy's line of defense, making way for the Host of Heaven to move forth to establish a new reign of righteousness and glory on Earth.

Cassius peered around the others hoping to see the action. *I want to get to Millbrook and meet Randal.* "Come on guys. You can do it." He got an idea. In a loud voice, even for heaven, he shouted, "Everybody. Let's help them. We'll worship really loud. The enemy hates that."

The trumpeting angels joined in. Even on earth some people heard the sounds.[8]

(1) Genesis 1:3, (2) Psalm 2:8, (3) Matthew 6:10, (4) Daniel 12:1, (5) Isaiah 61:1, (6) Psalm 108:13 (GNT), (7) Revelation 5:8, (8) Google- NASA confirms strange trumpet-like sounds in the sky.

Chapter 2

At the altar, Pastor Randy knelt to pray. He smiled as his knees touched the new royal blue carpet. *I'm so glad the board agreed with my choice of color. Blue has always been my favorite.* He ran his fingers across the plushness.

Randy disciplined himself to spend an hour each morning praying for his church. "Thank you, Lord, for the three hundred souls you've given me to pastor. Bless them. We're grateful for our newly remodeled sanctuary. The carpet's so soft, and it looks nice with the old pews and the wood trim all around. I like the new lighting, too. And thanks so much for that great sound system. We really needed it. Now, everything's fixed up nice. Thank you, Lord, that all the stress is off and I can enjoy being a pastor."

In the quietness of the building he felt an invisible heaviness settle in the atmosphere. *Is a storm brewing?* Something, not quite a breeze, entered the sanctuary. *Did someone come in to join me in prayer?* He looked around but saw no one.

That's strange. He turned back trying to refocus.

"Randal?" The powerful Voice rumbled with authority.

"Huh?" He turned, "Who's there?" *No one. Is someone messing with the sound system?*

"Randal." The Voice bellowed through the empty sanctuary again.

He jumped to his feet, waiting for someone to speak. Then he rubbed his eyes. They widened as a giant man appeared through something like fog. He was so tall he almost touched the top of the twenty-foot beamed ceiling.

A surge of power hit Randy. His knees buckled as he fell on

his face into the prized carpet. Fearful electric current passed through his body making him vibrate from the top of his head to his feet. When the shocking bolt subsided, he began to come to his senses. *What in the world was that? Be brave. Take charge.*

But he had no strength to get up, so with trembling words muffled by blue fuzz, he asked, "Who are you?"

"I have come from the courts of I AM. He wants me to prepare you for his great, glorious day. My name is Cassius. The Almighty has declared he is pleased with you. Therefore, today your life is required for the kingdom's purposes."

"Am I gonna die?"

The mighty angel burst into bellowing laugher as something joy-filled inside him escaped from unknown depths. The roar caused echoes to bounce around the hollow room.

Randy sat up to get a better view of the magnificent specimen. He had never seen an angel before. *Is this it? Get everything nice and then I'm gone.*

Hearing his thoughts the visitor responded. "No, no. I AM sent me to tell you his plans. I will prepare you for what's ahead. Randal, everything is changing. God needs his servants to move forward into the new day. Stop playing church. Don't you know demons are trying to take over here? And, they don't even have to work very hard at it. All they need to do is keep you busy with details and material things. Father God is waiting for his children to give him their lives so he can do great and mighty things through all of you. You have been distracted from enjoying his loving presence with activities and trying to look good."

Randy felt a bit embarrassed with the pride he enjoyed while reminding God of his successes earlier.

Cassius seemed to have an agenda as he pressed on. "Will you say 'yes' to the Lord?"

"Yes," Randy replied meekly.

"Are you really willing to say 'yes'?"

He froze. *What is the frightening Hercules asking of me? How do I answer?* His trembling voice was barely audible. "Yes."

"All right." the angel shouted in delight.

Did he actually slap his knee? I think he slapped his knee.

Randy sat on the floor quietly feeling the size of a speck. He noticed movement out the corner of his eye. Through blurred vision he saw angels in white robes with aprons wrapped around their waist. Many were moving throughout the room doing something he couldn't make out. Intrigued, he stared at them and asked, "What are they doing?"

"Many angels have been assigned to assist you in God's plans. We call these particular assistants *Exterminators*. They bring God's holiness when they come, which destroys every vile spirit who has made this place its home. You have demons stuck on the walls. The ones sitting in the pews whisper all sorts of things to the people, or they cause them to feel sleepy so they're distracted from hearing Father's voice. They've been in your sound system, too. We'll keep them out of this new one. The Evil One likes to fill churches with his own.

"The Exterminators are washing the slime off the walls where the demons stuck themselves. They're sweeping the floors of their remains, just like when you spray bugs and clean them up. You will notice a distinct change in the people when they come to church next time because it will be swept clean. The people won't feel tormented, frustrated, or even sleepy while you preach after today."

"Oh." His heart thumped so loud he was glad the angel shouted. With little understanding of what the visitor said, he tried to grasp the fact that a half visible clean-up crew was getting rid of demons. After all, he didn't even believe in the demonic or a place called Hell.

Seeing the man's shock, Cassius paused. "That's enough for today. Randal, it's nice to meet you. You better think about all this before I continue. I'll meet you again."

A sigh of relief came with the only word the young pastor

could speak. "Okay."

The angels disappeared from sight, but he felt they might still be at work. He dropped back to lay on the floor.

"Oh, God, what's going on? A giant angel? Really? This can't happen. It's impossible. Do I tell people? How would I ever explain to anyone? Oh, it wasn't real. Maybe it was my imagination. I don't understand. I'll just forget it. Why do I feel like crying?"

He rolled over and sobbed into the beautiful new royal blue carpet.

Chapter 3

Sunday morning indecision gripped Randy as he thought about the day's sermon. The reality of an angel's visit had faded. However, he did remember he said yes to the illusion.

Do I preach my sermon, or share what happened to me? Oh brother, can I go back to bed?

***

Pastor Randy Wright stood outside the church doors on a sunny Sunday morning. Tradition allowed him the privilege of watching his congregation as they came to church. His wife, Sherry stood dutifully beside him greeting people before she rushed off to help in the nursery. Young couples greeted each other while they hung onto their small children and herding the older ones into the building.

There's Gene. Poor man. The pastor watched him shuffle into the church knowing he would sit in the same place he and Dorothy always chose. His gray suit matched his gray skin which made him look older than his jet black hair revealed.

"Good morning, Gene. Beautiful day, isn't it?"

Gene's head was down with his chin tucked in. As if speaking to his shirt, he responded with something that sounded like mumble, mumble, as they shook hands. He moved on into the church.

Always the same. Randy sighed.

A chirpy voice quickly covered the gloom he felt over Gene as Barbara rushed up chattering. "Good morning, Pastor. What a day.

God is so good. He told me this morning he has great things planned for us today. I'm so excited I could hardly wait to get here."

"Morning, Barbara. Nice to see you." *This woman drives me crazy. She's always up, and tells me about her conversations with God, or what the prophets are saying. Why is there always one in every church?*

"Pastor, there's a city-wide prayer meeting Friday. Isn't that great? Maybe you can go."

He smiled and nodded. *Like I don't have enough to do. Last week she thought we needed to have meetings to pray for our nation and Israel. Oh brother.*

He looked past her. "Oh, hi, Jethro. Bless you." *Jethro, the in-house hippy. He always wants to get a group together and go street witnessing.*

He glanced behind the skinny, long-haired, bearded young man. "Jethro, there's a couple of guys calling your name."

"Thanks, Pastor." He looked over his shoulder. "Oh, that's Ken and Everett. They got saved last night in the alley behind the library. Hey, you guys sober yet?"

Oh great, more hippies. Randy turned, entered the sanctuary, and walked up the steps to the platform and sat in his chair.

Tony was directing the crowd in a lively praise song when suddenly he stopped and looked puzzled. He motioned for the worship leaders to play their instruments quietly. "I think it would please God if we took some extra time to worship him this morning." He glanced at Randy but didn't wait for permission.

Pastor Randy was nervous. *We don't do slow music in our church services. Lively, Tony, lively.* He twisted and turned uncomfortably in his chair.

Hallelujah seemed to be the only word necessary to create an awe of reverence. After a bit Tony began to repeat the words, "I love you, Jesus," continually.

Everyone joined in.

Oh, no, the hippies are coming to the front. All three look like grubby wise men bowing before the baby King.

The men dropped to their knees and began to quietly weep.

Of course. Here comes Barbara. She's not going to be outdone by those guys.

Prostrate on the floor, she sobbed like a calf bellowing for its mama.

Then everything was out of control. The whole congregation filed to the front, bowed to the floor and began to cry and repent.

As the muffled groveling continued, Randy tried to figure out what to do. Starting to stand, he realized he was frozen to the seat as if some supernatural glue held him captive. He struggled, but quickly all thought of taking charge vanished. His head bowed.

When he finally regained awareness and looked around, there were children scattered all over the floor with their parents.

After some time, the people quietly got up to leave. No one visited together, or said anything to their pastor.

Finally, Scott, the children's minister, walked over to Randy and whispered. "Pastor, the children started weeping and repenting in Children's Church as something like holy love covered us. I didn't know what to do except bring them to their parents. Everyone here was experiencing the same thing so we joined them."

Randy couldn't speak. He just nodded his head.

As everyone left Gene made his way back to his usual seat. Barbara pulled herself up to sit on the front row, and waited quietly. When most of the people were gone she walked up to Randy. "Pastor, there were four giant angels standing behind you this morning. Each was holding a scroll. Did you know?"

More angels? As if Cassius and Exterminators aren't enough. Finding his voice he responded. "No, I didn't Barbara. Thank you for telling me. What do you think the scrolls mean? Why would they be here?"

"I don't know. I'll pray about it."

"Good idea. Thank you." *Lord, I'm sorry for judging that woman. Maybe she's normal, and I'm the one who's messed up.*

She took off in her bouncy, excited manner.

Gene approached.

"How can I help you, Gene?"

"Pastor." His words sounded like he had marbles in his mouth. "Dorothy did da talkin' for me."

"Yes, I know, Gene. She was a fine woman."

The man struggled to speak slow and distinctly. "We worked hard an' saved. I waited thirty years to feel God again. This was best day a ma life since saved. God open ma heart today 'n' healed all the hurt from ma boy's death. I feel alive again. An …"

Randy noticed his skin looked suntanned peach. He appeared twenty years younger than when he came into church. "Gene, that's wonderful. I'm happy for you."

"What I wanna say is, I got money to help with what God's gonna do here. Whatever ya need don't let money hol' ya back. Okay, Pastor? We saved. I pay." He put his hand on the young man's shoulder.

Randy felt Gene's urgency to be understood. "Thank you, Gene. That's very kind."

"No. No." The man shook his head. "Not kind. This wha' God want, ya know?"

"Okay, I'll keep that in mind."

"Good. Good." Gene smiled as he turned to leave. This time the man held his head high with his shoulders back. He looked a foot taller.

Randy sat in the silence. *Whew. That was so strange. I had a really good message I didn't get to preach.* Frustration held him tight as he headed home for lunch.

Chapter 4

The next day, stubbornness and denial covered Randy as he entered the sanctuary. God's holiness lingered but the man's heart didn't soften as he climbed the altar steps and sat on his chair to pray. "Lord, was that you in the service yesterday? The whole thing was so weird. Aren't you a God of order? I tried to stop all the commotion but I was stuck, and didn't have any words."

A voice blasted through the building, "Good morning, Randal. Weren't you pleased with the Lord's presences yesterday? The people responded better than we expected."

Randy opened his eyes. Cassius sat on the air in front of him, his bright smile flashed with light as he spoke.

The pastor glared at the intruder. He wasn't afraid of him now, just annoyed. "You know Cassius, Sunday's service was a mess. People were scattered all over the carpet weeping and wailing. I wasn't able to preach, so they didn't learn a thing. That wasn't church."

"Oh, but it was. The Father did a deep work of love and forgiveness in the hearts of his people."

"Cassius, go away. I never asked for you to come. We were doing just fine without your interference."

Cassius disappeared.

"Ah," Randy sighed. "That was easy. Now for some peace and quiet."

"Just kidding," Cassius bellowed as he showed himself again. "I came to bring you the Father's messages, and you don't have the authority to send me away. I've been told to pester you until you submit, so take as long as you like. I warn you though rebellion against God can make life awfully difficult."

Randy squinted at the angel who was now more visible than before. He focused on the ancient-looking sandals bound to his giant-sized feet, suspended in midair. He studied the unrecognizable faded print of Cassius' humongous dark robe which was secured by a rope around his large waist. His face was blurred by something like fog. However, his annoying bright smile accented his mesmerizing eyes which were very clear.

Realizing he felt intimidated, Randy made an effort to show his boldness. "I am called Randy, not Randal. Randy, got that? Why are you wearing those clothes? I thought angels wear white robes and have wings. And the Bible says angels are neither men or women. Right?"

Cassius didn't blink. He stared at his pupil as if the man were a science experiment. "If I took this robe off I would blind you with the Father's light. Wanna see?"

Realizing he might have gone too far the pastor decided to keep quiet.

Cassius took his opportunity. "Okay, I've got your attention. It is true. We aren't like you, being male or female. We have the ability to appear to you in whatever way will help you feel comfortable with us. Anyway, I have much to tell you, so let's get started. Time has speeded up and the Father wants you ready for his new day."

"New day?"

"Yes. Heaven and earth are coming together. We're going to intersect, crisscross, unite, … kiss. Are those good words? It's all in your Bible."

"Whatever."

Cassius was not distracted. "Now listen. There's much to be done. Jethro, in your church, you know who he is?"

Randy nodded.

"He was created to be a great Evangelist. The enemy tried to defeat him, but he has found his proper path now. Encourage him,

20

help him, and go with him."

He paused to make sure the man got the message, then continued. "The Father's smile is bigger when he watches Barbara. She's one of many women who have been given the gift of prophecy. Make way for her. Receive what she tells you. She hears and sees many things in the kingdom. Don't forget, the Word says all should prophesy.[1] You also have other prophets awakening in your church. Don't dismiss them."

Randy felt dazed. To him, the words sounded like, "Blah. Blah. Blah."

"Are you with me? Pay attention. God's kingdom is arriving. It is a kingdom of love. You must be an example. You have a problem with judging others. That isn't God's will for you. If you repent and ask Father to fill you with his love, he will remove your judgmental attitude so love can reign in your life."

Randy felt himself wilt like a flower thirsting for water as Cassius continued. "Love is the final word in everything God does."

The angel paused as if considering what to say next. "Read about the New Testament church. Normal believers should be healing the sick, raising the dead, and casting out demons.[2] How many normal people are in your church, Randal?"

The giant didn't wait for a response. "Honestly, you run everything here like a business instead of a firehouse for God's glory. Your people have all sorts of talents waiting to come forth. Give Tony more freedom to lead worship. He knows how to follow the Spirit's leading. He will be called elsewhere if you don't let him grow in his gifts."

Cassius rubbed his chin, then presented his next question. "Have you ever experienced what you people call revival?"

"I'm not sure."

"Um hum. Did you know there was a hundred year revival once?"

"No."

"Google it." He flipped his wrist as if those words finished the discussion. "Anyway, we have come to help God usher in the greatest revival ever known to man. The whole world is going to shift supernaturally from death to life, despair to joy, and lack to abundance. You have been chosen to be part of hosting this mighty work."

Randy stared at his guest as he tried to grasp his words. "Why?"

"Why? Why is not the question," Cassius roared. "The Father wants to bring it to pass. He will use anyone who is willing to serve him. Although, I don't see you to be very willing."

He looked away, "Perhaps I have the wrong man. I've watched you, and you're good at trying to run away from your God-given responsibility. In truth, you became a minister because you thought it would be an easy job, and people would treat you with respect. Isn't that true?"

"Oh, please Cassius, leave me alone. I don't want what you're telling me. I have a ten year plan for my church. My sermons are prepared for the next three months. I've never prayed for revival, or any of the stuff that happened Sunday. This is my church. I'm the one who controls what goes on around here. There's no room for you or the others."

Cassius roared with laughter "You're in control? Are you serious?"

After a frustrated huff, Cassius pulled out a scroll and studied it. "Almighty God seems to find you usable for his kingdom purposes. I don't understand why. You're so stubborn and in total denial. If you refuse the Father's plans and hold on to what you think is ..." He held up his fingers as if adding quotation marks. "You being in control ...well ... that's the dumbest thing I've ever heard."

Randy shouted. "Go away."

The angel paused, as if waiting to be released. Perhaps, by someone Randy couldn't see. "Yes, of course. Just remember God loves you too much to leave you the way you are now. There's so much more." Words echoed from a distance as he disappeared. "Randal, don't let stubbornness and pride steal your destiny."

Anger took a seat in Randy's soul. *I hate that guy.* Hate found a place next to anger. *What guy. He's not a man, just a figment of my imagination.*

He looked around the sanctuary. *I hate this place. I hate this job. What am I doing here anyway? I could make a lot more money somewhere other than this stupid place.*

As he got up he swung his arm hoping to dismiss the whole building. He hit the chair so hard it wobbled wildly, but he was able to grab it just before it tumbled down the stairs. Stomping to the back, he pushed one of the doors open and let it slam behind him. At the office, he stuck his head around the door and announced to Glenda he would be out all afternoon.

She looked startled. "Do you want me to cancel your appointments for today?"

He was already gone.

(1) I Corinthians 14:5, (2) Matthew 10:8

Chapter 5

Sherry, the wife of Pastor Randy Wright, the successful leader of Millbrook Community Church, is happy to serve beside her husband in ministry, but her true pleasure comes from being a wife, mother and homemaker. After she spent time crying and repenting at church yesterday, her heart felt full of fresh joy and peace as she sorted the clean laundry. *I feel washed clean. Born again, again. Yes, that's it. I feel the way I did the first time I found Jesus to be real.*

She heard the children giggling as she walked down the hall with the folded towels. The sounds weren't anything needing her attention, but more a sweet draw in her spirit that made her want to join them. She stopped in the doorway and watched Olivia and little Amanda, now age four, as they sipped pretend tea. Really, their party consisted of the apple juice and the granola bars she gave them. They sat across from each other at their little wooden table, and busily talked to the empty chairs on each side. After nibbling a bite they paused and giggled with delight, as if learning the very best secrets from unseen friends.

Sherry wished she could climb into their imaginary world and join them. "Who are you girls talking to?"

"Olympus and Felix, Mommy." Four-year-old Amanda pushed back her blond curls and picked up one of the tiny napkins they created with half of a Kleenex to wipe away tiny crumbs.

"Oh, and who are they?"

Wise Olivia, age six going on twenty, and pretty certain she knew everything, gave the answer. "They're our angels that keep us safe."

"Really." *I've never told them anything about guardian angels. Wonder where they heard about them?*

"Um-hum." The girls answered in unison without opening their mouths.

"What are they telling you?"

Olivia's dark ponytail flipped as she turned her head to see if anyone else might hear. "We can't say. It's secret ... Oh, they said we can't tell you right now because you don't believe."

Sherry started to move on, but instead she stopped to ask another question. "What do they look like?"

Olivia stretched her hands as wide and high as she could. "Olympus is a really big guy." She pulled her arms down and looked at her mother with a serious expression, perhaps searching for the right words. "Like the ones who stop guys from moving the football in the games Daddy watches on TV. I feel safe with him around. He won't let any bad guys get near me."

Not to be outdone by her sister, Amada jumped up from her chair. "Felix is a giant." She stretched as tall as her little legs and tippy-toes could reach. "He has wings and a big sword, and he flies really fast."

"Well, Olympus can fly, too." Olivia announced.

Amanda settled back at the tea table. "I know."

"Okay, girls." *What amazing imaginations.* "Well, I'm going to have some quiet time now. Be good."

As she stepped out of the room their conversation zoomed through her mind. *That was strange. Olivia has never kept secrets before. What did she mean, I don't believe? Imaginary friends, do I deal with this now? I better keep a closer watch on them.*

After the clean things were put away she went into her bedroom and curled up in the comfy, oversized chair beside the window. Randy's mom gave her the hand-me-down piece which fit her and the room perfectly. The morning sunlight flooded in through the large window. She enjoyed her little sanctuary, the place where she quieted herself and invited the Lord's presence to fill her.

"I love You, Lord."

I love you too, my bride.[1]

She chose to believe those words were his response, and hoped she didn't just imagine them.

The angels of God stand around you, and they go before you.[2]

"I've never thought much about angels, Lord."

Get to know the angels, Sherry. Just as the Queen of England sits on her throne giving directions to her people, and they serve her with full enthusiasm, Jesus, the King, speaks and his angelic servants honor him.

Sherry quickly noted in her journal what she thought she heard. Then she sat silent again.

The angel's power and authority comes from Jesus, just as yours does.[3] **They see the kingdom realm, but you live by faith. Faith is the powerful virtue which makes it possible for you to see. Now your eyes will be opened.**

"Wow. Really? I hope I'm not just making this up."

My sheep hear my voice and they follow me.[4]

That's true. I know that scripture. I am hearing the Holy Spirit. Excited to learn more she searched her journal notes. "What else did he say? Oh, now my eyes will be opened.[5] What does that mean?"

*** *** ***

Across town, Gayle Watson loaded the dishwasher with the dishes she used to prepare a small feast for the Morgan family. Beth, the mother, is in the hospital and its Gayle's turn to take dinner. She prepared roast beef with vegetables, a salad, rolls and a cake.

I hope that will be enough food to feed five growing children and their dad.

The love and acceptance she felt in church yesterday

continued to warm her heart. She was grateful her children were beside her. "Lord, if only Dan was there. How do I share with my husband all that took place? I'm grateful he's such a successful businessman, but he misses so many special times with our family and friends because of work.

"Well, at least our children experienced the awesome event. Lord, I'm so grateful they know your reality. At fourteen Carl needs you more than ever. Even though Caroline is only twelve, she's such a beautiful young woman. Please protect her."

She wiped her hands and looked around the kitchen to make sure she didn't miss any dirty dishes. The hummingbirds buzzing around the feeder outside her kitchen window caught her attention. The tiny little clowns, with their silly antics and high energy always made her smile, and created a lovely distraction from her mundane chores.

I loved how the children's pastor brought the little ones to their parents, Lord. Even though Casey is only four-years-old she understood you were present. Thank you."

As a Bible teacher, Gayle contemplated, wanting to understand more about yesterday's supernatural experience. Words rushed through her mind. Revival. Visitation. Finally she grabbed one. "Holiness," she burst out. "It was holiness. No wonder none of us knew what to do. How do you experience God's holiness without a serious reaction? God's holy presence touched us all."

She walked back and forth developing the thought. To the teacher, that word was like finding hidden treasure. "We became conscious of how much we've failed to become the people God created us to be. His love wrapped us. We were challenged with new ideas and possibilities." Her eyes looked toward heaven. "We never wanted to leave your presence."

She felt a new longing for him in depths within herself she hadn't known existed before. How could she ever go back to life as usual? "You have ruined me, Lord, for anything but you. How does one live that sort of life?"

***

Randy sped down the highway in hopes the wind would blow his frustrations away. His 1964 Harley Panhead motorcycle saved his sanity whenever stress pressed him too much. Before he took off he stopped by the house for a quick lunch and told Sherry he needed some time alone.

She always knows when I'm upset. I'm glad she doesn't ask questions and just gives me some space. He mumbled while he rode along. "How can I tell her what's going on? I can't share this with anyone. It's too weird. God, why is this happening? I've done everything I'm supposed to do. I'm tired of dealing with other people's problems. Now you want to make changes. Demons? Cassius? Angels? Good grief. This is just too much."

He continued to rant as he took the curves, each time revving the engine for emphasis. After an hour or so into the ride, the bike seemed to find its own place to stop near Millbrook Stream. He didn't notice the old bridge that crossed farther downstream until a car rumbled over its rickety wooden planks. Trudging toward the edge of the water, he stumbled over a tree root which loosed his pent-up anger. He fired his helmet across the grass, then picked up a rock and skipped it across the water as hard as he could throw. Still frustrated, he leaned against an old tree that had branches so large they hung over the water's edge.

He barely noticed a fisherman walking past until he spoke. "Nice bike. That's a classic. I like the blue color. Where'd you get it?"

"My parents gave it to me when I graduated from Bible College."

"You're a preacher?"

"Yah."

"That's a strange gift for a guy going into ministry."

"It's the best gift I've ever gotten."

"Well, have fun." The man moved on downstream.

29

Sherry always says my wheels are my first love. She thinks a motorcycle makes a way for a grown man, with a boy's heart for adventure, to run away from home. That's true. At least I get to run away for a little while.

He turned and stared at the sparkles the sun created on the water as it moved. Self-pity partnered with anger like brothers who enjoy tormenting.

"What's going on, God? I've tried so hard to do what's right. I'm exhausted. Now none of my hard work has been good enough. Do you want me to change everything?" He paused to consider the possibility. "I can't. I don't want to. Maybe I should quit. You're never satisfied. I've got the building renovated. It's full of more people than I can care for. I don't have any more to give. I barely have time to see my kids. My wife deserves a better life."

Hopeless, he dropped his head and waited. Leaves moved in the breeze, water trickled along to unknown places. Another car banged boards noisily as it crossed the bridge. The fisherman walked back toward him carrying four large fish on a line. He held them up and smiled. "Great day to be alive. God is smiling on us."

Randy watched the man as he moved along whistling a tune that was familiar, but the words didn't come to him. *How did he catch all those fish so fast?* He stared at the ground. "God please show me I'm right about this."

When he finally raised his head, his face flushed red. "Nothing? Nothing? You've got nothing to say? You send an angel to upset my whole world, and you've got nothing to say. I'm through with you. Do you hear me. I quit! I quit!"

He grabbed his helmet, and kicked the ground in frustration as he stomped over to the Harley. The kick starter took the brunt of his anger while he continued to rage. Gravel hurled when he revved the engine to speed onto the highway.

(1) I John 3:1, (2) Psalm 34:7, (3) Luke 10:19, (4) John 10:27, (5) Acts 26:8

Chapter 6

After Gayle dropped the dinner she prepared for the Morgan's off at their home, she breathed a sigh of relief when she and Cassie climbed into the car. "Okay, honey, one more stop, and we'll be finished. I need to run in the hospital and pray with Mrs. Morgan. She's very sick and her family needs her to get well."

As she drove she remembered the day Beth told her she was diagnosed with Restrictive Cardiomyopathy. They knew something was seriously wrong because of the terrible pressure on her chest, and her heart beat erratically. She also had trouble breathing, and she often fainted. *We never considered it would be incurable.* The end results of all the tests concluded a heart transplant was her only hope.

Tears filled Gayle's eyes at the thought of losing her precious friend who now struggled for every breath. She felt her heart would break. *Lord, your Word says you are a God of miracles.*[1] *Five children need their mother.*

She thought of Beth's Kerry and Cassie playing together. Would the loss steal their young trust in God? She considered her friend's husband, Charles. He was barely hanging on, and seemed to have given up believing they might find a compatible heart for her. If it was even possible one would help at this point.

The memories of their shared dreams were sweet. *Father, Beth longs to be here when Micah graduates in two years. She seems to have fought this disease so hard for her children's sake. Please Lord, don't let her die.*

They entered the hospital and scurried through the halls, greeting familiar faces from town along the way. When they stepped into Beth Morgan's room, a handsome male in hospital garb was standing beside the patient.

"Oh, should we wait outside until you're finished?" Gayle inquired.

He glanced over, shook his head and motioned for them to sit in the chair near the bed. She stepped over and pulled Cassie beside her. The child seemed spellbound by what the man was doing. As far as Gayle could tell, he was only watching Beth. *I wonder if he's a doctor or nurse. I can't tell. Whichever, that is a good looking man. He must be the heartthrob of the hospital. Wonder if he's married.*

Cassie looked at all the wires attached to the woman, then cuddled closer to her mom. Sounding a little fearful she whispered, "Is she Kerry's mommy?"

Gayle nodded, and realized it had been months since Cassie was around her.

The attendant rested his hand gently on Beth's folded hands as he stood quietly over her. Finally, he patted them a couple of times and turned to Cassie. He stepped over and put his hand on her shoulder. Cassie looked up into his eyes. In the silence of the room, Gayle watched her child, who seemed frozen in time, stare at the impressive man. *Cassie is as taken with him as I am. He's so beautiful he almost glows.*

After what seemed a long time, but in reality was probably only a minute, he removed his hand from the child and smiled at her. She nodded and responded with her smile. When he left the room, Cassie turned to Gayle. "Momma, can I pray for her?"

Beth opened her eyes, and made an effort to raise her hand in greeting.

Gayle was surprised by the child's request. "Is that okay, Beth?"

Her friend blinked, and nodded slightly as a desperate whisper escaped. "Yes."

Gayle and Cassie stepped over to the patient and the child

reached her tiny hand up as far as she could to touch Beth's arm. She shut her eyes. "Jesus, you told me to pray for the sick and they will be healed. Momma brought me here to Kerry's mommy. She's really sick. I pray for her to be healed. Thank you for doing it. Amen."

Gayle laid a hand on her daughter's shoulder, then leaned over to kiss her friend on the cheek, knowing it might be the last time she would see her alive. "We love you, Beth."

The woman roused a bit and in a weak voice responded. "Love you, too," She focused on Cassie. "Aren't you ... Kerry's age?"

"I'm four. She's five."

Beth took a deep breath. "Thanks ... praying." She gasped for air then flinched as she tugged at her pillow.

"Let me help you." Gayle reached over to assist. "Are you trying to sit up?"

Beth acknowledged with a nod as she kicked the blankets around her legs loose. "Gayle, I felt a surge of ... something ... like energy." She gasped for air. ... "or life ... go through me" ... She motioned toward Cassie. "When she prayed. It felt so good ... as if love ... wrapped me. Ah." She breathed slowly as Gayle helped her lean against the pillows.

"Oh," the woman moaned with what appeared to be relief from pain. She closed her eyes. Tears ran down her face as she whispered, "Thank You, Jesus. ... Thank You."

Gayle took Cassie's hand and they sat together in the chair again. She thought perhaps the nurse gave Beth some new drug that was starting to bring relief. *We'll wait to leave until I know she's comfortable.*

Cassie sat quieter than usual so Gayle took time to admire Beth's flowers. She felt a little encouraged by seeing everyone's thoughtfulness.

As they waited the room filled with a golden glow. *Perhaps the sun setting has caused the effect. No, we're on the east side of the building.*

She checked on Cassie. Her eyes were closed and her face looked as sweet as a cherub. Gayle relaxed and shut hers, too. Relief washed over her and she yielded to what felt like floating. Beth stirred, so Gayle opened her eyes to see if her friend needed anything.

Beth's face was radiant. "Gayle."

"I know. It feels like heaven is in the room. The light is beautiful." Gayle searched for words to describe what was happening. She whispered, "I feel something glorious wrapped all around me. It makes me think of what it might be like to lay in whipped cream." She giggled.

Beth nodded and smiled.

"Just relax and enjoy this moment, Beth."

Gayle took a deep breath and yielded to the enveloping presence that could only be described as love. A startling thought went through her mind. *I wonder if heaven has come to take Beth home.* Tears began to flow.

After some time Cassie stood up. Gayle opened her eyes to check on her. The child was staring at the ceiling. She touched her mother's hand, and whispered, "Mommy, look."

"What is it, Honey?"

"Look. There's a big hole in the ceiling."

"A hole?" Gayle obliged and then looked back at Cassie. Light glowed from the child's face. She knew Cassie wasn't imagining whatever was there.

"Tell me what you see?"

"Mommy, look. The hole is letting heaven in. It's so beautiful. It's all so, so beautiful. Like. ... Like ... I don't know."

Gayle pulled her onto her lap. "Try to tell me, Honey."

"Look, Mommy. Can't you see?" A look of awe filled the child's sweet face as she continued to stare.

"Please. Tell me."

"Well," Cassie pondered. "You would love it. ... Like the

prettiest sunset you ever saw. ... So many colors. There's no crayon box with all those colors." She wiggled from her mother and turned in circles while looking up to see everything.

"What else?"

"Oh, can't you see it? Angels. ... Beautiful angels. ... So many."

Gayle reached toward her. "Don't get dizzy."

Cassie stepped over and leaned against her mother. "I know you're really big, Mommy, but the angels are big as you two times. Look, they're floating. ... So many are coming in this room. How can they all fit?"

Oh, please God. I want to see. Gayle looked up in hope.

As if a shade flipped open, the ceiling was gone and the glory of heaven revealed itself to a desperate heart. She saw colors and beauty beyond anything she knew. There was music more glorious than anything she ever heard before. "Wonderful," was all she had as expression. The shade snapped shut.

"I saw, Cassie." She hugged her daughter.

The child wiggled loose. "Can you see him, Mommy?"

"Who?"

"Jesus. Can't you see him? He's loving Mrs. Morgan."

"What do you mean?"

"Jesus is so, so shiny." She continued to stare at Beth's bed. "He's holding her hands like people in love do."

Awed by the child's words, Gayle squinted hoping she could focus enough to see him. She noticed Beth was resting peacefully.

Cassie touched her mother's hand.

"What do you see now, Honey?"

"Jesus just kissed her on the cheek and rubbed her hands." The child continued to stare, then smiled and wave toward the bed. She took a deep breath and slowly turned toward her mother. "Okay, he's gone," she announced as if she were ready to leave.

"Why did you wave?"

"Cause he smiled at me and waved."

Beth opened her eyes. "Could I have a drink of water?" She motioned to the pitcher sitting on the table at the end of her bed.

Gayle quickly got a glass of water and a bent straw so her friend could manage it.

"Thanks." She took a few sips. "Ah, that tastes so good. I feel much stronger. I think your prayer made me better, Cassie."

Cassie held one finger up to her mouth. "I know a secret. The angel told me to pray for you so other people will learn how to do it. Jesus heard me and he came to make you well."

Gayle asked, "What angel, Cassie?"

"The one who was in here when we came in."

"You mean the man who was here?" Gayle questioned.

"Yes. The angel who glowed. He was talking to Mrs. Morgan. Didn't you see him?"

"Yes, I saw him, but I didn't hear him say anything."

Beth responded. "He did. When he was with me I heard what he said in my heart. He showed me pictures in my mind, like I was watching a home movie. My family was having a picnic on a huge green lawn. The children were grown, and there were twenty grandchildren…. Twenty, Gayle." She smiled at the thought before she continued. "Charles had gray hair and we were so happy together." With a look of shock, she breathed deep and boldly declared, "Gayle, I saw the future. My future." She burst into tears.

Gayle joined in with her own tears, but now instead of sorrow, they represented relief and new joy.

Cassie's delightful giggle caused the women to laugh. Beth breathed deep and laughed, and then laugh some more. Pausing a second she spurted. "It's true; a merry heart is good like a medicine."[2] Then she erupted again with what could only be described as divine joy.

Doctor Parker came through the door and stopped abruptly. The women choked back their emotions trying to appear somewhat sane. He walked to his patient and smiled, perhaps he knew she was about to burst a button to control her laughter. "So how's my patient today?"

That did it. Beth's exhale sounded like the blast of air when a balloon escapes. With words wrapped in laughter she declared, "I'm fine. Great. I've never felt better." She pushed her blankets aside to sit up.

The doctor took her hand to assist. "Take it easy. Don't get light headed."

Gayle was trying to keep her laughter tucked inside, but one of Cassie's delightful giggles set her off again. "We're sorry doctor. We can't help it."

The kind professional waved his hand. "Don't mind me. I find this quite refreshing after all the sickness I have to face every day."

He began to study his patient. "Last time I was in your room you were … lethargic. So what brought this change?"

Beth was smiling from ear to ear as she tried to be respectful. "That child prayed for me. God healed me. I know he did. Look." She took a long deep breath. "Never thought I'd do that again."

The physician turned to look at the child. "Really?" Then he continued to check Beth's vitals and study the records on the monitor while the others gained control over their silly outbursts.

"This is unbelievable," he announced.

A young female nurse came in to assist him.

Beth questioned, "Where's the nurse I had earlier?"

"I've been your nurse all day. You didn't seem to be aware of my presence though."

Gayle and Beth's eyes met. They looked at Cassie, who shrugged. "I tol' you."

The women both put a hand to their chest and smiled, hoping they didn't cause another disturbance in front of the doc.

Looking at the doctor, Beth announced. "I've gotten a miracle. I can go home now."

"Well, let's not move too fast. We need to run some tests to confirm what you say happened to you." He continued to check her over.

Beth looked into the man's eyes. "No. Doctor, I need to go home. I know this is hard to grasp. I have received a miracle from Almighty God. He chose to give me my life back today. This will all be documented in the medical field with your name at the top. For now, I am going home to see my family and enjoy the life I almost lost. I want you to discharge me, and for goodness sakes, get all this stuff off me so I can walk around."

He nodded to the nurse, and she began to remove the equipment. After he checked his chart one more time, he spoke. "Madam, no doubt something wonderful has happened to you. To be honest, we had no hope for your recovery. I will be a happy man if I can declare you are healed, but I also have a responsibility to confirm what you've told me before I release you. Let me set up tests for tomorrow morning. If they show this unprecedented transformation to be a healing, I will be … cautiously delighted to discharge you." He and the nurse moved out of the room.

Beth looked at Gayle. "I want to go home now."

"I know."

Beth wiggled carefully out of bed while Gayle retrieved her slippers and helped her step into them. Suddenly, the door burst open. Charles's six-foot-six husky frame blocked most of the hall light. "What's going on? The staff's all talking about something. They wouldn't tell me," he shouted as he waved one hand toward the hall. He stopped as his mouth fell open.

His bride stood before him healthy and beautiful. "Beth," he gasped and dropped to his knees in front of her. Wrapping his arms around her waist, he pressed his head against her and sobbed. Beth stroked his hair and patted his head as the sorrow that held him captive washed from his soul.

Gayle took Cassie's hand and mouthed good-bye to her friend as they departed. She wanted the intimacy of those moments to be theirs alone.

***

Charles and Beth sat on the edge of her hospital bed holding hands. She was aware her husband was listening to her quiet breathing. All signs of the heavy pressure that continually tried to suffocate her before was gone. She didn't gasp for air one time as she shared everything that took place earlier.

Beth could almost feel her heart pumping like a fine machine as it sent blood flowing with new life through her body. Each steady beat seemed to bring more strength. When she inhaled, just for the fun of it, she reminded herself what a pleasure it was to have lungs full of air. With each breath she became more excited to find out what the doctor's test results would show because she had no doubt she was completely healed.

Dr. Parker entered. "Hello, Charles. I'm sure your wife has filled you in on today's events. I'm glad you're here so I can tell you both my plans for her."

Charles began to ruffle with agitation. "What plans? She's healed. We're going home."

Beth patted his arm. "Charles, I want to go home more than anything, but I've been thinking. They want to run tests to prove I'm healed. For us, this will confirm I've had a miracle healing. I think there's more going on here than our desires. God is showing himself to be mighty on our behalf.[3] We should let them document everything so we have a testimony that can't be denied. Our children will never forget God healed their mother. Everyone we know … all these people in the hospital who are still struggling to hang on, they will know God is their answer, too.

"I don't understand why it took so long. I wish I did. But then suddenly … remember us talking about all those scriptures that say 'then suddenly?'"

He looked at her and nodded.

"You go home and tell the children I'll be there tomorrow. Okay?"

He agreed as he squeezed her hand.

Dr. Parker slapped Charles on the knee, "Good man," then he vanished into the hall.

Looking at the floor, Charles confessed, "You know I don't like leaving you here."

"Yes, it's hard for me to stay."

The shy man paused in thought. "I made a deal with God before."

"Really?"

"Yep. I told him if he would heal you, I would be all in for him."

Beth laughed. "What does that even mean?"

He shrugged his shoulders. "I don't know. I really don't care. All that matters is I've got you back." He wrapped his arms around the woman he adored and kissed her with a passion so powerful he felt eighteen again.

Beth gasped. "My goodness. Even a girl who can breathe would swoon with that kind of kiss." They laughed and hugged as hope found its way home.

(1) Psalm 136:4-22, (2) Proverbs 17:22, (3) II Chronicles 16:9

Chapter 7

Several days of tension passed while Randy wrestled with his decision to quit his job. The sound of his motorcycle's rumble filled the garage when he drove in after another ride. Relieved no one was home he parked his bike and headed for the house. A few strides across the lawn took him through the kitchen door. He made himself a sandwich and stuffed it down as he headed back to clean and polish his prized possession.

Frustration gave him more energy than the job required. He focused on a little splat of bug guts on the front. *How do I quit my job? That church is my life. This has got to be worse than leaving other careers.*

Meticulously, he polished with his perfectly-sized little cloths. *I don't know who I am if I'm not a pastor. That's what I trained to be. I've lived the best I could to qualify. If I walk away it's all been for nothing.*

After a while, he stood back to admire his work, knowing by the time he completed his ritual the bike always looked ready for a showroom. *How can I tell Sherry I'm done here? Actually, she'd probably be relieved. My job hasn't been easy for her.* He stuck a soft brush in the tiny areas where particles of dust always accumulated as he considered the words he yelled at God. *Can I give up and still have God in my life? Yes, his Word says he'll never leave me.*[1]

He continued to polish already shiny chrome. *I was pretty happy with my job. If I'm not willing to change, that kind of narrows my options.*

As he moved around his man cave, really part of their

detached two-car garage, he was reminded of the comfort he found in having his own space the four years they've lived in Millbrook.

Strolling to his workbench, he shuffled around some tools he received as Christmas gifts, and picked one up. *Dad seemed to think I needed this. Hum.* He pushed the object, which had no directions attached, aside. As he reached for the tire polish he bumped the stool Sherry bought him at a garage sale. He grabbed the seat, and the book on it, before they fell. *What's a Bible doing on my stool? I didn't bring that out here.* He flipped the pages open. *Wonder what it says about angels. If they're real, does that mean demons are, too?*

The noise of a car pulling in the driveway made him smack the book shut as if he just got caught looking at a magazine with pictures of nude women. He covered it with his extra towel and sat it behind his cleaning supplies.

Chirpy little girls' voices sounded like a joyful flock of birds on the first day of spring as they burst through the door of his domain.

"Hi, Daddy." They rushed in and latched onto his legs. He bent over to receive their hugs. Harsh emotions cracked a bit. Looking up at his wife, his heart skipped a beat. The glow of her countenance took his breath away.

"Daddy, guess what? Guess what?" Amanda jumped up and down.

Sherry leaned over them and gave him a quick kiss. "Did you have a nice ride?"

"It was okay." He lifted Amanda into his arms. "I can't guess, Amanda. But it must be something good. You'll have to tell me."

"It was our turn to take dinner to Kerry's house, and her mommy's not sick now."

Confused by her announcement, he looked at Sherry. She smiled and nodded.

He sat Amanda down and stepped back to lean against the workbench. "Beth Morgan? She's home?"

The scene of his last visit with her at the hospital flashed through his mind. She didn't look good. Charles told him she was getting weaker daily and wasn't expected to live. He remembered how distraught the man was because the doctor told him he needed to prepare for the worst. Charles worried how he would manage caring for all their children, and was angry at the thought of their mother dying. He was heartbroken knowing he was going to lose the wife he dearly loved.

"What happened?"

Sherry related how Gayle and Cassie visited the hospital and the child prayed for Beth. "Cassie said an angel told her to pray for sick people so others would know God heals."

She became animated flinging her arms out to exaggerate the wonder of the situation. "The doctor took a bunch of tests and confirmed she's healthy. He said her heart looks like new. It's a miracle Randy. A real miracle right from heaven."

She crossed her hands over her heart and shut her eyes as tears welled up. "Randy, I can't describe the joy of walking into their home and seeing Beth." Awe-filled, she looked into his eyes. "The children are overjoyed. And their dad … Charles is a changed man."

Logically, Randy couldn't wrap his brain around the story. His mind tried to absorb her information but it was hard to believe. "The doctor said 'like new'?"

The girls were staring up at their parents as they listened to every word. They nodded to their daddy to confirm their mother's story.

Sherry continued. "Beth said all the heavy pressure lifted off her chest. She was so sure she was well she agreed to wait for the doctor's tests to prove her healing. Now she breathes easily, and you should hear her laugh. It's contagious."

The girls giggled as Sherry continued. "Isn't it wonderful?"

Randy's mind flip-flopped. "It's unbelievable."

Amanda gave him another hug. "The angels have come to help

us, Daddy." She and Olivia giggled as they took off toward the house, then stopped and yelled back in unison, "Mommy, we're hungry."

"Yes, we better have dinner. Are you ready to come in, Randy?"

"I've already eaten. I'll stay here and finish up."

"Okay. Love you."

Randy saw sadness cross her face. "I love you, too."

She turned away. "Come on girls. Dinner's in the oven. I'll race you."

A cushioned lawn chair sat in the corner of the garage den. Sherry brought it out saying he might as well be comfortable in his private castle. His heart softened a bit as he thought of his wife's concern for everyone else. He retrieved the hidden Bible and walked over to his private spot. Opening the book, he wandered through the pages in the same way he would stroll through a store when he forgot what he went for. *I thought I knew this book. I've studied it for years. What does it say about healing the sick? I guess maybe I don't know as much as I thought I did.*

***

Putting the girls to bed Sherry felt uneasy because Randy hadn't come in for those precious last moments of the children's day. She considered going out to see if he was okay, but that was his private space where he could blow off steam. *Something seemed seriously wrong with him tonight. I'm not going out there. It wouldn't be the first time he snapped at me when I got in his line of fire. I hate his harsh voice tones when he's upset about who-knows-what.*

Unity took a back seat as Division smiled.

(1) Hebrews 13:5

Chapter 8

Sherry woke early. She enjoyed the morning quietness of the house as she walked to the kitchen. Randy hadn't been told what their daughters said to her about the angels. *I wonder what he'll think? He'll probably say, "We don't want to encourage imaginary friends."*

Ready to get an early start, she shuffled through her recipe box and pulled out a stained card. *Apple muffins. Everyone loves them.* She gathered ingredients and placed them together on the table. *Oh, I'd better get those birthday cards while I'm thinking of it. I don't want to forget to put them in the mail today.* She wiped her hands and made the short trip to the bedroom to retrieve the cards. As she walked back she noticed the lights were on in the kitchen. *I don't remember turning the lights on.*

When she reached the door, she stood in shock. Brilliant light surrounded three breathtakingly beautiful feminine looking angels. She slid the kitchen's pocket door shut behind her as quietly as possible. They didn't notice her so she stayed motionless hoping for time to absorb such wonder. Long hair floated around them like it would in water. Their white gowns were almost transparent. The shimmering white fabric moved continually, as if it were alive.

What are they doing? She looked closer and saw they were reading her recipe and looking at the ingredients she set out.

"Oh," one gasped. They all disappeared. The bright light was gone.

Sherry flipped on a light. *That was weird, but I think I really saw angels just now. They were so beautiful.* After a pause, she went back to humming quietly while she measured and stirred the ingredients into the super-sized mixing bowl she enjoyed using because it gave her the feeling of being an accomplished chef.

"What kind of muffins are you making?"

"Huh? Who said that?" She looked toward the door to see who entered. No one was there. Though puzzled, she got out muffin tins and sprayed them so they were ready for the batter.

"Does your recipe call for nutmeg?"

Sherry whirled around and put both hands on her hips, ready to get to the end of the joke. "No! Who said that? This isn't funny."

"Oh, it adds another layer of yummy flavor, and smells so delicious."

Leaning against the refrigerator she waited for understanding. Three tiny, blurry female figures came into focus. Two sat on the counter, the third floated above. The chubby one looked like she loved to eat.

Curiosity took over so Sherry whispered. "Was it you who suggested the added ingredient?"

A sweet smile crossed the face of the intruder as she nodded her head. Sherry reached for the table and sank into a chair.

Her gaze turned to the one floating. The translucent material that resembled veils fluttered around her like the angels she saw earlier. *If that mirage were human she would probably be an actress on a red-carpeted runway somewhere.*

Amazed, she studied the others. *They're each so different. The third could pass for a schoolteacher with her book bag, hair in a bun, and wire-rimmed glasses.* She couldn't keep from smiling when the teacher's glasses floated off her face. Each time they drifted, she gave a little huff and snatched them back in place.

The supernatural guests remained quiet for a few moments, perhaps to give her time to adjust to their presence. When she didn't say anything, they all began to chatter. They examined everything in her kitchen, and didn't seem to know much about their new surroundings. Each questioned the other as they tried to understand how things worked. Several times the angel who looked like an actress sighed, as if pleased with Sherry's homemaking skills.

Am I hallucinating? The strange production reminded her of the three fairy godmothers from Disney's movie *Sleeping Beauty*. Except these visitors were real. She finally found her voice. "What are you doing here?"

They floated toward her, talking non-stop, telling her … who knows what. All their words ran together.

Ms. Book Lady whistled and silence fell. "The King has new plans. You have the honor of being part of them. We're going to assist you."

Sherry felt her eyes bulging. "But … but … I don't believe in ghosts. Or angels. Or other-world things."

The three looked at her curiously. The scholar seemed indignant when she spoke. "Not believing doesn't change the truth. Wait a moment." She pulled a book from her bag and read to herself. "This says you're a Bible believer."

"Yes." Sherry frowned as she tried to understand what that had to do with anything.

The angel pulled her glasses back on her face and peered over them. "Then why don't you believe in us? We're mentioned over 200 times in your Bible."

Sherry's mind took off like a rollercoaster ride. *This is crazy. What's wrong with me this morning?*

The wise teacher didn't seem to have time to wait for Sherry to figure everything out.

"Angels we have heard on high."

"That's a song," Sherry responded.

"That's Bible. It's truth. Read Luke 2:14. The angels of the Lord camp round about those who fear him. Psalm 34:7-9. Are not all angels ministering spirits sent to serve those who will inherit salvation? Hebrews 1:14."

"Oh, my goodness, that's true! I guess I've ignored those

verses since I didn't believe they were real. I didn't understand what those words meant."

"They mean what they say. There are myriads and myriads of angels." She pointed her finger. "That's Revelations 5:11. They're coming here right now to transform the earth for the King's kingdom."

"But I thought angels wore white and had wings."

"We can take on many forms, but you caught us unprepared when you surprised us earlier. We didn't want to scare you when we introduced ourselves, so while we watched the movie your daughters called, 'Sleeping Beauty' with them, we decided looking like the fairies wouldn't frighten you too much when we revealed ourselves."

Sherry laughed. "That was so kind of you. Yes, I was shocked enough with you tiny visitors."

The three smiled sweetly, and again their voices filled the room with contagious excitement. Then, as quickly as they appeared, they were gone. Sherry sat stunned in the silence of her kitchen. She rose and moved slowly to the cabinet, pulled out nutmeg and added some to her mixing bowl. *Hum. It does smell extra delicious.* Once stirred in, she poured the gooey batter in the tins and popped them in the oven.

I need my morning coffee. Strong coffee. Angels are real.

Chapter 9

Charles, Beth and their children sat around the table enjoying dinner together. Micah, the oldest, was proud to have his driver's license which came in handy while his mom was sick. He taxied his brother and sisters everywhere they needed to go to help his dad out.

The young man marveled at the fact things seemed normal again. His mother was sitting in her spot as if she were never ill. *How could that be possible?* They told him it was a miracle. Well, he had to agree because seeing her healthy was more than he could have hoped. Relieved, he sighed as he remembered the heavy tension in the house the past year.

He studied his dad. *How did he survive all that? I guess like we all did. One day at a time.*

His mother smiled at him. He could see her pleasure in being with her family again.

Micah took a bite of food and swallowed. "Dad, could I use the car tonight? Some of the guys are getting together at Evan's house."

Charles looked concerned as he questioned his son. "Are his parents going to be there?"

"Yes, I made sure they would be home when he invited me."

"What do you think, Beth? I'm not sure this is a good idea."

Beth nodded showing her concern as well. "I don't know Charles. You'll have to decide what's best. He has been a big help and deserves some fun, but I don't know all his new friends."

Micah could almost see a war going on in his dad's head as he chewed his food while trying to make the decision.

"Okay. But only Evan's house. If I come by, you better be there" Charles fished in his pocket and pulled out the car key.

Micah took another fork full of food before he jumped up to take his plate to the sink. "Of course, Dad." He retrieved the key. "Thanks. Do you need me to put gas in it?"

"No, I filled it yesterday. Have fun and be careful."

"I will Dad. Don't worry."

"Everybody worries when they have a sixteen year old driver." Charles smiled. "Love you, Son."

"Yah. Love you guys too." He scooted around the table and gave his mother a kiss on her cheek. "I'm so glad you're home and well, Mom." He vanished.

The couple looked at their food and remained quiet while the other four children kept the room lively.

***

Much later, Micah slipped quietly into the house. Darkness convinced him everyone was asleep. He took off his shoes and set them on the stairs, felt his way to the kitchen, drank a glass of milk, and headed back to the front hall to go up to bed.

"It's after midnight, Micah. You broke curfew. What have you been up to?"

Startled, the young man froze while mumbling under his breath, "Not again. I sure don't need him yelling at me right now."

He turned and entered the front room. "Dad, what are you doing up so late? Don't you have to work tomorrow?"

"That wasn't the question. Why are you staggering? Turn on the lights."

Micah obeyed and squinted as the light hit his bloodshot eyes. He slowly worked his way to the sofa trying not to bump into furniture, and sat down across from his father. Evading the question about staggering he replied, "The time just got away from us."

"Curfew is a community law as well as our house rule.

Right?"

"Yes, sir."

"Who were you with?"

"Just some of the football guys. You know ..."

"You've been drinking?" Charles confirmed more than questioned.

Micah looked at his feet as he considered his options. *Should I lie? Who really cares what he thinks. He'll give me a lecture. I'll promise to change. But I know what I'm doing. Will he ever quit treating me like a kid?*

"We went to Evan's house. His dad has a bar in their basement game room, so we checked out the different stuff. Everybody was doing it."

"Where was his dad?"

"He was upstairs. Evan said he didn't care if we had some drinks. He's cool." Micah was going to explain how some dads thought teenagers should enjoy all of life's experiences, but his father interrupted.

"What else?"

Oh, get off my back. You don't really care what I do. Let me go to bed. Micah yawned as he looked at his father, hoping for reprieve.

"What else?" his dad insisted.

"What do you mean?"

"Micah, you smell like a smokestack, and it's not a tobacco odor."

"Oh, ... Matt had some marijuana."

"And you had to try it?"

Feeling a little hopeful, Micah thought his dad understood. "Right." He shrugged. "It's legal now."

Charles sat forward in his chair, and spoke softly. "Not for you. You're sixteen years old. Did you forget you're captain of the JV football team? They expel students for drinking alcohol and using drugs?"

"I didn't think about that."

"No. I guess you didn't. As a leader, did you consider all the other guys who will be expelled with you? No." His father paused seeming to choke back rage, but continued in a low voice. "This is why your grades were so bad. You couldn't concentrate."

"Oh, that stuff doesn't affect grades."

Exasperation wrapped his father's words. "Micah, get real. When drugs or alcohol are in your system, it affects everything. I've known you were sneaking out at night. I let it slide while your mother was sick, but we can't make excuses for your actions any longer."

The teen slapped his knees as he stared into his father's face. "Dad, I'm sorry, but I'm tired. If you want me to talk, okay, but you haven't got a clue what's going on in the world. You're so wrapped up in your work, Mom and the kids, and church stuff you can't even see what's going on around you."

His father took a deep breath, and stared into space. Micah tensed while he waited for the booming voice that would spit out an angry lecture. His dad's words shocked him.

"Well, why don't you tell me about it then?"

Relieved by the opportunity to tell the secrets he kept, Micah allowed the floodgates of his emotions to burst forth. "Dad, I'm tired and I have a headache, but if you want me to talk, okay, I will. This is a small town. Booze and drugs flow through here like Millbrook Stream. Marijuana is nothing compared to some of the stuff available. I've stayed away from that. But what's wrong with a little fun?" He didn't really want a response. "A lot of the guys get really wasted. We spend half the night getting them home. And the girls."

"Girls?" His dad looked concerned.

"Dad, come on, you're not from the dark ages. There's no secrets about girls and sex and all that. Look at television. It shows us everything. You think we're not going to try it? I guess you never considered there might be some senior girls who want to be the first to have sex with the football players."

His father looked at him in shock.

Micah jumped up. "Oh, I can't talk to you about this stuff. I'm going to bed."

Charles sprang to his feet. "You sit back down and cool off."

Micah huffed, but sat and crossed his arms in defiance.

"Son, how bad has this gotten for you?"

Micah shuffled his feet, "I'm okay. Fine."

His dad continued, "Bad enough to be kicked off the football team? Bad enough to let your grades slide until you throw away any chance for a college scholarship?

"Oh, son, what are we going to do? I've had so much going on with your mother's illness. The bills are unbelievable, so I'm working extra hours. I know you got stuck taking care of the other children too often. I'm sorry. I depended on your help too much, and didn't take time for us to hang out like we used to do. I'm so sorry."

Surprised by his words, Micah looked at his dad. *He's apologizing to me. Sure, I helped out. No one asked me if I was okay with that. I needed a life too.*

Charles said, "You need to stop before you can't quit."

"Maybe, it's too late."

Those words seemed to crush his dad.

That felt good. In your face, old man. You just don't get it. "All of us guys spend most of our time trying to figure out how to get our next buzz. Some of the parents help us by letting us experiment at their houses."

Micah watched anger flash through his father's eyes as he said, "I don't suppose you want to give me the parent's names?"

The boy shook his head.

Charles paused before he spoke again. "Well, we need to get you some help. I don't know how I'll ever pay for it, but if I have to get a second mortgage, I will. Would you go if I find someone who can help you?"

"I'll think about it."

"You'll really think about it?"

"Sure," he shrugged.

"Well, for now you're grounded. Give me the car key. I don't want you driving while intoxicated. Fortunately, there's no school right now. You'll miss football practice. No outside activities until we feel we can trust you again."

"You won't let me drive?" he whined. But, he reached in his pocket and tossed the car key to his dad.

Pain etched his father's face as he continued. "Micah, after your mother was healed I wanted to do something to help other people. I met a guy named Jethro at church. On Friday nights, I go with him to some down-and-out people, and we help them. The experience has been eye-opening. I want you to go with me next Friday. You will stay in this house every day until then. No football practice. No friends. Give me your phone. No text or calls. I'll be up to get your computer out of your room. You have been shut down. Got it?"

Micah sobered. *How am I going to get around this?* "Yes sir."

"I mean it, Son. It's for your own good. Try to clean out your system. Think about what kind of future you want. If you sneak out, I will know. This stops now, do you understand? You won't like the repercussions if it doesn't."

The teen nodded and tossed his phone to his dad. He stomped out of the room, grabbed his shoes, and climbed the steps to his bedroom. *I'll figure this out in the morning. I'm too tired right now.*

***

Charles considered their conversation. "Lord, help me. Help my boy. My heart is breaking to think I'm losing my son. What am I doing wrong? My wife went through hell with sickness. I'll be paying those expenses forever. Now, Micah is slipping away. How

54

am I supposed to pray?"

He paused and waited in hope he might hear something, anything. "I remember when I finally quit fighting for Beth and gave her to you. You came through. I forgot about doing that. Okay, Lord, in the same way Abraham gave his son to you[1], I put Micah into your hands. Free him from all the things that are trying to steal his future and life."

Charles thought about their conversation. *Why did I tell him to go with me and Jethro? It's dangerous down there, and drugs are everywhere. That's certainly not a place for him to be right now.*

***

When Micah woke up, the sunlight shining in his eyes was blinding. He squinted and grabbed his head. "Oh. My head aches." He stretched and listened to the quietness of the house. *What time is it? Wow. 11:30. The house is so quiet. Maybe no one else is here.*

As he opened the bedroom door to make sure the house was empty, he noticed his computer was gone. He headed down the stairs. *Everybody's gone.* In the kitchen he took several aspirin from his mother's kitchen supply, and grabbed some leftover toast.

Climbing back up the stairs, his normal three steps at a time, he closed the door so he could search the room. In the closet he pulled down a box of baseball cards. *Good place to hide grass. It's so messy no one will notice.* Shuffling through the cards, he came up empty. *What? I'm sure this is where I stored it.* He dug in his sock drawer. *I didn't roll those socks and place them in rows. Who's been in here? Did they find my bottle?* He tossed the bundles around digging to the back of the drawer. *It's gone. Did one of the kids find it?*

Dropping to the floor, he searched under the bed. Sure enough, an empty bottle was still there. He pulled it out, rolled over, and tried to pour a few last drops into his mouth. *Nothing.*

Panic struck. He jumped up and went through all the pockets of his jeans, and coats. *Nothing. No nothing.* Finished there, he pulled out the other drawers which only revealed underwear and junk. Next, he checked his desk. *Oh, I remember. I did hide some in here.* He pulled a drawer out and dumped it as he turned it over. There on the bottom was the tape he used to hold a small stash of marijuana. A note replaced the little bag.

We are helping you give up the things trying to destroy you.

"Are you kidding me? Who did this?" *My brother and sisters know better than to come in my room. It had to be Dad or Mom. I'm not sure Dad wants her to know. He did it.*

Throwing himself across the bed he yelled, "Now what?"

His stomach cramped, and his head throbbed. "Oh, I'm going to be sick." He rushed to the bathroom.

When he returned he fell on the bed and held his head. The silence soon seemed louder than the normal confusion in the house so he decided to go outside to get some fresh air. When he turned the door handle, it didn't budge.

He wasn't aware many angels had come to fight for his freedom. Some of them held the door closed. He tried to open it again. Then swore and yelled, "Who's out there holding the door? This is crazy. Let me out." *Well, I'll show them. I've been out that window and down the drainpipe so many times they wouldn't believe it.*

More angels moved quickly to secure the exit. He pushed the window frame but it didn't budge. *Someone must have sealed the window shut so I can't get out. This has gone too far. I could die in here.* He picked up his football and threw it at the wall. It wobbled into the closet. *No one could find everything I hid in my closet.*

Back to the closet again, he tossed boxes as he rummaged through them, then pulled all his pants off the hangers in his desperate search. His head still throbbed as he slid down the wall, sat on the floor, and watched his hands shake.

He didn't see the angels, who were assigned to him, standing in each corner of his room. There was no way for him to know they were protecting him from his enemies' destructive enticements.

After, what seemed like forever, he heard his dad's voice.

"Micah, I brought us hamburgers and fries for lunch. You hungry?"

The teen got his feet under him and pushed himself up the wall. He was ready to bang on the door and tell his dad what he thought about being locked in, but the angels opened it. He stuck his head out to see who was there. *That's weird.* "Dad, why did you lock me in my room?" he shouted as he moved toward the kitchen.

Charles came to the door. "What? I didn't lock you in your room."

"Well, somebody did. And they messed with my stuff. That's not right."

"I only took your computer from your room, just as I told you I would. You were sound asleep so you didn't hear me when I came in." His father pulled their lunch out of the bag and sat it on the table. With a puzzled look he said, "Micah, your bedroom door doesn't have a lock."

The teen plopped in his chair as he tried to figure out what happened, but his dad interrupted his thoughts.

"I took a long lunch break to see if you want to come with me this afternoon. Maybe you would enjoy being outside doing some manual labor."

"I don't know. I've got a headache."

"There's nothing like fresh air and hard work to make you forget your problems. You always liked swinging a hammer. We're going to put the studs in a remodel. You know how to do that. I'll even pay you an hourly wage."

Micah's sulking voice agreed. "It's better than being stuck here all day."

"Great. I've missed the times we did things together. It's kind of hot, so better put something cooler on, and you'll need work boots on the job site."

They both concentrated on their lunch as if they were starved. When they finished eating they discussed the work project, while last night's encounter grew distant.

Micah jumped up when they finished. "Okay, I'll get dressed and be back in a minute."

His dad rumpled all the wrappers as he cleaned up their mess. "I'll get water for the cooler and meet you at the truck."

Lumbering up the stairs to his room, Micah noticed a breeze blowing the curtains through his bedroom window. "I know that window wouldn't open." He stepped into the closet to find some old jeans and his boots. Everything was hanging neatly, all the stuff from the floor was back in the boxes on the shelves. He grabbed his jeans and boots and turned toward his bed which was perfectly made. The room was clean. The dust that almost qualified as antique was missing. *What is going on? No one in my family would do this.*

Angels lounged around the room as if exhausted.

Chapter 10

Micah's week of discipline was finally over. When he went to work with his dad, he felt sort of sick, but didn't know if it was withdrawals or the flu. Each evening, when they got home from work, he stomped to his room in defiance, and refused to eat. By Wednesday, he joined the family for dinner. His brothers and sisters cheered when he came to the table.

Friday night finally arrived. His night to meet with friends and have fun. Instead he was walking with his dad from the police department parking lot where he liked to park, to meet his new friend to do good deeds. *What a waste of a weekend.*

They approached a tall hippy standing in the shadows of the old Grand Hotel. The man's face was covered with a stringy beard, and his hair looked like he hadn't used shampoo, or seen a barber, in a long time.

"Son, this is Jethro. He's our leader tonight."

Jethro stretched out his hand. "Nice to meet ya, Micah. Your dad told me you were coming with us." As they stood eye-to-eye, the hippy's piercing gray eyes seemed to look into his soul. "Glad to have a tall dude join us. I need to look down at most people, except for your dad, of course. You ready for some excitement?"

Micah shrugged. He felt helpless and longed for reprieve as he scanned the dark empty streets.

Jethro laughed, "Oh, you'll be surprised at the activity around here later."

Ken and Everett joined the group. They laughed and cut-up as they introduced themselves to the new recruit.

A couple of bums? What are they so happy about? I remember them from church. They're weird.

"Everybody ready?" Jethro inquired and looked around. "Yep. I see full backpacks. Charles, are your pockets loaded?"

Charles patted his bulky sides and smiled, "Ready."

"Then let's get going."

Micah wanted to run off, go home, do anything but spend Friday night with these guys. He was startled when the men moved so quickly. *Where are they headed in such a hurry? Why don't we just drive?*

They walked through the streets of an old neighborhood he hadn't seen before. The large houses, that were probably a hundred years old, where now apartments in disrepair. A few times they heard people arguing, mostly everything was quiet. Something kicked a can over between the houses. Micah jumped as a cat sprinted across in front of him.

Ken and Everett slowed down to walk with the young man. They both chattered as they explained to him that the place they were going was their home until Jethro came and found them. "We were both drug addicts," Everett explained. "What Jethro told us gave us hope and a purpose. It's the only way to live." The men bumped knuckles and laughed.

***

While they talked to Micah, Jethro took the opportunity to speak with Charles. "What a fine boy, Charles. He's tall like you, and must have his mother's good looks." Charles smiled. "No really. His blue eyes show right into his soul. He has such a good heart and a heavy call of God on his life. No wonder the enemy is trying to trap him. I pray he experiences something life-changing tonight."

Charles nodded. "Oh, Jethro my heart pleads for him continually."

"I know," he patted the father on the shoulder.

***

Streetlights ended near the railroad tracks. Only seldom passing cars gave any light. The group moved into the darkness of something like a cave. Micah looked around. *Oh, we're under the railroad bridges.*

Jethro moved back to him. "Okay, Micah. Stay right with us. You could get lost in this maze."

The teen nodded. He shook his trembling hands as he tried to adjust to the darkness.

"Around here," Jethro directed.

They all followed him along a curved wall. Firelight flickered in a few spots. Micah squinted to see the ground so he wouldn't step in a hole or something. As they got closer to the light, the musty moisture and diesel fumes made him cough. A hunched man walked by, he reeked of alcohol. Ken leaned close to Micah. "That's why we quit drinking."

Jethro approached a small group around a fire. "Evening folks. Nice fire. You guys doing okay?" Several mumbled a few words.

"You want coupons for breakfast?" The men held out their hands without a word. "There you go. Don't forget God loves you. We're here to help if you need somethin'."

Everett opened his backpack and handed a new pair of thick socks and a tube of ointment to one of the men. "Here you go, George. This should help your sore feet."

"Thanks, I hope so." George responded.

Ken whispered to Micah. "Everett has become our doctor. He finds out what will help their symptoms and gets it for them. They don't have no health insurance or nothin'."

Micah nodded and watched with interest as the two men moved off to some of the others who were resting on mats laying on the hard ground. Charles touched his arm. "Jethro wants us to go with him." The two stepped over to join Jethro as he finished a conversation with a grubby looking man. "God loves you, Clarence. See you next week."

When they moved forward Jethro tripped over something. He looked down. "What's this?" He jerked out a small flashlight. "A body," he announced in surprise. He ran the light back and forth. Seeing it was an unconscious man he checked his throat for a pulse. Then he shined the light in his eyes and leaned into his face to feel him breathe. "Nothing." He scanned the body again. "Look here." Charles and Micah peered over at the sprawled out man. A needle was hanging in his arm. A strip of rubber was tied tightly just above it. "Overdose." He shined the light into the ashen face. "He's gone. Look, he's just a kid. Poor guy."

Charles and Micah stared at the young man. Micah watched his dad clench his hands in anger. He had seen that before. *His blood pressure must be getting really high.*

Charles shouted, "No. No. This is not God's will."

Jethro reached out to him. "Sometimes these things happen. If we got here earlier we might have helped, but it's too late now."

"No. I don't believe that." He jerked away. "If God can heal my wife, who was almost the same as dead, He can bring this kid back." He looked at Jethro. "Do you know his name?"

"David, I think."

Ken joined them, so Jethro asked him. "Is that right?"

Ken's face showed the despair he felt. He nodded.

Charles squatted down by the corpse. "David, I'm going to ask God to bring you back to life. Do you hear me, David?" He looked up into space. "Death you cannot have this young man. He will live and not die. Do you hear me? Let him go!"

Those in the darkness stirred and moved away from the disruption.

Jethro patted the man's shoulder. "Come on Charles. It's too late. We'll call the authorities."

Charles growled like a crazy man. "Get away from me. This kid will live." He grabbed the boy's jacket collar, and lifted David from the ground as if he were weightless. Looking directly into the lifeless face he shook him as he prayed, tears flowed with his words. The young man's head flopped back and forth. "God please, bring Micah back to life." Let him live and not die. Don't let drugs take my boy."

Micah stood in shock listening to his father's cries for divine intervention. "Dad. Dad. That's not me." Micah reached down trying to bring his dad to his senses.

Charles jerked away. "David, your parents are praying for you. I can hear them. Come on. Fight. Get back into your body. Life is worth living."

Micah was in tears. "Dad. Please don't. I get it. I won't do that stuff anymore. I won't die like he did. And I'll tell my friends what I've seen, and explain way we can't mess around. It's okay. Let's go home."

Charles looked at Micah, as if hearing him for the first time. He loosed one hand from the collar and grabbed Micah around the neck. "Good son, good. Now help me. God wants him alive. This is not his time to die. I know it isn't."

Micah studied his dad's face. He knew that look. The man was fighting a God-given battle and he would not fail. Throwing all common sense aside he joined his father. Charles returned to shaking the jacket collar, and demanding the dead one to come back to life. Micah pleaded with Jesus, asking for him to put breath back into David's body. It was a ridiculous scene the other three men chose not to be a part of. They decided to go and finish their rounds.

When they returned sometime later, David was lying under a dirty blanket. They had taken off his shoes and socks for some reason, and were now praying quietly.

Jethro looked at the exhausted prayers. "Sorry guys. You gave it a good try."

"Hush." Charles whispered. "Don't bring doubt in here. Look." He pointed at David's feet.

Jethro looked at Ken and Everett and shrugged.

Charles saw the response so he pointed toward the bare feet. "Put your light on his feet."

Jethro pulled out his light and shined it down the corpse's legs. The man's feet were turning pink. He flipped the light to his face. Still gray. Then back to his feet. Pink.

Charles spoke in a matter-of-fact tone. "Life comes back into a body through their feet. I studied this stuff while Beth was sick, thinking I might have to bring her back to life."

"Really?" Jethro questioned.

Charles nodded. "Help us pray."

Faith rose in the others. They dropped to their knees around the young man and prayed.

"Look Dad. His fingers are changing color."

Charles held an arm up. Yes, his arm is getting warmer as I hold it. "Come on David. Come back to us. We will help you. God has plans for you here on earth. It is not his will for you to die today. You have a long life to finish."

A gasp was heard. David sat up as air filled his lungs. He looked around and tried to focus on the others.

Charles beamed as he spoke. "David, you overdosed on something and died. We called you back. Your parents are praying for your return. I heard them."

David looked around in disbelief. "I don't remember when I saw my parents last."

"That's okay. Let's see if your body is working. Can you move your feet?"

He wiggled his toes and bent his knees.

"Good job. How about your arms?"

David lifted his right arm and turned his wrist. As he tried to lift his left arm it wouldn't move. He took his right hand and lifted it.

"It's still dead." Micah suggested.

"Seems to be," was Charles's response. "Come on guys. Let's

finish the job." They all laid their hands on his arm and asked God to bring it to life. David began to roll that wrist and bend his elbow.

"Great. Thank you, Father." Jethro shouted.

They helped David to his feet. "Can you walk?"

David carefully took a step, then another, and another. Strength flowed through him like an engine building up steam. Charles grabbed him and they cried together.

"I was being pulled into hell." David sobbed. "I was screaming to get away but they were so strong." His whole body trembled. "It was horrible." He looked like he might throw up. "Horrible." Pausing, he looked around. "Thank you," he gasped. "How did you get me out?"

Charles wrapped his big arm around the kid and Micah asked. "Did you hear us telling you to come back into your body?"

David stared ahead. "I'm not sure about that. But I felt something really strong pulling me. That terrible pit of fire was drawing me with a force I couldn't fight, but another power just as strong wouldn't let me go." He looked at the guys. "It was you. I did hear you calling me to come back into my body. I remember saying, 'Yes. I want to come back.' That's the last thing I remember before I woke up."

"So hell is real?" Micah asked.

The grateful one nodded. "I never want to see it again."

Charles jumped in giving hope. "You don't have to, David. I know your parents are praying for you. We were just agreeing with them. We can take you home. Is that were you want to go?"

"They don't live here. I can't let them see me like this."

Listening to the conversation, Jethro replied. "We know people who can help you. You can stay at the shelter tonight, and tomorrow they'll connect you with them."

Micah moved next to the guy knowing the emotions of feeling lost, hopeless, and unable to get past something that held him more strongly than he could fight. "Jethro, can I go with him and get help?"

Jethro look at Charles. "What do you think?"

The father was so choked up he couldn't speak. He only nodded.

Micah moved over and hugged his dad. "This is what it's all about, isn't it?"

Charles smiled. "I'm so happy you got to see this. And we're only starting to know how to help others."

Micah rubbed his hands together. "Can't wait." He stepped back to David and wrapped his arm around the filthy resurrected kid. "We're going to be champions like Ken and Everett, aren't we David?" The boy gave a crooked smile, but looked like he had no idea what Micah was talking about.

***

Charles watched the others move on. Bewildered, he asked, "Father, how did you do all that in one evening? We experienced raising the dead. It sounds like I might have my son back. Ken, Everett, and, of course, Jethro, are called champions. Life is continually amazing. You really do create 'signs and wonders,'[1] don't you."

---

(1) Mark 16:20

Chapter 11

Pastor Randy entered the sanctuary with his Bible under his arm. He turned slowly as he moved down the aisle toward the front, and then paused to admire the warm wood beams above.

"Cassius are you here?"

A voice roared in the silence. "I'm here, but I haven't seen you lately."

"I know. I've been … distracted."

"Yes, I heard."

"You heard? Are you stuck in here all the time?"

"I have been assigned to assist you with the great and glorious days ahead. If you do not choose to participate, I wait until you change your mind, or I will go when I'm called elsewhere."

"Well, I'm not convinced I want to … as you say … participate. But I do have questions, and I think you might have the answers."

"I will gladly help where I can."

Randy opened the pages of his Bible and held it out. "I was up all night reading. Now, I have more questions than answers. I realized most of my understanding of the Word came from Bible school, where I was taught what other men believed the words meant. Really, I think I've always skimmed over, or dismissed, many of the scriptures I didn't understand."

Cassius revealed himself. He sat floating on air before the young man. "I see."

"Ah, there you are. Thanks for … showing up." He smiled at his own words.

"How nice to see a smile. So what concerns you?" Even with

effort to quiet his voice, Cassius' words echoed as they bounced off the walls.

Randy noticed his controlled words as he continued. "Strange things are taking place, and I have no grid for them. No understanding. But it seems to be God's work."

"Yes," Cassius nodded.

"I read all the scriptures about angels. You've been right here, and I never connected you with the stories in the Bible."

"We were before time."

"Before time." Randy picked up an old bulletin and grabbed a pencil from the back of a pew. "I think I better take some notes." He scribbled around the edges of the print as he spoke. "When was before time?"

Cassius watched closely. "I am pleased you've decided to learn. An unteachable man is useless to the kingdom. There's a large note pad and a pen right over there." He pointed to the piano.

Randy stepped over to retrieve the paper and rewrote his question, then said, "Great. Okay, I'll get back to that question. What can you tell me about angels?"

"Well, that is a big subject." Cassius leaned back as if sitting in a reclining chair, put his feet up, and hands behind his head. "What did you learn when you read?"

Full of new knowledge Randy fired information like bullets. "I noticed you seem to show up just before something awesome happens. Like when Jesus was born. I found you guys all through the book of Revelation. It sounds as if we each have at least one guardian angel." He paused in thought, and then continued. "There are a lot of you. Some are warriors, others are ministering angels. Sometimes you appear as humans." He looked at the relaxed giant. "What kind of angel are you, Cassius?"

"Today I'm a mentor, or teacher, who assists the Holy Spirit in preparing chosen vessels for kingdom purposes. You have all been given the authority to do great exploits. Father is going to do something big on earth at this time. He has heard the prayers of the saints, and sent us, some who have waited all through human history, for this time, to help you.

"Mighty angelic warriors have come to assist those he is empowering to fight the good fight of faith.[1] The evil one will be cast down."[2]

Randy wrote as fast as he was able. "Wow. The evil one will be cast down. Okay." He dotted the last word, and then stared at his companion as he contemplated.

"That brings up another question. I realized if angels are real, maybe demons are too?"

A look of disbelief crossed Cassius's face. As if trying to control himself, he floated up until his head went through the ceiling. After a few seconds he opened his hands wide at his side, and settled back into the room. He sat on air and looked curiously at the man. "Seriously? Are you kidding?"

Randy looked a bit embarrassed. "I just wanted to ask."

"Of course, they're real," he said in an overly controlled voice. "Didn't you hear me when I told you how many of them were living in here before we banished them?"

Randy stared at Cassius while trying to remember their first encounter. "You did say something about that, didn't you?"

The angel shook his head. "Did you read where Satan was cast down with his angels because they rebelled against God?"

Randy paused and looked at his Bible. "Where does it say that?"

"Isaiah 14:12. That really happened, you know. Those lost spirits were doomed so they established their own kingdom. They know Father God is bringing his kingdom to Earth now. They're doing all they can to stop his coming. The evil ones entice, capture, and destroy as many people's lives as they can. That's why you're seeing all the killings and random shootings on the news today."

Cassius paused, took a deep breath, and looked up. "Father, help me explain. Okay, those who fill their minds with murderous thoughts and bloodshed are most likely to be taken over by the evil one's powerful deception. Many young people have yielded to the tormenting voices, and followed their destructive guidance to kill themselves, or other innocent people. Your leaders think they can make laws to fix the problem, but they have no idea how to deal with the spirit world. The church doesn't either. They seem helpless, and yet the answers are all written in your God-given manual. Remember? It says you are to cast out demons."

"We're … supposed to cast them out?"

"Oh, man is your head made of wood?" Cassius slapped his palm over his mouth. Softly, he said, "Sorry. Allow me to continue."

"Pastors don't seem to understand political personalities aren't the chosen leaders of their cities. The pastors are. If you actually stood your ground and fought for the truths found in God's book we could really change things."

Randy plopped onto the altar step. "Oh dear God."

***

Cassius waited patiently through the rest of the pastor's prayer hour. The man seemed to be searching his heart. Was he willing to move forward, find his true calling, and become who he was created to be?

Finally, Randy spoke. "I have much to do."

"Yes. Are there any more questions?"

"Well, I did want to discuss healing but I guess that's possible too."

Cassius spoke in what he probably considered a whisper. "Father's book says, 'He healed all their diseases.' He is using children to prove it to you. There is no sickness in God's kingdom. You have the privilege of living in his kingdom right here, right now. Your mandate is to heal the sick, raise the dead, and cast out demons."

"Where's that scripture?" Randy put his pen on the paper.

"Matthew 10:8. Randal, you're not alone. You have a whole church full of people wanting to follow you. Jethro can help you get started."

"Jethro? The hippy?"

"Yes, he has a passion for God we rarely see."

"Jethro. Okay." He tore his notes from the pad and put it and the pen back on the piano. Without looking up he spoke. "Thank you, Cassius." He took a few steps preparing to leave, and then stopped and looked up at his mentor who sometimes reminded him of a combination of Hercules and a teddy bear. "Do you pray?"

"Continually."

"So you will be praying for me as I face all this change?"

"Yes. It is God's will for you to be successful. We are here to help."

***

Cassius watched the man leave. *I think that went well. It's the first time he asked questions and really listened.*

(1) I Timothy 6:12, (2) John 12:31

Chapter 12

The sun announced a new day in Millbrook. Randy decided to go along with the angel's suggestion and meet with Jethro. At least, that would delay telling Sherry he wanted to quit; at best something good might be ahead.

He hadn't bothered to get acquainted with the hippy, and didn't know where he lived or if he had a phone, so after church Sunday they agreed to meet today at Maggie's Café.

While he jogged into town, he heard a familiar voice in his mind, so he slowed to a walk. He wondered if Cassius joined him, but his mentor had a hardy laugh, and sounded much louder. This voice came as a whisper.

"Look around. I'm giving you this city."

Well, that's definitely not my thought. He turned to see what he was being given. Well-maintained houses lined clean streets where mature trees canopied over blooming flower beds.

"Look again."

He paused to gaze, then scanned the horizon as someone would look through a submarine telescope. More cars than normal were parked in driveways. *Is that because people aren't going to work?* He looked again. Realtor signs, lots of them. Some said foreclosure. *How come I didn't notice this before? These people may be having a hard time. It's possible they will need to leave town. But what can I do to help?*

"Listen to Jethro. He will help you. He is an evangelist who will bring many people to me."

Moving downtown, he observed Main Street's charm with pride. The hundred year old red brick buildings showed loving care. Business owners agreed to make the needed repairs to keep the historical facade of the shops. He liked the way the updates inside had modern comforts mixed with the old pictures people donated of places and events from the past.

What a privilege to be part of this community.

He passed the cleaners, video store, and hobby shop. "When did they close their doors? "All those good people are out of work. Guess I wasn't the only one who didn't use them much," he mumbled.

A newspaper dispenser on the street caught his eye. The headline read, THE NATIONS DEBT PROBLEMS CAN'T BE SOLVED.

That's why we quit taking the paper. They never print any good news.

As he passed Peachtree Street, he spotted Jethro leaning against a light pole. "Morning, Jethro."

"Hi, Pastor. Nice day."

"Yes, I really enjoy summer."

"Me too. It's a lot better than going out to help people in the winter."

Randy looked puzzled. *Who needs help? Oh, guys like Ken and Everett.*

Inside the restaurant, they headed for a booth in the back. Randy hoped to be isolated from the morning rush so they could talk freely. Nostalgia wrapped him as they entered and walked past the same tables and chairs with chrome legs and red Formica tops that were new in the fifties. A row of booths along one side gave evidence of a soda shop, once the hangout of teenage girls wearing poodle skirts and bobbysocks, and guys with slicked back hair and turned up collars.

Sliding into their booth, they scanned the menu. A young waitress in jeans and a Crayon pink T-shirt with the word's *Maggie's Café* on the front, came toward them. Her dark ponytail flipped as she carried a coffeepot.

"Morning, guys. Coffee?" Receiving two nods, she filled their cups with the fragrant, black, steamy liquid. "What can I get ya?"

Jethro glanced up in response to her question. "Oh. Hi, Helen. Good to see ya. This is my pastor. Randy Wright."

"Hello, Pastor. Jethro's told me so much about you. He thinks you're the best."

Randy looked up into beautiful sparkling green eyes and a million dollar smile. "Thanks, Helen. Nice to meet you."

"What'll ya have this morning?"

Randy nodded to Jethro to go first. He ordered the special of eggs, bacon, sausage, hash browns, toast, coffee, and orange juice.

She turned to Randy for his response.

"Yes, the $4.99 deal sounds good. I'll have that, too. Make mine scrambled eggs please. Let's have a basket of breakfast rolls, too." He hoped those might give Jethro's skinny frame a few extra calories. The waitress moved off quickly to place their order.

Jethro added cream and three heaping spoons of sugar to his coffee. Randy watched with interest. *I've heard people with past addictions substitute sugar. Wonder if that's his story.*

After a sip of the syrupy concoction Jethro set it down slowly. "Helen's doing really good. She used to work the streets. We talked with her a lot, and she got saved. Maggie gave her this job, and she was able to get her little boy back. They live in the apartment upstairs."

Surprised, Randy responded. "I would never have guessed. She looks like she's got it all together. Does she go to church anywhere?"

"Can't. She works Sunday. It's one of their busiest days. But she comes to our Bible study Tuesday nights."

"Really?" The pastor's interest piqued.

"Yep. There's been so many who've met Jesus, we needed a place to meet. Maggie lets us come here after it closes at eight. There's thirty-five or forty of us now."

"Interesting." Randy leaned forward. "Who leads it?"

"Well, I have to. I've been saved the longest. And I'm the only one who goes to church. Most churches don't want us. I teach them what you preach on Sunday."

Randy laughed, feeling proud of the thought his messages were being repeated. "And what did you teach the week I didn't preach and everyone cried?"

"I taught them how to get quiet before God and repent and cry. It was just as good the second time, but even more happened that night. A bunch of other people wandered in off the street and joined us. They cried and repented, too. Boy, preach'n and teach'n is really easy, ain't it?"

Randy hadn't found that to be true. However, he wasn't just repeating what someone else already prepared. The food arrived, he blessed it, and Jethro dug in. For the first time the pastor really looked at the man sitting across from him. He gazed through the scruffy beard and long unkempt hair. He tried to see past the skinny frail looking body, the rough skin, and crooked teeth.

Lifting his fork he said, "Tell me about yourself, Jethro. Where do you work?"

"I have a job sometimes. Ya know, Pastor, I got in trouble when I was young. I was with a bunch of guys. We robbed a jewelry store. It was so stupid." He shoved a fork full of hash browns through his beard, chomped twice, and swallowed. "I had this girl I wanted to give a gift. Not a wedding ring or nothin'. Just something to impress her. So we robbed the store, and I got her a sparkly necklace. Didn't know it was worth over five thousand dollars. I just thought it was pretty. She liked it, too. Didn't take long for the cops to get wind of it." He took a swig of coffee and leaned back. "I landed in jail. Did my time. Now I've got a record. Not easy to get work when you're a convicted felon, but Mr. Shipley, you know from church?"

Randy nodded as he chewed his food, hoping the *but* meant a turn for better.

"He hires me to work at his garden store. I plant trees and do a lot of the heavy lifting for him. He also tells me if someone calls for lawn mowing or other yard work. I don't need much money. I stay at the shelter, so when I work I pay a few dollars a night, and help out any way I can. Lots of needs there.

"I eat at the food kitchens. Not so much cause I want to eat, but those places are where the people who are hurting and need to hear that God loves them are, ya know?"

The pastor nodded. "So it sounds like you're doing well personally."

"Yeah, I'm great." He wiped his mouth and set his napkin beside his plate. "I'm right where God wants me. If I had a better job I couldn't stay up all night to help the homeless people." Jethro filled his mouth again.

"Did you finish school?"

He choked down the bite. "Finished junior college. Pretty much made a mess of that. Didn't get saved til I was in jail. I'm so thankful for the people who did what the Bible says, and came to prison to tell me about Jesus's love. I'm saved cause of one of them."

"That's great." Randy paused as he remembered the words he heard earlier. He took a sip of coffee, and then asked. "What do you see as a need in our city? What would you do if you had resources to make changes?"

Jethro's eyes lit up. "Oh, don't get me started." He leaned back as he wiped his mouth again, then contemplated before he began. "I don't know if you know this, but we've got a serious drug problem here. I'd love to see people set free from that monster. It sucks the life out of 'em. Their gifts and talents are goin' to waste cause somethin' besides God is their master." He paused, looked at the ceiling, then brightened as he leaned forward and grabbed a roll.

"I guess that would have to start with prayer."

"Yes." Randy pulled out his phone and typed a note about drug problems under, "Prayer Requests" for the ladies. "I'll get the prayer group going on that."

"Great." Jethro was just getting wound up. The roll headed for his stomach as he moved closer to keep what he said private. "Because of drugs and other stuff a lot of women solicit. Don't misunderstand. Ya see, they're like my sisters. It hurts to see them live such dangerous lives, plus it darkens their souls. A lot of them leave their kids home by themselves while they try to make some money."

Randy couldn't imagine such a problem in the community. But really, he knew it went on everywhere. "Do you have a solution?"

Jethro pushed back and grinned. "I have a dream. The old Grand Hotel sits empty five blocks from here. The city owns it." He held both palms face-up in front of his chest. "What do they need it for?"

He waited for the pastor to answer, and then continued. "If they'd give it to us, we could make the rooms homes for women and their kids. Then they could be off the streets at night. Jobs are hard to find right now. Wouldn't it be great if the gals were trained to have good jobs that don't put them in such danger? With that, and knowing God's love, they could have better lives.

"Think what their kids know and have seen. God can't be happy we've ignored them."

The inner Voice spoke again. **"I'm giving you this city."**

Randy lost his appetite. *I don't really want it, Lord.* He pushed his plate back, picked up his spoon, and stirred his coffee even though he hadn't added anything to the cup. "Interesting. What else?"

"Ya know, Pastor, you're really the leader of the city, you and the other godly pastors in town. The government isn't supposed to fix all this stuff. God has given his people the wisdom and power to do what needs to be done."

Randy remembered pushing those same words away before. His head started to pound. *God must be stretching my brain. It hurts. I gotta get out of here.* He glanced at his phone. "Oh, good grief. The time has sure flown. Jethro, you've given me a lot to think about. I want to be able to help."

The inner Voice struck again. "**Do you really?**"

"Jethro, God told me you're an evangelist. From what I've seen and heard you're doing a great job. Would you allow me to go with you sometime?"

What just came out of my mouth? I don't want to go out there.

"Pastor that would be great. How about Friday night?"

Randy grinned in spite of his fear. "Okay, let's do it. I'll meet you in front of the Grand Hotel. I'd like to look at it up close. What time? Nine?"

"Nine's good," Jethro agreed.

As Randy paid the check, Jethro started gathering the rolls from the basket into a napkin.

The pastor spoke quietly "Wait a minute." He glanced toward Helen and she looked over. "Do you have a plastic bag?"

She noticed what was happening and quickly brought a bag to the table. Jethro loaded it with the sweet rolls, then reached over and added the buttered toast they hadn't touched.

"People under the bridge at the train yards will love these. Thanks for breakfast, Pastor."

They slid out of the booth. Jethro stood a good five inches taller than Randy but the pastor reached up and patted his slim, yet muscular, shoulder. "Thanks for being you, guy. You're really something."

Jethro gave a crooked smile that revealed a once broken uneven nose. "See you Friday night."

They moved out of the café and said good-bye. Jethro headed south, probably to deliver breakfast to those hiding for whatever reason.

Randy looked around the area again as he walked north, and turned the corner to go up the hill to work.

Chapter 13

Friday night Randy parked at the police station. *The car should be safe here. I wonder if Captain Dennison is working. I'll check.*

Inside, he spotted the balding, somewhat overweight, uniformed man talking with another officer. The Captain nodded at Randy, said a few more words to his co-worker, and then headed over to him.

"Hi Pastor, what are you doing here?"

Randy took a breath before he smiled. "Hello, Dean. I'm going out on the streets with one of the guys from my church. I hope it's okay to leave my car in your parking lot."

Concern crossed the Captain's face. He eyed Randy up and down, perhaps, checking his appearance. "Sure, that's fine, but you be careful out there. We've got a couple of gangs in town, and they're lookin' for trouble." He paused and shook his head. "Some kids have no conscience. They'll shoot you just for sport. We hear the gangs want to kill each other off. But they're not very smart. So far they haven't done any harm. Who are you going with?"

"Jethro." He realized he didn't know the hippy's last name.

"Oh, good. He knows how to avoid trouble. Got a cellphone?"

Randy nodded.

The Captain took a solid stance with his legs apart and hand on his weapon as if ready to assist. "Give us a call if you see any trouble."

"Thanks. I appreciate what you guys do."

They shook hands, and Randy headed out the door. He walked to the old Grand Hotel on the corner of the next block. The architecture of the building, where people once came for the healing waters of the local springs, was still regal. *No wonder there's been talk of restoring this building as a museum. It's beautiful. If God is giving me this town, I wonder if it might really be possible to use this place to help people.*

"Hey, Pastor." Jethro shouted as he approached with Ken and Everett right behind him. "Let's go heal some bodies." Though grubby, the guys looked well rested, and wired for excitement.

Pushing past the fear that surged through him when Jethro mentioned healing people, Randy responded. "Hi, guys. This building is something special, isn't it?"

Jethro nodded. "Can't you just see it, Pastor? When it was new it was a place for people who needed to heal their bodies. Could we make it a place to heal souls, too?"

"Great idea, Jethro."

Ken and Everett agreed.

Hoping to look like he fit in, Randy wore his favorite old jeans with the frayed hems and worn knees. He decided his scruffy hiking boots were a good idea, and he put his lightweight jacket on over a tee-shirt. In one pocket he carried his small Bible. His cellphone rested in the other.

The group turned and marched through the streets like soldiers moving into a territory where they planned to plant a victory flag. Several times he heard one of the guys behind him whisper the name "Jesus" as if in prayer.

Randy noticed the area seemed to get darker the further they walked. *How can that be? Oh, there's a bunch of streetlights out. No.* He realized what he felt was more than missing lights. *It feels like darkness is covering everything like thick humidity would.*

Jethro scanned the area ahead as they walked across Seventh Street. "Not many out yet. We'll come back here later. The john's don't show up till after their families go to bed. Pastor, if I told you who some of the guys are that pick up the girls you would probably explode."

The thought made Randy cringe. *Oh, Lord, I don't want to know.*

The ever-present voice responded. **"Get your head out of the sand, Randal. It's time to grow up."**

He took a deep breath.

Jethro looked over at him. "Ya know Charles Morgan from church, Pastor?"

"Sure."

"Well, he's really excited because God healed his wife, so he has been going with us lately. Last week while he and his son, Micah where along we found a dead guy."

Randy stopped and stared at him in disbelief and fear. Jethro and the other guys stopped, too. "The needle was still hangin' in his arm. Now you know Charles, he's a big guy."

Everyone agreed. Ken and Everett listened as if hearing the story for the first time.

"When he saw the kid layin' there like that. I don't know. Something happened to the man. He grabbed the dead body by the collar and demanded the kid to come back to life."

Jethro shook his head as if he didn't even believe what he was telling. "It was weird. His son jumped in. They talked to the body like it was a liv'n person. Us guys went on to help some others. When we got back the dead guy's toes had turned pink. I saw them. He was one-hundred percent dead, no pulse or nothin', and his toes turned pink."

Ken and Everett nodded confirming the truth of the story.

Jethro continued. "So the rest of us joined them in thank'n God that it's his will for the dead to be raised to life. As we praised God, pink moved up his legs, then his arms, and into his face."

Everyone stood captivated as Jethro looked into each pair of eyes, like he was ready to tell the end of a ghost story. "The guy came too, sucked in a big gulp of air, and opened his eyes. He didn't say nothin'. Just looked around like'n he was in shock. He tried to move his arms. The left one was like paralyzed, but all his other parts seemed okay."

Randy realized he was standing in the middle of a Raising the Dead 101 class, so he listened carefully as Jethro finished. He had an uncomfortable feeling he might need the lesson.

"We kept thank'n God, and then the guy joined us. Sure enough, his other arm started work'n too. We got him to his feet, and he walked around. I never saw nothin' like it before.

"Seems he got a clear understandin' of hell when he was dead, too. He was real quick to want ta get his life right with God. Charles took him ta Westbury where they have a good rehab center for drug addicts. I heard he's doing real good."

Randy let out the breath he was holding. "Wow."

"Yep, it was fun." The other guys agreed and took off walking again. They seemed excited to see what God would do next.

A chill ran down Randy's spine and his hands began to sweat. *Oh, dear God, what am I doing here?*

As they approached the area where they would go under the bridge, Jethro paused and leaned close to prepare his sidekick in the ways of another world. Urgently, he spat out instructions.

"Okay, this ain't no place to socialize, but trust me there's souls here ready to be free." As if giving the newbie the lay of the land, he continued. "These people live in cardboard boxes. Some are out in the open. Those who are lucky might have a tent. Others are the mentally ill who fell through the cracks when the mental hospital closed. Several are homeless vets. There's even a college professor gone bad. God wants to redeem them. Just stick close. They all know me."

Randy listened carefully. Understanding he was totally out of his element, he didn't want to miss a word. They entered to the stench of rotting garbage, urine, and dirty oil. Randy gagged. Remembering how to survive baby diapers, he breathed through his mouth. People moved about quietly, as shadows wandered in aimless patterns across the graffiti on the walls. Dim flickering light came from a barrel that crackled from wood burning. A few people stood around its warmth but most stayed to themselves.

Randy hadn't noticed Jethro's backpack before. He saw the other guys carried them, too. Jethro introduced a woman named Cat, he guessed for Catherine. After she greeted the group, she and Jethro stepped away for a little powwow. When he returned, he was ready to move.

"Okay, let's go. Lots to do tonight." He led them to the first dirty alcove under the bridge. A pitiful man lay on a raggedy, dirty sleeping bag. "Randy, this is Marshal. He was a sergeant in Viet Nam. He's an American hero."

Randy appreciated Jethro not calling him pastor as he usually did. "Marshal, I'm honored to meet you. Thanks for your service. Is there something we can do for you?"

"Hmm." The man frowned and grunted, "Not unless you can get this shrapnel out of me. I can't stand the pain. It's gotten a lot worse."

Randy responded, "I'm sorry to hear that. The doctors didn't remove it?"

"They said it would kill me if they tried to get it all. I might as well be dead. This ain't livin.'"

I've already messed up. This is impossible. Doctors couldn't even help him.

Ken started bouncing from one foot to the other. "Well, can we pray for ya? If Jesus can raise the dead, he can certainly remove shrapnel."

"Whatever." Marshal scrunched into his bag.

Jethro spoke above the noise of the cars passing overhead. "Randy, you pray."

"Okay." He knelt and looked at the pitiful shadow of a man. Once a mighty warrior, he was fallen in the streets of his city. Randy's heart felt crushed to think of all the gifts and talents God instilled in the man's life that now lay wasted. Words began to come without effort.

"Marshal, God loves you. He never wanted you to struggle

with these issues. He is so sorry for your injury. We have come tonight to pray for you to be healed."

Heaven seemed to open over Randy. He felt a flood of peace wash over him as he heard words in his heart. "**Randall, I have heard Marshal's prayers. I will heal him through your hands.**"

A surge of excitement flashed through Randy. "In Jesus name, be healed."

Waiting for Marshal's response, Randy pondered the words he just heard.

Jethro moved forward and bent down." Come on, man. See if God healed you. What couldn't you do before?"

Marshal slowly turned over and sat up. "I can't use my legs. The shrapnel's near my spine."

Jethro nodded. "Well, try doing something you couldn't do before."

Marshal wrapped his arm around his leg to lift it, and then looked surprised as he realized the leg was strong enough to raise itself without help. He lifted the other leg and began to squirm and stretch his spine. "Everything's working." A big smile spread across his face. "The pain's gone. Totally gone."

He looked at Randy, and with awe in his voice he whispered. "I'm free." He leaned his stinky body against the pastor and cried into his shoulder. Randy joined him with his own tears of joy, gratitude, and more love for a stranger than he ever felt before.

"Now this is cool. I'll tell Cat." Jethro took off to give her the good news.

When the two returned Marshal was talking. "As a kid I knew Jesus, but after I got hurt, life seemed hopeless. My whole future was wiped out. I prayed and prayed, but decided I couldn't count on God for help."

"Oh, yes you can." Jethro grabbed the man and gave him a bear hug. Then he and Cat explained to Marshal they would like to take him to a shelter to sleep and then help him get a new start.

Marshal agreed to go with them, and asked if he could join

their little band of men as they continued through the area. Pleased to have him, they all moved on together. Marshal walked with a grin of his face as wide as a Cheshire cat's smile.

The group moved through each filthy alcove handing out things from their backpacks. They started with coupons. Everett explained, "They're McDonald's gift certificates. We never give them money."

Some of the people had asked for toiletries. There were small bags filled with the needs Cat requested for others. Everyone got a little treat to remind them they were special.

Randy watched as Everett presented a red rose to Ms. Brown, a little lady with stringy hair, wearing layers of soiled clothing. The pastor's heart melted as he watched the woman standing in dim light, who looked old enough to be Everett's grandmother, blush and smile shyly as a young girl would.

"What's going on there?" Randy inquired.

Everyone glanced over to see what he was asking about. Ken answered, "She's the woman who took care of him when he was down here all strung out. She's been kinda like a mother to him."

They moved quickly through the grounds, as they tried to avoid oil slicks, trash, and disgusting puddles of … who knew what. At least a hundred people hid in the ugly damp environment. Jethro paused when he noticed his companion was missing. He walked back to check on him. Compassion held Randy captive as he asked, "Aren't we going to pray for all of them?"

Jethro explained, "We only do what we see the Father doing. Cat's our eyes. She knows who needs his touch the most tonight. Pastor, we're totally at the mercy of the Holy Spirit. We can only follow his lead or we waste too much time."

In awe, Randy considered Jethro's words. "Wow." *That was profound. I need to learn that lesson.*

Randy moved quickly to keep up. As they continued, Jethro introduced him to many of the people. The Holy Spirit seemed to engrave their names and faces into the man's heart. He would always pray for them. Every one of them would be added to the prayer list for the ladies at church.

Next thing he knew, they were out of the stench and on the streets again. They all headed for Seventh Street with Marshal, who chattered continually about God's amazing love.

Chapter 14

Fear grabbed Randy as they passed Thirteenth Avenue. He looked both ways to see what was wrong.

"Keep moving, Pastor. We don't wanna be part of what goes on here at night."

He quickened his steps to match Jethro's stride. They took Marshal to the shelter, introduced him to the workers, and made sure he was comfortable. Before leaving, Jethro also assured the man he would be back to see him the next day. Randy was impressed by the efficiency and dedication of the people who helped them. Hope stirred as he realized others were already at work meeting the needs of people in their community. The little group of warriors said their good-byes and left for the streets again.

When they turned the corner to walk down Seventh Street, Randy noticed at least twenty women standing along the sidewalks. He was enticed by the pairs of long legs that ran from tall platform heels to the edge of some of their short skirts or shorts. Their colorful getups and glittering additions were the only bright spot in the area because the shops were closed and dark.

As the guys moved forward, Randy recognized one of the young women. He reached out and grabbed Jethro's arm. Shocked he asked, "Is that Iris Barnes? Doctor Barnes daughter?"

Jethro squinted to see who he was asking about. "Yep. That crazy girl. Her dad gave her everything, and she comes down here to see what trouble she can get into."

A black Jaguar swung to the curb next to her. While the engine purred, Randy saw the man who leaned across the seat to open the door for her. She smiled and jumped in. Randy stared in disbelief. "Was that Bill Grant, the city treasurer?"

"The one and only."

As the car roared away Randy looked at Jethro. "He's old enough to be her grandfather."

Jethro shrugged, then walked over and leaned against a building. Randy assumed it was time for more strategy so he joined him.

"Look at this, Pastor. All those women are selling their souls for money, and this is just a few of them. I know every one of their stories. Most would come off the streets if they had some help to find a better life. They need to know how much God loves them."

He nodded his head toward the other side of the street. "Juliet, over there, has two little kids sleeping by themselves in their apartment. She'll lose them if social services finds out. She wants to be a good mom. Her kids deserve better."

Jethro dropped his head and motioned slightly. "Karen, that classy looking tall woman is a man."

Randy's heart sank as Karen quickly jumped into someone's car, and they zoomed away.

Jethro nodded again to point out another without being obvious. "Dezerea was fourteen when her dad kicked her out cause she got pregnant. She dropped out of school and has supported herself and her kid this way the last couple of years. Candy, the girl with her, was raped by her dad. She came to Millbrook when she ran away from home."

The man Randy called a hippy shifted to look at his companion. "But it's not just the girls. My heart hurts for the guys. They're in bondage, too. That lust is going to destroy them and their families."

Questions fired through Randy's mind. "Can't the police do something?"

"They come by and hang around sometimes. They know all the girls by name, of course. Things slow down while they're here but nothin' changes. I know this goes on in most towns, but surely

90

God has something better. He loves these people."

Randy heard The Voice again, **"This is the city I have given to you."**

Dear God, what can I do?

Another car pulled to the curb near several women. Ken poked Everett, "There's Lewis, let's go talk to him."

The men rushed over and started a conversation with the guy, who everyone knew, had other plans. "Hey Lewis, good to see you. How ya doin? Nancy and the kids good? Isn't Ricky in the baseball league? …"

An attractive woman in a very short skirt, fishnet stockings, and a blouse with a plunging neckline started walking toward Randy and Jethro. The pastor stared at the woven black threads that wrapped her legs. *Those are different. I like the way they make her legs look.*

***

An alarm in heaven sounded. The host of angels traveling with Randy listened. Their orders were announced by the leader, "Stand Back." All they could do was watch as the seductive spirits, that controlled the woman on the streets, enticed him.

***

Marcy smiled and walked so close to Jethro, he backed up. "Hello, Jethro," she cooed. Tonight's your night with me." She put her arm through his. "Shall we go?"

"Oh, Marcy, you know I never carry money. You don't want me."

"Sure I do, I'll give you credit."

Randy watched the seductive ritual with interest. He was aroused by the idea, and wondered how Jethro resisted her so easily.

"Oh, gotta go." The young woman ran as fast as her six inch

heels would carry her and jumped into a waiting car.

Leaving Ken and Everett with Lewis, the two men walked on slowly, watching for opportunities to speak to others. An older woman stepped forward to greet Jethro.

"Well, Jethro, long time no see." As she approached it became obvious there was nothing appealing about her. She wore thick makeup and bulged out of her under-sized dress. The forty-something woman must have had some hard years. Approaching Jethro, she moved close to his ear.

"Don't my girls appeal to you? Maybe you'd prefer a master. I can do things for you that are worth dying for."

As if noticing Randy's shocked look, she moved even closer to Jethro and rubbed up against him. "I can …" She spoke words Randy had never heard before, but he felt the draw. She described a type of adventure he didn't know, and he wanted what she offered. He wanted the ecstasy of a night with a woman that could physically rapture a man.

Jethro shook his head and moved off to check on Ken and Everett. The woman looked over at Randy. She smiled like a sweet school girl. Coy words flowed like liquid fire from her lips. "Oh, I see you're interested. Well, come on, boy, I'll make you the man you always wanted to be."

Randy felt frozen to the ground. He couldn't move or think. All he knew was he wanted to go with her. He didn't care how old she was, or that her life revealed a crust of harshness. He wanted what she offered, and he did have money in his pocket.

***

The angels watching at a distance became agitated. Finally, their leader gave the signal. Several surged toward Jethro and gave him a push toward Randy.

***

Jethro looked back and rushed over. "Oh, Mia, leave the guy alone. Come on, Pastor. Let's go." Jethro gripped Randy's arm and led him away from Seventh Street. "I'm sorry, Pastor. I shouldn't have let you get into that situation. There's a powerful spirit of lust and seduction in the area."

Randy felt dazed, as if waking after being knocked out. He spotted a bench in front of a shop and staggered over to sit down.

Jethro joined him. "You okay?"

The pastor placed his elbows on his knees and put his face in his hands. After a few minutes he looked over. "Jethro, I really wanted that woman. I would have gone with her if you hadn't stopped me. I've never felt such a pull to do something I knew to be totally wrong. It was like a magnet drawing me and I had no resistance."

He bowed his head again. "Oh, God, I'm so sorry."

"Jethro," he continued. "She wasn't even pretty. I didn't think about Sherry and the girls one time. I just wanted what she offered. I'm a total failure."

Jethro leaned back as he considered what to say to the man he admired. After some time, he broke the silence. "I think maybe God wanted you to feel the power of lust and deception that makes men fall. He created us with our sex drive and the desire for adventure. But the enemy takes what God meant for good, and deceives us with things that will never really satisfy. Once welcomed, its addictive nature doesn't let go easily. A spirit of lust and seduction owns that section of town. It's fed nightly, so it grows."

Randy was scrunched down on the bench like a wet noodle that missed the spaghetti sauce. "How do you do it, Jethro? How do you go there night after night and not give in?"

"It's a strong spirit all right. I know that personally. But God wants men free. And that's the real way to get those women off the street. Some things only change through fasting and prayer,[1] so I only eat breakfast and fast the rest of the day. I don't know how it works, but prayer and not eatin' gives me the strength to stand up to women coming on to me. Plus, knowin' you're dealing with demons[2], not women, opens your eyes."

Jethro put his hand on Randy's shoulder. "We're the ones who can break the stronghold."

He looked into Randy's face. "I don't think you saw what happened when Ken and Everett went over and talked to Lewis. They reminded him of his wife and kids, and the loss he would face. They sorta brought him to his senses, cause a seducing spirit[3] had him wrapped like a fly in a spider web. I guess they were breaking the chains that bound him. You probably didn't see him drive off after they talked with him."

Still feeling deflated and defeated, Randy responded. "I didn't know I was so vulnerable."

Looking at him, Jethro replied, "Really? I've never known a man your age that hasn't been seduced by a woman before."

"I've always had Sherry with me. When I watched guys get involved with other women, it looked like a lot of trouble to me. Good grief. When I've counseled men messed up with lust and affairs I didn't do a very good job helping them. I didn't get it."

Jethro sat up looking a little more encouraged. "Maybe you'll be a better counselor now that you understand the pull of lust."

Randy sighed in agreement. "That's for sure."

Jethro stood. "I'm sorry I brought you down here. I wasn't thinkin' about what you'd be facin'. Guess I got used to it. I should've warned ya ta fast and pray before we went. I better remember that. Don't want teenagers vulnerable when they go with me. Ready to go home now?"

Randy nodded, relieved to be finished. With new compassion and respect for Jethro he replied. "I guess we both learned something tonight."

"Always do." Jethro smacked his pastor on the knee as he got up. "I better get back and check on Ken and Everett."

"Thank you Jethro, for everything."

"Thank you, Pastor. You're the best." Jethro's long legs carried him back into the spiritual war zone.

***

After midnight, Randy walked through his quiet home and looked in on his children. He picked up Olivia's doll from the floor and placed it in her arms. In his bedroom, he paused to admire his wife sleeping contentedly. He moved to the shower in hopes of washing off the stench of the evening. Finally in bed, he thanked God for the peace and quiet of his sanctuary. Exhausted, he fell asleep.

Without disturbing him, angels fill the room.[4]

(1) Matthew 17:21, (2) James 1:14-15, (3) I Timothy 4:1, (4) Psalm 34:7

Chapter 15

Exhausted from the stress of his experiences on the streets, and his weekend responsibilities, Randy walked through the sanctuary, and dropped to his knees at the altar. Before, this place was where he dumped all his problems, and brought the people's needs to God. Now, with the nagging intruder, he dreaded coming. He paused and listened to the silence. *Ah, no one is here to bother me. That sounds crazy. Who would believe some angel is the source of my frustrations?*

A voice that sounded delighted about something, roared, "Good morning, Pastor. Isn't it a wonderful day to be living in God's kingdom?"

The man's arrogance, mixed with feelings of intimidation warred within. *Oh, no, not this morning.* He sighed, "Hello, Cassius. What do you mean by living in God's kingdom?"

"Don't you know? We are here together. Isn't that amazing? You prayed for his kingdom to come and it has."

"Really?" Randy responded with no real interest. Oh, he was curious but felt compelled to control the situation as much as possible.

"Yes, indeed!"

"I don't get it." The pastor turned and sat on an altar step.

Cassius was standing on the floor. His body filled the area like a wall. He folded his arms across his chest and nodded his head as he spoke to confirm the truth of his words. "The kingdom of God is a spirit world where God's manifest presence dwells. God's people prayed until the prayer bowls[1] in heaven are full. He promised he would answer. They asked for the Almighty One's kingdom to come to earth as it is in heaven.[2] He answered. Here we are."

"Then why are things such a mess? I could spend all day praying for the needs."

The joyous voice continued. "True. Well, for one thing, when the people of God focus on their troubles instead of God's solutions, they empower the enemy. They give him open doors to continue his destructive ways. If they would focus on the truth of who God really is, and what his plans are, the enemy would scatter.[3] Some people are learning that skill or discipline. I'm not sure which. It comes naturally to us."

"Pastor," Cassius's voice sounded as gentle as the glorious one could probably control it. "These are the days of God's grand shift."

"Grand shift? What's that?"

The giant looked puzzled. "You know."

"No. I don't."

Cassius puffed up until his head went through the roof. He shouted. "It's all in your manual."

Randy tried not to show insecure feelings. He shouted, "I've never read 'God's grand shift' in my Bible."

"Of course you have. God's Word explained how to handle every situation with the evil ones. The Saints respond by using their God-given authority to declare the truth of his Word. The light of truth drives out lies and darkness which defeats the enemy. Heaven and earth shift. Simple."

"Well, it feels more like the enemy does stuff, we pray, and nothing changes."

"That's why these days are so grand. The Father allowed the enemy to test people to see if they would love and follow him no matter how hard things got. His people prayed. The time has come for the fulfillment of all things. He is bringing the glory of his kingdom to earth. Oh, the tormentors will still throw fits. They see the movement of God's heavenly host as they come forth, so evil will try to attack even more. But God's love and glory is too powerful. Watch. Just watch and see. Open your eyes, Randal. Look past all those prayer requests. See the answers." Cassius's voice trailed off as he vanished. "And don't forget to thank him."[3]

Randy felt helpless. He tossed the papers with the prayer requests across the altar. "Lord, I'm so tired. I can't do this anymore. I can't quit, and I can't go on. I don't have the courage to tell Sherry what I'm feeling. I give up."

As if a vise loosened off his mind, the tormenting pressure lifted. "Is that what you want? You want me to give up?"

The words of an old song ran through his mind. *I surrender all. I surrender all. All to Thee my precious Savior, I surrender all.*

"I surrender," he whispered.

The reality of God's presence rested on him. Heaven's glory caused a groan to come from someplace deep inside him. The sound was so powerful it became more like a lion's roar as it echoed through the hollow sanctuary. He felt as though the very depth of his soul was being extracted. Randy collapsed onto the floor in exhaustion. "Father, I do surrender," was all he had strength to utter.

In the silence, angles hovered over his emotionally emaciated body. As he lay there, feeling flat as a pancake, something, perhaps the Breath of Life,[4] filled all the emptiness inside him, and Love's warm coziness covered him like a blanket.

While quiet, the feeling of a pleasant breeze moved around him. Soon, it became a powerful whirlwind of delight. He felt he might burst with joy. He began to laugh. And laugh. And roll on the floor. And laugh.

He wasn't aware invisible companions spontaneously joined his laughter.

***

Dan Watson ducked his head as he stepped through the doorframe of the church's office. Glenda looked up, and couldn't help but notice the handsome forty-something man's great build and dark wavy hair. To her, he resembled a Greek god.

"Hi, Dan. Nice to see you." *Well, it is nice to see him. He looks like a beautiful sculpture. Good job, God.*

"And you, Glenda. You bring a needed radiance to this room. Don't be bored with your job here. It will be much more challenging shortly."

She notice he looked embarrassed after saying those words. "Okay," she responded curiously. "How's your family. I heard about Casey praying for Mrs. Morgan. She's only four, isn't she?"

"Yes. They're good. Carl will be a freshman this year. Doesn't seem possible. Is there any chance I could see Randy?"

"He is here. Let me see if he's free. Oh, he's on the phone. Can you wait?"

"Sure. I'll go to the kitchen and get coffee. Want some?"

"No thanks." Embarrassed by her feelings, she settled back in her chair. *No, that wasn't lust. His whole countenance just kind of takes my breath away. He said I brought radiance to the room. What a line.* She rehearsed his words again, wanting to believe they were true.

When Dan returned with two cups of coffee, Glenda noticed the light for pastor's phone was off. She walked over and knocked on his office door, then stuck her head in. "Dan Watson is here. He'd like to meet with you. Do you have time?"

"Sure." Randy sprang up and came out to greet him. "Dan, good to see you. How are things going?" He noticed Dan looked wearier than his normal vibrant self. Maybe he hadn't been sleeping well.

"I'm okay." He held out a cup. "Are you ready for afternoon coffee?"

"Sure, come on in." Randy accepted the cup, and the six foot four man followed him into his office. The pastor settled in the chair behind his desk. Dan chose one of the wingback guest chairs across from him.

"How's business, Dan?"

"Good, really good." He paused as if questioning how to proceed. "You know, I don't usually talk about business, but I consider you a trusted friend." He took a sip of coffee and set it aside. "I'm just going to tell it like it is."

Randy was pleased he didn't feel intimidated by the man's success anymore, and realized the wonderful experience while in prayer must have freed him from his insecurities. He felt happy to think someone like Dan considered him a friend. "Of course."

"You know, I bought that first little company. When it took off, we bought another. We set up Gayle's home decorating business. She's doing great. Now, I just closed on my eighth company. It's ridiculous. I don't know how it happened. The last two places called me, asking if I'd buy them out. They said they knew I could make their businesses thrive. Randy, I just do what I know."

Randy leaned back in his chair and laughed. "I know you do, Dan. God has given you almost supernatural skills in business. And look at how many jobs you've created to help get people back to work."

Dan was quiet for a moment. "I guess that's true. They're really good workers, too. I don't even need to show up. So far they run the companies for me."

"So how can I help you?"

Dan moved to the edge of his chair. "Well, something's been happening and I'm concerned. I've been having dreams that are so real I think I could video them if I were awake. They're disturbing dreams. I don't know what to do. Do you know about this kind of thing?"

Randy stared at the man he knew to be successful in every way. *Dreams. Don't know about dreams. I can talk to you about giant angels. But dreams ... nope. Don't know much about that.* "Have you talked to Gayle about them? She has a lot of wisdom."

"No, I'm not ready to share this with her."

"Okay. Do you want to tell me about them?"

"Yes. I need to discuss this with somebody so I can try to make sense of it all. Several times while I'm dreaming, it seems as if light fills the room, and someone is standing in front of me. The voice I hear is the same as I know the Holy Spirit's voice to be. I'm not sure who the ... vision is." He paused as if hoping to be understood.

Randy responded. "What does he say?"

"That's the part that's eating at me. He tells me I've been called to be a prophet to the nations. What in the world is that? All I know about prophets is they were killed in the Old Testament if their words didn't come true. Is this guy some spirit lost in a time warp?"

Randy quickly rolled his chair from behind his desk and moved over close to Dan. "Let's talk." Dan stared at his pastor while he told of visits with the giant angel. He finished by saying, "I've been told we're moving into the time God revealed to Daniel, when he told him to seal the message for a later day.[5] Everything around us is in upheaval because God is ready to rearrange, and restore the earth, and manifest his kingdom here.

"So," he paused looking for words, "Dan, I don't know any more about being a prophet today than you do. But I do understand God is up to something exciting, and we don't want to miss it. The only thing I can offer you is that Barbara Claymore talks to me regularly about what the prophets are saying. She might be helpful. Cassius, my giant friend, says I'm supposed to help her get some training because she's one of God's chosen prophets for the days ahead."

As if the words pumped oxygen into Dan's lungs, he let out a big sigh. "Thank you Randy. That's a big help. I'll talk to her, and I'll go on-line to see what's available there on the subject."

"Good, think about this. If God is calling you to the nations, he has already set you up with those businesses and good employees so you're free to do whatever he has for you. God knows you want to serve him. He is ready to promote you to a new thing, and it will probably be more exciting than anything you could imagine. And look at Gayle. She's right there with you, fully mature spiritually. Carl will be in high school this year, and Caroline's almost grown. The only one still small is Casey, and who knows what God has planned for her. All we need to do is try to understand what he has for us and then do our part."

Dan smiled for the first time.

Randy laughed. "That's sure a lot easier to say than do. Dan, we need each other. I don't really have anyone else I can share these things freely with either. I've always tried to hide the fact I feel totally inadequate for my job. Now, I'm starting to realize God likes me that way. Then he gets the praise when good things happen. Can we banter this stuff around together again?"

"That's a great idea. I appreciate you as my spiritual leader, and value your input while I figure this all out. I wonder if it would be possible to talk to the guy in my dreams when he comes."

"I'm not sure you're dreaming, Dan. Jesus, or one of his ministering angels, may really be there. The invisible kingdom is becoming visible. Sure, you certainly can talk to him."

"All right. Thanks for your time, Randy. You've been a big help Let's see where this is headed." He rose from his chair

"My pleasure, Dan. Oh, one more thing. Tell your wife what's happening. You need to be united in this."

Dan nodded and headed out the door.

Smiling, Randy leaned back in his chair. "Thank you, Lord for preparing me for Dan's visit earlier this morning. Your touch freed me so I didn't feel intimidated by him. I love to counsel people with your help. I learn so much. I'd better study the book of Daniel." He paused as if someone was speaking to him. "Okay, Lord, I hear you. I need to tell Sherry what's happening."

---

(1) Revelation 5:8, (2) Matthew 6:10, (3) Psalm 68:1, (4) Job 33:4, (5) Daniel 12:4

Chapter 16

Cassius felt like having fun with Randy when he came in for prayer. He sprawled across the top of the ceiling, under the beams, and looked down at the young pastor as he came in for prayer. "God is love," Cassius announced in his loud, and he hoped, best Father God imitation.

Randy jerked and looked around but saw no one. His eyes widened as he considered the possibility of the voice of God speaking to him.

"Gotcha." The angel laughed as he floated to the floor.

"Oh, Cassius, you scared me. I didn't know what was happening."

"I couldn't resist. At home, we enjoy trying to sound like Father. Did I?"

"I don't really know what he sounds like, but I was thinking maybe …"

Cassius slapped his knee. "Great," he laughed. "Anyway, the words I said are true, and that's the subject I've been given for my student today. Love."

Randy responded. "Love? I see. Okay, I'm listening."

Cassius took the position of a very large instructor up front so Randy sat on the front row.

"Are you ready?" the mentor inquired.

Randy nodded and the tutor began. "Love is who God is. Everything about his kingdom is wrapped in love." Those words filled the angel with joy which caused him to rise as he exclaimed, "Oh, I can't wait for you to know its fullness yourself." He paused and dropped his head in thought. Settling closer to the floor, he pointed his index finger in the air as he continued, "I've got it. His love is like air, or the water in the ocean. That's it. Yes, the ocean. Someone wise once said, 'You should be consumed in God's love like fish live in the ocean.[1]'

"Humans have shrunk love into an emotion or feeling, but love is much more, it has substance. When Father is in you and you are in him, love manifests."

"Sure, I understand."

Cassius looked at him as if questioning his words. "Really? But you're not living as if you know it. What would Sherry say about your love for her?"

"She knows I love her."

"What would you say about her love for you?"

Randy smiled, "She really loves me."

"How do you know?"

The man felt bold as he explained. "She tells me often. She does everything to make me happy. She forgives me when I mess up." He searched for more words. "She didn't even hesitate to come here with me so I could pastor this church."

"You mess up?" Cassius asked as if surprised.

Randy lowered his head. "I do. When things get too challenging and I'm frustrated, I take it out on her."

"What do you mean?"

The pastor looked up. "She says I shout at her. I just want her to understand what I want."

"How does she respond?"

Sadness covered Randy's face. "Sometimes she cries. She told me she can't hear me when I yell. What does that even mean?" He looked at Cassius to see if he had an answer. The angel didn't respond so he continued. "She says I don't speak to anyone else the way I do to her. What is her problem?"

"How about the children? What do they do when you get loud?"

Randy shrugged. "Usually they aren't around."

"Maybe they're hiding. Or perhaps you choose times when they aren't present to show your frustration to Sherry."

The pastor jumped up ready to fire back sharp words, then, with a questioning look he paused and responded. "Do you think so?"

"Did your parents love you?"

"Oh yes, they loved me very much. They did everything possible to give me a good childhood."

"How did you respond?"

Randy got up and walked across the front of the church with his head down.

Cassius asked again, "How did you respond?"

Randy clenched his fist and blasted. "Basically, I was a strong-willed, controlling brat."

The calm voice continued. "So you weren't loving with your parents?"

Randy tried to remember a time he showed love to his mother and father. "When I went to college, I told them to get off my back because I would do things my way. I've done fine without their interference."

"Are you sure?"

Randy glared at his instructor. "What are you trying to say? You're such a nag."

The teacher held a well-worn Bible that looked tiny in the palm of his hand. "The Word says to honor your parents so it will go well with you.[2] Perhaps you've worked hard to accomplish a measure of success on your own, but it's all for nothing if love isn't at the center of everything you do.

"Randal, I happen to know your wife is in great pain. She came from an abusive background, and your harshness with her is causing scars that will go too deep to recover if you don't choose the path of love. Your children are aware of your temper. They love you now, but soon you will be attacking them, too. That will damage those precious little girls."

Not to be intimidated, Randy shot back. "What is love anyway? It's just caring for one person more than others."

"Didn't you hear me before? Love is the foundation of everything you are meant to teach. You can only do that if you know it personally. Haven't you memorized I Corinthians 13:4-8? Love is patient and kind, it doesn't envy or boast. It isn't proud, or rude, or self-seeking. It is not easily angered." Cassius paused. "Have you learned that one?"

As the words brought conviction, Randy crossed his arms in defiance.

The tutor continued. "It keeps no record of wrongs. It always protects, trusts, hopes and perseveres."

After a pause, the angel looked as if he just remembered the perfect words to explain what he was trying to teach.

"Love never fails. All those virtues only come as you allow Father to fill you with his love. Your lesson now is to learn to love."

"How do I find such love? I guess I need to read all the scriptures on love now."

"That would be a good start, but just ask God for it. He wants you to know how great his love is for you. Once you know his love, you can share it with others."

Cassius gave the man a little time to think. Then he said, "I'll leave you now so you can talk with our Father."

Randy nodded and dropped to his knees. "Father, it's tough when you put your finger on the things I need to change. I'm supposed to be a person who helps other people, and I don't even like some of them. I've treated my wife badly, and ignored her tears and disappointment. She probably feels like I treat her more like a servant than my bride.

"I've been around loving people all my life, but I've used them. I never learned to love as they have. How can I change?"

He waited for an answer. "Lord, I give you my life. Obviously, I can't do what's needed. Will you help me love my family with real love? Your kind of love?" He stopped abruptly.

"Oh, I just remembered, your love lays down its life for others." He sighed. "Will I ever learn?"

Suddenly, hope filled his heart. "I surrender everything in me to your love, Father."

When he finally stood he felt peaceful. The voices that continually called him a failure were silent.

(1) Tozar, (2) Exodus 20:12

Chapter 17

Thursday evening Randy was alone. Sherry took the girls with her to girls-night-out. When she decided to go she explained to him it was really moms getting together so the children could play. He agreed it was a nice idea, and knew noisy kids wouldn't slow those women down one bit when it came to talking together.

He decided to take a walk. With the long summer days it wouldn't be dark for another hour or so.

His Bible reading filled his mind with new thoughts. The constant question became, *When did they put that scripture in here?* God's love really did flow through the whole book. He continued to find references to angels and demons. How had he missed them before? The words of Matthew, where it said to heal the sick, raise the dead, and cast out demons, sounded like an extra commandment. Before, he pushed those words aside as impossibilities, therefore he considered them irrelevant. *God forgive me for taking your Word so lightly.*

As he walked the streets of town, he enjoyed the wholesome feel of the Midwest community. The scenery along the walking path by the creek, where the old mill stood idle, was always changing. He listened as the katydids serenaded. The trees, abundant with dark green foliage, made a canopy as he moved along. *Not much water in the creek with the summer heat. Last spring when the rains hit it was out-of-control. Must've been six feet deeper then.*

He smiled and spoke to all the folks along his path, and waved as drivers went by and yelled, "Hi, Pastor."

As he reached the edge of town, the descending sunlight burst out around the clouds. Gold outlined the white billows and an array of soft colors looked as if God himself was painting. When the sun moved lower, light spears shot through the sky. The glow held him with its overwhelming beauty. He imagined angels might be moving on a glorious staircase. A scripture came to mind. *The heavens declare the glory of God and the firmament shows his handiworks.*[1]

Awestruck, Randy stood watching as the beauty dissolved into the shadows of late evening.

Back to reality he admired his church on the hill. The big expanse of property behind the building filled his mind with possibilities. Some cars were in the parking lot. *Did I forget a meeting? Wayne Smith's white Chrysler is in its usual spot. He has keys. He must have let everyone in.* With long strides, he rushed up the hill and through the foyer doors.

How strange. No one's moving around. No kids yelling in the youth hall.

Quickening his steps to the sanctuary, he opened the door and stopped. People were scattered around on their knees. Some sat quietly in the pews. The only sounds he heard were words of thanks being spoken reverently. He scooted into the last row to watch.

Mrs. Anderson was on her knees at the altar. Her eighty-two year old shoulders trembled as she wept into her handkerchief.

How did she get down on her knees? Her arthritis is so bad. Her health has been failing. Sure don't want to lose another prayer warrior. That woman loves to pray.

The Robinsons sat huddled together with their family. "Thank you, thank you," seemed to be the only words coming from their lips. Even their son Todd, now eight, who was born with one leg three inches shorter than the other, sat quietly giving thanks.

As Mrs. Anderson stood, Randy starred. *She looks so … spry.* She began to dance around the alter seeming somewhat mesmerized while waltzing with an invisible partner. *What a beautiful sight. She doesn't seem to be in the pain that often shows.* After a while she opened her eyes and looked embarrassed when she saw others watching her newfound agility.

Two heads popped up from the front. Hillary and June, her prayer partners for decades, joined her and they quietly rejoiced together.

Wayne walked back to where Randy sat. "Pastor, God is doing amazing things. It looks like Mrs. Anderson's body might be healed. The scripture that says we will rise up on wings as eagles, run and not be weary, and walk and not faint[2] is really happening.

"And the Robinson family, they're new here, God healed their son. His short leg grew three inches longer while he was sleeping. They said when he woke up and got out of bed he screamed. They ran into his room and found him laughing and jumping from one foot to the other. He's excited to start doing all the things the other boys get to do without any handicaps. They're the ones who called and asked if they could come to the church. The boy wanted to give thanks to God for giving him a miracle."

Randy stood up. "I see. I've never heard of anyone having a leg grow out before." Slowly moving forward, he was surprised so many people were there quietly enjoying being in God's presence.

Wayne walked beside him. They passed a couple curled together on the floor thanking God. "Matt got a job today. It's been two years. They almost lost their home. His new salary is double what he made before. They'll be able to get on top of things quickly."

He motioned to another couple holding each other, and giving thanks. "Meredith and Gary just found out she's pregnant. They were told ten years ago they would never have children.

"Pastor," he whispered, "I think we need to keep the doors open in the evenings so people can come in. This happened last night too. Is that okay?"

"Yes, of course. This is God's work. Let's make way for him."

Randy walked out the door overcome with awe at what God

was doing, yet remorseful for being so unaware of what was happening all around him. *Father, forgive me. How could I dare think I was in charge of anything? Have your will in this place.*

(1) Psalm 19:1, (2) Isaiah 40:31

Chapter 18

After another week in the church office, Glenda Johnson was happy to be home to enjoy her Saturday off work. She looked across the green rolling fields and wondered what wild flowers she could find. Wearing a sundress and summer slip-on shoes, she pushed the kitchen screen door open and headed for the meadow. Her dark hair blew softly in the breezes as she walked along picking a bouquet of colors. Breathing deep she settled under the shade of an old oak tree. The birds seemed to be singing just for her so she closed her eyes to enjoy their songs.

Her thoughts turned to the fact she never expected to be back in Millbrook after she graduated from college. But, her parents needed her help with their farm, so that's what daughters do. She remembered how overwhelmed they were by the success of their home grown organic products, and grass fed buffalo. It was good she was able to help them get their business organized on the computer, and create a website for them.

She opened her eyes and watched the buffalo roaming through the south field. "Who would have thought buffalo would be so desired on the dinner table?"

I'm pretty sure I've done the right thing. The farm is stable now. I needed to make some money, and the church didn't have a secretary or bookkeeper. It all made sense. She pulled a leaf from her hair. *The work's rather boring now that things are sorted out, but I'll wait until God shows me what he wants me to do next.*

Pulling her knees up to rest her chin on, she let her mind wander. *I want a family and home of my own someday. Maybe church is the place to meet a good man. But not just any man. My man. The one God has for me. Maybe someday.*

Sorting through the few single men from school who were still in town, she didn't find a possibility, so she sighed, "Yes, maybe someday."

She brushed those thoughts away, and relaxed against the tree trunk. With complete concentration she tried to figure out each note of nature's beautiful melody. Perhaps she dozed.

Suddenly, a male's voice startled her. "Wake up pretty girl."

Her eyes popped open as she wiped slobber off her mouth. "Oh, hi Brett. What are you doing way out here?"

The man bent down to sit by her. He scooted close. "Oh, I just took some back roads on my way home from the city. I wondered if you might be around."

She looked at him puzzled. "Why?"

"I've missed you Glenda. I'm so glad you're back in Millbrook."

"I've been here a year already."

"Yes, I know. It's taken me some time to get the courage to come see you."

"Why?" He was making her nervous.

"Oh, Glen, I've really missed you. I just wanted to see how you are."

"I'm fine." She straightened the skirt of her dress and picked up her flowers.

He waved across the field at a sharp little convertible parked along the road. "What do you think of my new wheels?"

"It's nice."

"Would you like to go for a ride in it?"

Glenda looked at him still questioning. "No thanks."

Brett moved closer. "Oh, come on Glenda. Don't you want to pick up where we left off when you went away to college?"

"Didn't you get married, Brett."

"Yes, sure I did. You didn't stick around. Things aren't working out with Marsha. I was hoping maybe we could spark something new."

Glenda turned red faced as she huffed and started to get up. "You've got to be kidding."

He grabbed her arm and pulled her back down. Having a strong hold, he pushed her back and forced a kiss.

"Get away from me," she shouted as she pushed him with all her might.

He didn't release her. "Oh, come on girl. I know you want me."

She struggled to get away. "Are you crazy?"

A voice came from a short distance. "Hey, Brett. What are you doing with Glenda? Your wife's probably at home waiting for you."

Brett loosed his hold and jumped to his feet, rage crossed his face. "Mind your own business!"

Andrew pushed past him and helped Glenda get up. "Hi, Glenda. You okay?"

She felt embarrassed, but nodded and smoothed her hair.

Andrew dropped his head shyly and suggested, "You probably want to go up to the house."

"Okay." She stepped into her shoes while hugging her bouquet, and moved away quickly.

Andrew looked at Brett. "I see you have a new car. How fast will it go?"

Brett turned from watching Glenda leave. "Oh, I've had it to a hundred. It almost flies at that speed."

"Nice," Andrew responded. You want to show it to me. My bike's right there beside it."

"Sure. It's a honey."

Andrew glanced back at the house to check on Glenda just as her dad walked out on the porch with his shotgun.

Chapter 19

The next week, while walking home for lunch, Randy considered all the new things taking place at the church. Then his thoughts turned to his marriage. *These secrets aren't healthy. I need to talk to Sherry. A date. That's a good idea. We'll go on a date and I'll tell her everything.* He picked up his pace and jogged to the house. When he burst through the kitchen door he stopped abruptly. almost toppling over his wife's backside as she pulled a salad from a low shelf in the refrigerator.

Startled, Sherri looked over from her bent position. "You're home." She retrieved the dish and set it on the countertop while closing the refrigerator door with her foot. "What's wrong?"

"Nothing. I just wanted to ask you on a date."

Sherry pushed a strand of blond hair behind her ear as she looked into his face. "A date?"

"Yes. We haven't had any time together and I miss you. Can we find a few hours to go someplace where we can be alone?"

"Oh, that would be so nice." He could almost see his wife's mind sorting through their tight schedules. With all the activity they barely had time for meals together. She took a breath, "When were you thinking we could do that?"

"Maybe daytime would be easiest. Would you mind checking with Glenda and see when I'm free. We could run off and have a picnic somewhere."

He saw her puzzled look vanish as she said, "Okay. I'm sure the girls can play at someone's house for a few hours."

"Great. I love you." With a quick kiss on her forehead, he was off to spend a little time with his daughters.

As he left the room he heard her say, "Love you too."

***

Randy walked into Glenda's office. "Hi, Glenda, Sherry's going to call you. Will you set aside some time on my calendar for lunch with her? Also, tell her not to fix food. I'll take care of it."

"Sure, I can do that."

"Thanks." He turned to leave, paused and faced her again. "Would you mind calling the new Bistro? What's its name? Ask them to fix up something really fancy and ... sophisticated. Is that the word I want? Maybe classy. But for a picnic. Okay?"

"Sure, Pastor. Are you getting the reports of what's going on around here? It's as if God dumped heaven in our laps. People are being blessed in all sorts of ways.

"Oh, here are your messages, and Lewis Spitzer asked to meet with you. He owns the field out back. The top note needs a call right away."

I just want a date with my wife. "All right, thanks for all you do." He headed to his office.

***

Three days later, Randy felt just as he did in college when he picked up Sherry for their dates. He stopped by Lara's Bistro, and admired the box lunch wrapped in impressive, romantic looking paper and a bow. The enticing aroma was something only a gourmet chef could create. *Those women worked magic. How do they make paper and ribbons look romantic?*

As he pulled in the driveway, Sherry rushed out to meet him. The skirt of her sleeveless, pale yellow dress floated in the breeze as she moved. He smiled thinking they were about to enjoy something memorable. *She knows this isn't a shorts and tee-shirt date.*

He jumped out of the car and ran around to open her door. When he reached her, he wrapped his arm around her waist, and

120

pulled her close. After kissing her he declared, "You look beautiful."

Blushing, she slid into the car while a smile covered her face. "Thanks."

He banged the hood of the car with one hand and danced to the driver's door. Inside, he took her hand in his and paused to stare at her beauty. Then he tenderly kissed her hand. "I love you."

Looking shy she responded, "The neighbors will see."

"Oh, I hope so. What better example could a pastor set for people?"

Feeling he knew his wife pretty well, Randy could tell she was delighted with his efforts, and she would tuck every happy detail away to remember and enjoy later.

As Randy backed the vehicle out she remarked, "The girls are excited to be with Hillary this afternoon. She'll teach them some new games, and tell them stories about Scotland when she was a girl."

"That's great."

Soon Randy was cruising along the road by the stream he knew so well. "There's a nice spot out here about a mile before the bridge." A quick shadow made way across his mind as he thought of the frustration he left there before.

He pulled in, and they paused to enjoy the beauty of the water flowing past. The breeze moving through the mature trees seemed to beckon them forward with an invitation of cool shade along the banks. Sherry started to get out but Randy asked her to wait. He went around and opened her door. Face to face they smiled. Emotional tension from busy schedules vanished like a bubble on the water, and in that moment they were one again. They embraced, and after another kiss he took her hand and led her to the trunk to reveal all his surprises. There was the beautiful box lunch, a bouquet of flowers tied with a ribbon, a blanket, and two pillows to prop behind them.

"Oh, from the new Bistro," she cooed.

He smiled, pleased she was impressed. They carried the things into the shade. Each took corners of the blanket and flipped it a bit before they laid it on the grass. After arranging the pillows, Sherry admired the bouquet of summer flowers and put them on the blanket for their centerpiece.

Randy lifted the box lunch and sat it in front of Sherry. "I have no idea what we have to eat."

His wife smiled as she removed the bow carefully and laid it aside. "I hear everything they make is delicious." She opened the lid. "Wow. This looks like a lot of food." She sat out plastic plates which looked like china, and shiny silver plastic forks and knifes. Pulling out containers, she said, "Oh, they put the names on top of each dish. That will help." They both smiled.

"Look Randy, these are the drinks. It says, 'Pineapple cooler with lavender and lemon.' That sounds good. The stemmed glasses have lids. The girls will love these. I'll save them."

Randy watched his wife as she continued to be intrigued by their lunch time adventure.

More containers emerged. "There's enough food here for a week. Surely they don't always pack so much. This one says 'Shrimp with melon cucumber wrap', and the other is 'Radish Tartines'. Want to try them?"

"Sure." He reached over to take the dishes and opened the tops. They paused to thank God for their lunch, and then Sherry put them on each plate. She savored every bite. Randy ate his and waited. "That was good."

Sherry nodded. "Oh, my goodness, and I don't even like radishes but that was delicious. Who knew shrimp and watermelon went together. Those people at Lara's are amazing. What's next?" She peaked into the box again. "Here's one that says fruit and cheese. I bet it's really good. Do you want to save it for later, and try the other things first?"

"Sure." His heart filled with delight as he watched his wife enjoy her surprise. The job pressures and frustrations disappeared.

Back in the box, Sherry pulled out Apricot Prosciutto Focaccia, Mozzarella Red Pepper and Bacon Skewers, Deviled Egg Potato Salad, 5-Bean Summer Salad, and Grilled Buffalo Chicken Sandwiches.

After eating Randy fell back on a pillow. "I'm stuffed. Lara outdid herself with this scrumptious feast. It was delicious."

Sherry began covering containers and putting them back in the box. "This box is lined with some kind of cold insolation. There is so much food left we can share the rest with the girls for dinner. Oh, I missed this one." She read the lid. "Strawberry hand pies. You want one?"

Rubbing his stomach he answered. "No, no. Save them too." He watched her finish packing up. She took the bow and put it back around the box. Finished, she lay down beside him.

Relaxed, the couple laughed at the silly characters they saw in the clouds and talked about anything and everything. Well, not everything. Finally, Randy turned toward his wife and leaned on his elbow. He reached over to touch her golden hair. "I love you."

"I know."

"We really needed this day."

Sherry's eyes filled with tears. "Yes, we did."

Randy continued. "Honey, you're wonderful. You have an impossible task as my wife, and you do it with such grace."

"Thanks for saying that."

He paused, hoping to find just the right words. "I've been a little distant lately."

Not wanting to distract him, she forced herself to stay silent in the same way she would when she didn't want to scare a rabbit away. "Um hum."

"I need to tell you why."

Hope leaped within her, but fear of the unknown stood right behind. "Okay."

"Something strange has been happening. Of course, you know the good things. Beth's miracle and so many others have good news. Well, just before those things started, I had a visitor."

Sherry rose to lean on her elbow and face him. Her brow wrinkled. "A visitor?"

"Yes, now you're not going to believe me so just go with this, will you?" She nodded in agreement. "I was praying in the sanctuary when a giant angel appeared. He was so tall he touched the ceiling."

"Really?"

"Yes."

"Were you afraid?" she asked.

"Yes. But I was angry too. I didn't like the things he said. He told me everything was going to change. You know how hard I've worked on what we've already accomplished?"

Sherry nodded as Randy continued. "The angel said he was appointed to help me because I am one of God's leaders for our town. I have no idea what that means. Sherry, I can barely do what I'm doing now. I didn't understand half of what he talked about. He really confused me."

Trying to find the right words, Randy added. "As if that's not enough, the scriptures have been literally flying through my mind. I feel like God took his Word and threw it in the air. When it comes back I understand what it means in ways I've never heard anyone else preach. I don't know what to do with that."

Frustrated, he sat up and stared at the sparkling stream as the rippling water moved along.

After remaining silent for a few minutes, Sherry scooted closer to him, put her arm across his shoulders, and started playing with his ear. "It's okay, Randy, if it's God," she whispered. "God is always good no matter what things look like, or how they change. We can still have faith in his character, even if we don't understand his ways. Look what's been happening since the angel came. The Morgan's have Beth back. All the healings have been wonderful. Lives are being changed for the better."

They sat silent. Finally, Sherry spoke gently. "Randy, you're a born leader. That's why you're so good at what you do. But, it seems God wants you to quit leading and follow. I would think that's a hard transition for you. Maybe, it would also be very freeing. Perhaps, God is up to something too big for us to touch with our restricted human abilities."

She quieted to give him a chance to chew on the thought. Then it was her time to share her secrets. "I've had visitors, too."

She had his attention. He looked at her with hope in his eyes. "Really?"

"Three angels have been in my kitchen. Not often, but because I've seen them I sense they're always around. Shall I tell you what they looked like? They're so different from yours."

"Of course. I want to know."

"Well, the first time I saw them they looked like beautiful women in white flowing gowns. The fabric moved continually, and their hair floated instead of lying on their shoulders. When they saw me, they vanished."

"Wow."

"Yes, but that's not all. I went on cooking and they showed up again. This time they reminded me of the three fairies in the Disney movie, Sleeping Beauty. They said they took that form because they saw the fairy's while watching TV with the girls, and thought if they looked like them I wouldn't be afraid."

Randy laughed. "So they can change their appearance?"

"It would seem so. They were tiny enough to fly above the counters. One dressed in a flowing gown like an actress at the Oscar awards. I call her Ms. Actress. I named another one The Book Lady. She wears glasses she can't keep on her nose and always has a book with her. Mostly the Bible. The third is chubby and so delightful. She suggests what I should make and gives me hints on how to improve the recipes."

"That's funny."

"I know. And it's fun. Life is meant to be fun, Randy." Her smile had a twinkle he hadn't seen in a while.

With laughter in her voice, she said, "You know, I think I'll tell the girls about each dish in our box. Maybe the angels will hear and give me the recipes."

Randy laughed with her while saying, "You've always been a great cook."

"Thank you, honey." She paused, and then spurted, "Olivia and Amanda have been entertaining angels, too. I didn't tell you before because you had so many other things to deal with. Their angels' names are Olympus and Felix. The girls say they're guardian angels. The four have tea together. When I asked what they looked like they described them so clearly I couldn't doubt. The angels also tell them secrets."

Randy questioned, "Like what?"

"One message was that they are to pray for people to be healed so their parents can learn how it's done. Olivia said Gayle's little Cassie was given the same instructions by her angel."

Randy looked shocked as he jumped up. "Dear God. Sherry, we're sitting right in the middle of God's kingdom coming and we didn't even know it."

"I think so. But Randy, it won't be any fun unless we share it with each other. Please, let's keep talking. I know you're tired when you finish your day, but I long to know what you're experiencing too. I think if I share with you as well, we can work through the whole process more quickly. God put us together to be united. We'll be stronger if we stick close to each other. Okay?"

Randy reached out for his wife's hands, pulled her up and embraced her. "Definitely, okay. I don't want to take a step without you at my side." Their long kiss sealed the deal.

Letting go of her, Randy yelled over the noise of the stream, "Thank you, God, for my wife."

A flock of birds in the trees took flight.

Chapter 20

Charles was washing up after mowing the grass when his phone rang. He answered and heard Micah's panicked voice shout, "Dad, we need your help. There's a car flipped upside-down. Kevin Baker is lying outside it bleeding. I called 911."

His father's heart skipped some beats as he shouted, "Where are you, Micah? Are you guys okay?"

"Yes. Travis and I were driving back from training camp. We're at the big curve on Millbrook Road. But Dad, I think Kevin's dead. He looks like a ghost and there's blood all over him."

Charles grabbed the car keys and his wallet as Micah continued.

"I don't know how long it'll take to get help out here, but if we don't pray him back to life before an ambulance comes, we won't be allowed near him."

Micah's father stopped. His mind flashed back to their discussions. When they found Matthew 10:8 in the Bible, which said to heal the sick, raise the dead, and cast out demons, and experienced bringing David back from death, the question became, "How do we get to the people to pray them back to life before others stop us?" So far, their only answer was, get to them first.

"Okay. I'll be there as soon as I can. You guys start praying. You know how to do it. Talk to him and demand his life to come back into his body. Bind the spirit of death. And thank Jesus for the answer. This young man will not die on our watch."

He stuck the cellphone in his pocket, scribbled a note for Beth, and slammed the door behind him.

***

The sunbathed countryside around the accident was peaceful. Birds sang their chirpy tunes and the stream gurgled. Otherwise, everything was silent. The complete opposite of what churned in Micah and Travis's minds.

Micah pocketed his phone. "Let's go." They moved closer to Kevin. Even from a distance they could see his wounds were serious.

Travis paused. "I've never seen anyone covered with blood before. This looks hopeless."

"I know. I haven't either. We'll just get as close as we can." Micah lifted his foot as he crossed broken glass. They moved forward slowly. An odor made him pause. "Keep an eye out for gas." He bent over to look under the car. "I don't see any on the ground. Do you think we should move him farther away?"

Travis took a sniff. "Yeah, I smell it, but I don't think we're supposed to move someone who's injured."

Micah considered the thought and changed his focus. "Okay, Travis. Then are you ready for battle?" He paused, "We better pray first." The teen did his best to remember how his father prayed when they saw the man under the bridge brought back to life.

"The Word says we have the power living in us to heal the sick, raise the dead, and cast out demons. Father, show us how to pray for Kevin. Amen."

Travis nodded in agreement. He took a step closer and looked sadly at Kevin. Trembling, he spoke, "By the power of Jesus' blood, I command this body to be healed."

Sparked by those few words, Micah nodded. "Wounds close, body be restored in Jesus' name. Kevin, God has plans for your life. It's his will you live and not die. He has gifted you with talents that must be used. Thank you, Jesus, for bringing Kevin back to life."

Boldness entered with each phrase. Tension caused them to

yell into the quiet afternoon. "Every death angel within a hundred miles, I bind you from taking Kevin's life. He is God's child. You can't have him. Thank you, Jesus, for healing Kevin."

Travis joined the bold words. "Kevin, we command your life to come back into your body. We demand you live and not die. Thank you, Jesus, for healing him."

Charles skidded to a stop and jumped out of his car just as the emergency vehicles arrived.

"You boys okay."

"Yes," they responded with hoarse voices after all the shouting.

Kevin's face was ashen as the ambulance workers examined him. Not finding a pulse, they began CPR while preparing the boy for transport to the hospital.

Seeing how shaken the boys were, Charles put his arms across their shoulders. "Come on guys, I'll drive you to the hospital. We'll come back for your car later."

***

After a few moments, Charles' car zoomed into the hospital parking lot. He dropped the boys off at the emergency entrance so they could be close when Kevin was carried in.

The rushing medics were all business. "Out of the way, we've got a pulse."

Micah and Travis stretched forward to see their friend. Travis turned with hopeful concern on his face. "A pulse? Did he still look like a ghost?"

Micah replayed the image that just passed. "I don't think so. We've got to get people praying."

Charles joined them, and Micah told him the news. They all pulled out their cellphones and ran their thumbs over the face, as texts flowed out.

***

Three days passed. Micah couldn't wait any longer. He heard it was a miracle the way Kevin's wounds were healing, so he decided to stop by the hospital and see what he could find out. When he got to the nurse's station, he smiled at the woman behind the counter.

"Hi, I'm Micah Morgan. I'm a friend of Keven Baker. I wonder if you can tell me how he is today?"

"Oh, Micah, you're on his visitor's list. Would you like to see him?"

Surprised, and feeling as if he just got by with something, he nodded.

The nurse came from behind her work space. "Let's go to his room and see if he's awake. You know they didn't give the family much hope. His brain went without oxygen for some time but there's no damage. Isn't that wonderful?"

Micah listened and nodded in agreement.

She continued as they moved down the long hall. "Even though he was in a serious car accident, none of his vital organs were injured. He's a lucky boy. Here's his room." She tapped on the door, and then opened it. "Kevin, you have company."

Micah felt relief as Kevin looked up. "Hey Kevin. You're looking a lot better than you did three days ago," he kidded, then walked over and sat in the chair beside his bed.

Kevin gave a weak grin as he turned toward his friend. "How was the rest of football camp?"

"Well, everyone was so concerned about you, I'm not sure we accomplished much. Coach tried some of the guys in new positions. The whole thing looked more like clowns in a circus act, than a scrimmage."

Kevin smiled. "So what's the line-up now?"

Micah filled him in on all the details of new plays and positions. When he finished sharing, they both became quiet. He thought Kevin might be tired so he decided to say good-bye.

Instead, Kevin sat up a bit and pushed his pillow in a bunch to support his head better. "I saw you and Travis praying for me."

A thrill ran through Micah. Not wanting to miss a word, he moved to the edge of the chair.

"Micah, I think I was dead because I was outside of my body and my skin was so pale. There was blood all over me and on the ground." Kevin paused to catch his breath. "I saw when you guys drove up and ran over to me. I heard you tell your dad you had to bring me back to life."

Micah eyes widened. "Really? Neat."

Kevin nodded. "When you started to yell those prayers, it felt as if a magnet was pulling me back into my body. You were so busy praying, I don't think you realized I stopped bleeding. I could see my blood stop running on the ground." He took a deep breath. "Thanks, Micah."

Micah jumped to his feet. "This is great. This is so great." He shot a glance at Kevin, "Oh. You're welcome."

There was a long pause as Micah paced, and the two young men considered the wonder of it all. "I knew we had to pray for you. God's voice inside me kept telling me you were to live and not die. I remembered all the plans you have for when you finish high school, and how good you are with math and chemistry. There was no doubt in my mind God wants you alive. You just had to live."

"Cool." Kevin responded. "Will you teach me how to do that? I want to help people come back to life, too. If I'd known to pray like you guys did, my dad might still be alive."

Micah's heart sank as he was reminded Kevin's father died in the same hospital four years before from a brain tumor. How should he respond?

"We didn't know then, Kevin. I'm sorry. But we do now. I'll be happy to tell you all I can. We've only started to understand. Jesus said he only did what he saw the Father doing. Maybe that's what I heard when we prayed for you. God wanted you to live."

That set off a conversation about David dying from an

131

overdose, and how he and his dad prayed for him and he came back to life. He shared how they were trying to find ways to get to people who die so they could pray for them, but it wasn't easy.

"You need permission to cross the tape at accidents. The morgue won't let us in without the family's permission. Maybe being close isn't even necessary."

Their conversation lasted until the nurse came in to care for Kevin. Micah left so excited his feet seemed to barely touch the ground. *Wait till Dad and Travis hears this.*

***

There's a key that comes with victory. One victory brings others. When people realize they really are meant to heal the sick and raise the dead by the power of Jesus living in them, the successful experiences are contagious, and create an unquenchable passion to be fully used for God's purposes.

Chapter 21

When Randy entered the church for morning prayer, Cassius's massive body was sprawled across the pastor's prized carpet. Surprised he felt pleased to see the annoying angel, the pastor shouted, "Making yourself feel at home?"

The illusion sat up and smiled before he roared through the quiet room. "I hear you've gotten over yourself, and decided to join us in these great and glorious days."

"I can't believe Glenda doesn't know you're in here. Surely, she can hear your voice."

"No, you're the only one who can see or hear me. One day we'll be visible enough to be considered aliens, just like others who aren't citizens, but live among you."

Randy stopped and considered that idea. "How would that work?"

Cassius gave him a puzzled look, as if he didn't believe he asked such a question. He huffed and touched his chin. "You can see me."

"Yes. I haven't figured out how that's happened either."

"Well …"Cassius rubbed his chin. "Hmm ... with eyes of faith, of course. Remember the day I introduced myself to you."

"Yes, it seems like some time ago now."

"You didn't believe what you were seeing. I was a … a disruption to your status quo."

Randy shook his head. "That's for sure. I was content with what I knew. You have really messed with my mind, you know?"

"But our Father has great plans and we must fulfill his purposes."

"Please explain," the confused man asked.

"Let's start from scratch. Earth is full of humans. God's kingdom, which is everywhere, has many different types of creations. Each for explicit purposes. We were created before time, but move into certain periods of human history as our Father leads. I have come to serve you. You with me?"

"Yes. I guess so."

The angel opened his palms. "Most people haven't been aware of our presence because it wasn't time for the fullness of his glory. But now, there has been a great shift in heaven. God is sending the end-time host forth to assist his people on earth. The days ahead will be like none you have ever seen or heard of before. That's why I've come to help you."

Randy looked surprised. "Does that mean other people are having giant angels teach them, too?"

"Probably. Many came when I did. As people break free from religion, and realize Father God is our ever present reality, their eyes will be open to see the thousands, probably millions, of angels waiting to assist them in fulfilling his plans." Excitement filled the mentor's voice. "We can hardly wait because we have seen what's ahead. Randal, the future isn't gloom and doom as some predict. Oh, there will be great challenges, but when the King's kingdom manifests, heaven's glory comes."

It seemed as if Cassius couldn't resist challenging his student further.

"In the same way you overcame the division of different races living together, the manifestation of God's kingdom on earth will liberate people, and free them to integrate with the host of heaven naturally. But we won't live in houses or anything.

"It'll take a while for you to adjust to the way we zoom around though." Cassius flowed through the room to demonstrate his agility. "Everyplace will probably feel crowded until you become accustomed to the way we move through you." With a quick swish the mentor passed through Randy and settled in the air in front of him. The pastor jerked back at the shock of Cassius coming at him.

"You only felt a flutter of my presence, didn't you?" "Humans are so grounded by gravity, and they sure move slow." He cocked his head. "You know it's your privilege to visit the King in his kingdom throne room anytime?"

"No, I didn't know. How could that happen?"

"As you learn to live by your spirit instead of your flesh you can also walk in the spirit and easily meet with the King.[1] He longs for you to recognize you belong beside him.[2] You can go many places when your spirit unites with the Holy Spirit. Remember how the Spirit of the Lord caught Phillip away to another place?" His flesh yielded to God's spirit in him and he was there."

Randy flipped through the pages of the Bible. "That's in Acts 8:39-40. *The Spirit of the Lord snatched Philip away and Philip found himself at Azortus.* I've always wondered how that happened."

Cassius said, "Usually we just think and we're there, although when I came here we all marched together like warriors into battle.

"Anyway, what did you think of all the new people here Sunday? Have you noticed they're showing up in the evenings just to be close to our glorious King? Heaven is open over this area. The hearts of the people are being drawn to the Master."

"But I've never prayed for this. I just wanted to be a good shepherd to my flock."

"And you've done well. But God does abundantly above anything you could hope or ask.[3] He has many others to bring to you."

Randy shook his head and looked down. "Honestly, I feel maxed out. I can't do any more in a day."

"What did Moses' father-in-law tell him?"

"Assign leaders."

"Oh, you do know his Word. Yes, that's right." Cassius was gone.

Did he really leave? Randy stared into space. *I wonder if I really can learn to see into the invisible realm.*

Teasing words bellowed through the room as the mentor revealed himself again. "Well, isn't your faith growing? Wanting to see the unseen realm wasn't even on your radar a few months ago. Human logic will never accept the things which are only received by faith.[5] To be the powerful hands of Almighty God extended to others is *the* most glorious privilege."

"I believe you're right, Cassius. Will you be the one to help me learn?"

"I'll do what I can. You already know all this stuff, and you hear the voice of the Holy Spirit. You just got stifled by lies and deception. Those are real spirits, you know?"

"I didn't know that."

"Yes, they're as real as me. And they're a nasty lot. They never play fair. Anyway, what are you going to talk to the people about Sunday?"

The thought gave him pause. "I don't think I need to say much at all. God's presence is so powerful the people are hearing from him personally."

"I told you it would be easy. Let Tony loose with worship. Don't think too much about your sermons. Just share whatever the Holy Spirit gives you. You'll be surprised. It will be fun."

"Oh, that does sound like fun, but I'm not one to leave things to chance. I'll think about it."

Cassius smiled and drew closer to the man. "Just say, 'yes.' Otherwise, you'll struggle all week trying to come up with something."

Randy looked up into the relaxed being's face and snorted. "No doubt. Okay, I've got plenty of other things to do anyway."

"Great." The giant clapped. "But don't forget your motorcycle rides. That looks like fun. The kingdom is fun, Randal."

A smile crossed the man's face as he realized how much he liked the guy he once thought annoying.

***

Glenda stuck her head in the pastor's office. "Your dad's on the phone."

"Oh, thanks." Concerned, Randy reached over to pick up the receiver. He hadn't talked to his dad in months. "Hi Dad. Is everything okay?"

"Real good, Son. I was praying for you this morning and couldn't get over the feeling I needed to call and tell you something."

"Sure. What's up?" Randy had been very vocal about telling his father he didn't need any of his advice in the past, so he knew this couldn't be an easy call for his dad to make. *Man, have I been a jerk.*

"Well, this morning I was led to the story of Moses, the part where his father-in-law told him to assign leaders to help carry the load.[4] As I read it, I realized the whole story was the same as laying out a business plan for people. Then I felt I needed to call and remind you that many hands make work light." His dad paused a second. "I know this sounds rather strange, but I couldn't think about anything else. I felt compelled to call."

"Dad, thanks. I need those words. I know I haven't respected your wisdom in the past. You had a know-it-all son. I'm sorry. Some things have been happening here, and I've realized I don't know much of anything. But it's all good."

He got excited as he shared the news with his father. "There are so many new people coming to church. We're seeing miracles. Dad, it looks like what happened in the book of Acts. You've got to come experience this."

"Wonderful, son. So that's what's happening. Your mother and I have felt we were supposed to take a few months off. We didn't have anywhere we wanted to go, but we knew we should arrange everything to be away. This must be the reason. Would you call it a revival?"

137

"Maybe. It might be more like … there's more. Angelic encounters. Supernatural manifestations. It's all very strange, but good."

He could hear his father … whooping … yes, definitely whooping, on the other end of the phone. In a bit, as if the man came back to his senses, he started talking.

"I've been praying for this for years. Thank God I've lived to know it's happening. Just to hear the change in you is a miracle for me. We'll be there soon, Son. And don't worry about finding us a place, or taking time for us. We're coming to help. I gotta tell your mom. Bye."

Randy stared at the phone. *Well, that was fun. It'll be nice to have them around. The girls will love having their grandparents here.*

He checked his schedule. "Oh, I need to talk to Tony."

(1) Galatians 5:25, (2) Ephesians 2:6, (3) Ephesians 3:20, (4) Exodus 18:17-23, (5) II Corinthians 4:18

Chapter 22

Randy stood at the door of Tony's office listening to him sing as he played the piano. He felt God's holy reverence, and thought he would violate something special if he crossed the threshold.

The music minister finished what he was playing and bowed his head. When Randy felt free to step inside, he spoke. "Tony, that was beautiful. Did you write it?"

The man looked around and smiled. "Thanks. Yes. But not really. God gave me the words. The notes seemed to flow through my mind like they were coming from heaven."

Coming closer, the pastor put a hand on the musician's shoulder. "Can you repeat what you just did?"

"I hope so."

Randy pulled a chair next to the piano and sat down. "I've come to apologize to you."

Tony gave him a questioning look. "Really, for what?"

The pastor put his hands in his lap, and whispered, "I've been too controlling with this church. I confess I thought I was responsible for everything that happens here. To be honest, I didn't know the Holy Spirit wanted to be an active part of what we do. My attitude probably stifled your creativity. I'm sorry.

"As I listened to you just now, I realized how good God has been to send us a mature worship leader who knows how to welcome heaven here. Thank you."

Randy cleared his throat and swallowed hard to get the next words out. "I am freeing you to lead worship however you feel the Spirit leading. If he wants us to worship all morning, I'm okay with it."

The questioning look remained on Tony's face. "Really? Thank you. I confess, sometimes I've needed to repent after church for not following the Holy Spirit. But, I know I'm under your authority, too."

"Yes, you've shown more maturity than I have. In the future, I'd like us to be more like partners in the church services. Hopefully, you will use this new song God gave you."

Tony smiled and said, "Great. Can I share a few things with you that I've been thinking about?"

"Please do. I'm sorry I haven't spent more time with you."

"No problem. I would like to start something similar to a choir. I know you want to be contemporary, and the worship team is great. This would be different. We could have musical productions for the community to enjoy. There could be a children's choir, too. People always enjoy children when they perform. And wouldn't an orchestra be great?"

Randy liked the ideas. Not wanting to give Tony too much instruction, he replied. "There's nothing more important than to bring the worship of heaven to the people, and help them respond. Do you agree?"

"Definitely. These ideas would be more for the community."

"Yes, I understand. Sounds good. Although, after hearing you this morning, I think God wants to use you as a song writer, too. Perhaps you should pursue writing music above the other things you've mentioned."

Tony nodded. "Yes, in fact, I've been writing a musical production. It's totally original. The music and words just keep flowing through my mind. I'm very excited."

"Great. I'm glad I stopped by. Follow the Lord's leading and we'll see where he takes us."

"Yes, I will," Tony smiled. "I keep asking the Lord how the ideas he gives me can ever really happen, and here you are encouraging me to go for it." He paused, "Where is this all leading, Randy?"

The pastor shrugged, "I don't know. We don't need to have all the answers. We'll just follow the Master. He knows."

***

As Randy left Tony's office he considered the words he just spoke. *We don't need to have all the answers. We just follow the Master. Those sure weren't my words. Father, is that true?*

Barbara rushed down the hall to meet him. "Pastor, I have information for you. I prayed about the four angels with the scrolls in church a few weeks ago. They were so amazing. Glorious light flashed from inside them. Anyway, the Lord led me to Revelation chapter seven where it talks about four angels coming to bring destruction. However, one commentary said they come to hold back *evil* until God choses *his* day to bring judgement."

"Hmm. Very interesting, Barbara. I hope the last reference is the correct one. What do you think?"

"Well, I think the angels are here to protect us from the enemy because God has great plans ahead. Perhaps the scrolls hold the blueprints for what he wants to do here. Isn't that exciting?"

"Um-hum." He remembered he was told to encourage her, but felt like something unseen was trying to choke him so he couldn't speak. He shook his head, hoping to break free, and uttered. "Thank you for your research, Barbara. You have a wonderful gift for seeing what others can't."

She smiled, "Thank you, Pastor. What a nice thing to say. I've always felt like you thought I was nuts." She turned and waved as she hurried on. "See you Sunday."

Randy moved toward his office. *What is that gift? Maybe she is a Seer, like in the Bible, or even a prophet like the Word tells about. I guess I better pay more attention to what she says.*

***

When Randy returned to the church after lunch, Andrew was locking his bicycle near the door.

"Hey, Pastor. How's it goin'?"

"Good Andrew. How about you? Are you enjoying your time off this summer?"

"Sure am. Just rode thirty miles. I was hoping to get to talk to you."

"Okay. I'm free now. Let's go into my office."

"Sure."

Glenda greeted the two as they entered. "Pastor, you had a call from Dave Bruner again. It seemed urgent."

He glanced at the message. "Oh, The mayor. I wonder what he wants. I better call back. Excuse me a minute, Andrew."

"Sure. Go ahead." The young man turned to Glenda.

"How are things with you, Glenda?"

"Good." She tried to control her breathing, hoping not to show any emotion to imply she was interested in one of the few single men her age around the place. "What's going on with the youth group?"

He brightened. "Wow. It's growing. There's real excitement in the kids. I have some ideas I want to talk to Pastor about."

"Nice. Well, if you need any help, maybe with the girls, I'm available."

Andrew smiled. "What a good idea. I'll keep you in mind."

After they chatted a bit the pastor opened his door and waved. "Okay, Andrew, come on in."

He nodded and said, "See you later, Glenda."

Inside the office the thin young man sat across from his pastor. His long legs almost banged the desk, and his broad shoulders rubbed the edges of the wingback chair.

Randy wasted no time. "What's new? School's starting soon. What are you teaching this year?"

Andrew pushed his studious glasses back on his nose, and then swiped the short spike of hair above his forehead. "They've got me teaching history and science. With budget cuts caused by so many people moving away to find work, the history teacher lost his job,

142

so I'm up."

"You're certified in both subjects?"

"Yes, I love science and history. When I couldn't decide which I wanted to teach I got certified in both. It was a lot of work. The challenge to teach two subjects will keep me busy, but ..."

Andrew looked serious. "I wanted to talk to you about what's happening here."

"Sure, what's on your mind?"

"Well, after Micah and Travis were part of praying Kevin back to life, the youth group started growing. We had forty-five kids last week. They asked a million questions, and had me on my toes trying to remember scriptural answers and where to find the passages to confirm them. I'm just a volunteer. They need a real youth pastor who could spend time with each one of them."

"Well, Andrew, it's good those kids trust you for the answers they're seeking."

"Yes, it is, but I feel so inadequate. I never went to Bible school. I just know Jesus is real and loves them unconditionally. Anyway, when I ride, no one else is around so I hear the Holy Spirit better. I've been thinking about the laws saying we can't teach from the Bible in schools. I don't believe those laws are really constitutional so I'm thinking of breaking a few. Our students are talking to others. The young people have a fierce hunger to know God. I'm convinced history and science would be excellent subjects to teach Bible truths."

Randy stared at the quiet young man as he shared the actions he was considering. He had never heard more than ten words out of him before.

Andrew's thoughts seemed to be formulating as he spoke "I'm thinking I can teach the true meaning of our national holidays in American history. I can do the same in world history by having the students write reports about God's part in establishing nations. There are wonderful historical books that include God's presence in one miracle after another all through our country and other nations' history."

He took a quick breath. "Of course, science is a great place to reveal the grandeur of someone greater than all of us. He established the laws of nature and the moral code for mankind. I'm telling you, these kids want to know this stuff. They'll thrive as they realize the depths of God's intricate presence in everything around us."

Randy leaned back hoping for wisdom. "You know you could lose your job if you go too far with this."

It was obvious the young teacher wouldn't be distracted by such concerns. "True, but that will probably happen with my next idea. I'm thinking of using the Bible as one of our resource materials. It is just wrong the greatest book in human history isn't allowed in classrooms. I may get fired, but so what? I could be cut from the budget just as easily."

Randy could almost see fire flashing from Andrew's eyes. He leaned forward. "I do think you're up to the fight, but as your pastor I'm afraid I need to pour a little cold water on your enthusiasm. The students need you at the school. They're looking to you for answers. You can be much more affective working with them, than taking a heroic stand for your views and getting kicked out."

Andrew sighed and dropped his head, "Pastor, I feel like something bigger than I am is driving me to take this opportunity. I can see if I'm bold and successful an entire high school could be empowered to become who they were created to be."

He took a breath. "They just need to know the truth of God's love for them. Some are so lost and alone it makes me hurt. Drugs, sex, gangs, the violence in computer games, and now the confusion about their gender, is trying to destroy these young people. None of those things will help them find who their hearts really wants to know."

Randy nodded, "I understand, but aren't there things you can do in the school to help them without blatantly coming against the establishment?"

"I don't know. I'm thinking I'm probably not the first teacher to try this. There may be resources available to help me."

"Ask Glenda to see what she can find. She's always checking resources for me."

Andrew smiled. "Good idea." He stopped as if lost in thought. "I know I can use the students to write the reports I mentioned. They still have a right to free speech, even if I don't in the classroom."

"Yes." Randy agreed. "And God has given you love for the students. He will help you know what to say and do. Plus, they are hearing about what's happening in our youth group and starting to come to check it out."

The teacher perked up. That's right. We may need a bigger place to meet. Our room is maxed out."

Randy agreed. "I'll look for a quick solution, so don't worry. If we need to we'll put up a tent, or rent a place."

Andrew responded, "That sounds good."

***

After Andrew left the office, Randy relaxed. Each conversation with the people earlier ran through his mind. He remembered the choking he felt while trying to encourage Barbara. "Lord, that wasn't right. What happened?"

He was surprised to hear an answer so quickly.

"In the past the spirit of pride and judgment bound your ability to be an exhorter. You were created to see the good in people and encouraging them.

"With Barbara, you felt choked because the enemy does not want anyone to recognize the strong anointing on her life. She is my mouthpiece. Normal life is hard for a woman who sees what others can't. She is always an outsider. The evil one attacks her continually with his degrading words."

"Oh, God, I didn't know. Please empty me of the hindrances of pride and judgment so I can praise others freely. Will you replace those things with your love?"

"It would be My pleasure."

Chapter 23

Sherry opened the door and the girls ran out yelling "Grandma, Grandpa." The older couple left their car doors open while they embraced their grandchildren. Sherry joined them with Randy close behind. One conversation stacked on top another as they tried to make up for lost time.

"We're so glad to have you here. Come in, come in," Sherry finally said. "I've made lunch. After that we can take you to see the house we found for you."

"Perfect," Mother Wright responded.

***

After taking a long lunch to visit, Sherry checked her watch. The afternoon was moving too fast. Randy and his dad were head to head discussing all the things happening at church. Mother Wright was in the girls' bedroom. The children were chattering non-stop while their grandmother shared their excitement.

"Randy, it's getting late. Don't you think we better help them get settled?"

"Oh, of course. Girls, bring your Grandma, and let's take them to see their new house."

Quickly the little covey of females emerged with Amanda announcing. "We fixed it up all pretty." Then she whispered to the women, although everyone heard, "We put flowers on the table for you to look at and smell."

Olivia looked shocked and whispered back. "You weren't supposed to tell. It was a surprise."

Grandma responded secretly, too. "Oh, darlings, that sounds wonderful,"

Everyone laughed as they headed for the cars. "Can we ride with them?" Amanda questioned.

Sherry looked at their car. "The backseat is full of their things, girls. Maybe next time."

Grandma agreed. "Yes, next time. We brought you some surprises we will give you after we get all our things inside."

Olivia and Amanda smiled at each other.

***

Back at the church, Glenda was pleased when Gayle stopped by her office. She asked her if she had time to talk a few moments. The woman paused and checked her phone.

"I feel like I'm always on the run. Sure, I do have some time, and I'd love to get to know you better, Glenda." She took the seat closest to her desk. "You must really be busy with all the new activity, and added office work. And, now you're mentoring the teen girls. too."

"Yes, I am." Not wanting to waste a minute of Gayle's time, Glenda jumped right into her question. "I need an answer to something, and I know you're a Bible teacher. Maybe you can help me."

"Okay, I'll try. What's your question?"

"How do you know if you're really hearing God's voice?"

Gayle smiled. "Why do you ask?"

"I've been having thoughts much bigger than I would normally consider. Ridiculous ideas come to my mind about things I could never accomplish."

Gayle scooted closer to her desk. "That's what they said about putting a man on the moon, and hundreds of other things." She looked at the pretty face which was so serious with concern. "Wonderful girl, hopefully I can help you. I've found when I have

148

thoughts that are much smarter than I am, I can trust I'm hearing God. Oh, the words sound like my own voice, but they're always more challenging than anything I'd come up with on my own."

"Yes, they're like that."

Gayle nodded. "Then, when I pray about the thoughts, a scripture often comes to mind to confirm the truth of what I'm hearing. If that doesn't happen I write the thoughts in my journal and watch for confirmation through other scriptures I haven't memorized, or from all sorts of other ways God speaks to us."

"That's what happened to me. I said, "Holy Spirit, if that's really you talking, give me a scripture to prove it. Instantly, Philippians 4:13 came to mind. 'I can do all things through Christ who strengthens me.'"

"Exactly. Isn't it amazing?"

"Yes and strange." Glenda added. "That's why I offered to help with the teen girls. I kept seeing them confused about their identity. They're sucked into thinking they need the latest fashions, make-up and hairstyles to fit in. It's so sad. I remember struggling through that too."

"I know," the woman said. "I'm so pleased Caroline is in your group. The pressure on young people is overwhelming. They need to be in an environment that helps them find God's answers to their true identity."

Glenda smiled as hope-filled thoughts joined her confusion. Feeling safe with the godly lady, she decided to share more. "People have started coming in my office just to hang out. I can hardly get any work done. Ever since I began mentoring the girls they come in with questions, or just to share their day with me. Andrew often stops by to 'bat ideas around'."

Gayle seemed to be studying her. "Glenda, do you have any idea how beautiful you are?"

"What? I'm not beautiful. I know I'm a Plain Jane with office skills, but that's okay. God loves me."

"Oh, my dear, I agree God loves you, but the rest of that is totally not true. Of course you're not a super model. Who wants to be? But you are a head-turner."

Glenda blushed and looked at her lap as the woman continued.

"People are drawn to you because you shine like a bright star. The glory of God glows from inside you. In truth, you are rather captivating. The girls are trying to find out how to get what you have.

"Andrew is too absorbed with helping the students, to figure out he is completely infatuated with you. Everyone else can see it."

"Really?" She blushed again. "That's hard to believe."

"I know. Give him time. You don't want to run ahead of God's plans anyway."

Embarrassed by the thought, Glenda quickly changed the subject. "It's nice, and fun to have him and the girls around, but I have so many new projects, I can't keep up."

"Yes, yes." Gayle jumped up from the chair. "Isn't that the truth? I'd better get."

Glenda was shocked. "Oh, I didn't mean that you needed to go."

"I know. But we both have much to do. I've really enjoyed our chat. We must talk again soon." Gayle headed toward the door, but paused and turned back. "You're an awesome woman of God, Glenda. We're blessed to have you here. Bye."

"Goodbye. Thank you." Gayle's healing words washed over her.

Angels smiled as they watched the beautiful one they were sent to assist continue her work.

Chapter 24

Jethro and Charles emerged from the darkness of the bridge area after another successful night of serving the weak and needy. They followed Ken and Everett, who were taking three more people to the shelter. Jethro shook his head in amazement. "God does more good stuff every time we go. He is pulling people out of darkness physically and spiritually. Soon there won't be anyone who needs to live there."

Charles nodded while keeping in step with Jethro's lanky legs. They moved quickly along Thirteenth Avenue in hopes of finding more souls ready to receive God's love.

Before they reached Seventh Street, five men sauntered toward them. The darkness obscured their faces, but even at a distance the flashes of steel in the hands of the two in front showed clearly. They rushed forward, weapons extended, vile words flowing. Two of the others stopped a few steps back and pulled their shirts open to reveal revolvers stuck in their baggy pants.

They parted like they were the security team for their leader who pressed to the front. The night was dark but one streetlight shone on the face of the man who looked as if he just took center stage. A four-inch scar ran from his temple down his left cheek.

Jethro cringed. *Nate Grady. I was hoping not to meet him. They say he wears hate like a badge of honor.*

The gang leader faced off as best he could with the men at least a foot taller than him. "We let your other guys go on by. You won't be joinin' 'em tonight." His black eyes flashed with a spark of light.

Black eyes. Light flashes. Looks like we've got demons. An involuntary chill ran down Jethro's spine as he glanced at Charles.

Oh, I wanted to avoid this He stood totally still while trying to remember what he heard about the young man who looked hard as stone. *He came to Millbrook when he got out prison because his mother lives in town. He was arrested for robbery, selling drugs, and there was something about putting someone in the hospital after a brutal attack. Obviously, he didn't come out of the fight too well by the look of the scar.* He recognized those with him from town. *They're just a bunch of misdirected troublemakers.*

What now, Lord? He hoped with all that was in him he would hear an answer.

"Arrogant spirit.[1]"

Really. I wouldn't have guessed that. I'm seeing hate, and maybe murder. But if you say so. Arrogant spirit. They think they own the world. Come at them with the opposite spirit.

Jethro humbly dropped his head. "What do you want?"

The assailant jigged around like a trained boxer ready to attack. He seemed even more excited his opponents already surrendered.

The cackle of his voice sounded diabolical. "We want blood."

I told you it was hate and murder, God.

Jethro could hear fear in Charles' voice as he whispered, "Jesus. Jesus."

Father, you've got to get us out of this. Charles' kids and wife need him.

A scripture came to his mind. Quietly, he said to Charles. "At the name of Jesus every knee will bow and every tongue will confess that Jesus Christ is Lord.[2]"

Speaking God's words quieted his spirit. The street evangelist listened again.

"Arrogance will want you to know who it is that's so powerful."

Okay. I'm trusting you, Lord. With head still humbly facing the ground, Jethro slowly put his thumb and forefinger on his chin and twisted the hairs of his beard. "Don't think I know you guys."

Nate announced, "You jerk. We're the Gladiators. We're taking over this town." The others shrugged their shoulders while swearing, and declared how stupid the guys were for not knowing about them. Nate banged his clenched fists together. "You'll remember us when this night is over."

Even bowed, Jethro was tall enough to look down into their eyes. "Hmm. I don't think so. You see, God is taking over this town. He has sent his mighty warriors to fight for his land."

God, what did you just have me say?

Jethro saw Charles's bowed head jerk from the gang to look at him. He heard his companion whisper, "Oh, God get us out of here. Thank you, Micah couldn't come tonight." Jethro shared his concern, but knew their only hope was to follow the Spirit's lead. He waited quietly.

Nate continued his intimidation. "I don't know why you guys keep coming into our territory, but this is your last night here. You got that. Whatever you're up too, it stops now. We own this land and everyplace around here. You're not welcome."

The other Gladiators pulled their weapons and moved slowly closer. Their eyes reflected fierce hate and murder as evil seethed through them like bloodthirsty wild animals.

Jethro and Charles couldn't move. They felt paralyzed knowing if God didn't show up these would be the last painful moments of their lives.

The possessed rebels were so close they could smell their stinky breath as they poured profanities like a sewer over God's faithful servants.

Jethro burst out. "Jesus save us."

Nate seethed. "Jesus ain't real. What can he do? God has no power to save you. We have all the power here."

Words flew out of Jethro's mouth without a thought. "I will call upon the Lord, who is worthy to be praised. So shall I be saved from my enemies."[3]

Shocked by a scripture he didn't remember knowing, flying out of his mouth, he tenses.

Suddenly, the five rebels squinted as if someone blasted them with bright lights. They covered their eyes and moaned. Then the gang grabbed their middles and wilted in pain. Their bodies contorted and their spines convulsed. The vile language continued to flow. There was no doubt the evil holding them was powered from the pit of hell.

Jethro and Charles jumped back in surprise and banged into something large. Warmth, like a hot furnace penetrated their backsides. They were grateful for whoever came to help, but didn't dare turn away from the group to see who was there.

Feeling a bit more secure, they watched in amazement as grown men seethed and hissed. Jethro observed the scene like a scientist doing research. He whispered to Charles. "I've seen demonic manifestations before but these fiends are really showing off. They don't want these guys to be free of their control."

The men watched the poor souls writhe and moan while they tried to figure out what to do next. Involuntary words flew out of Jethro's mouth again. "You're being tormented by the demons you let into your life by your wrong choices. You thought the things you were messing around with gave you power. That power has turned on you. How do you like it now?"

Guttural curses and growls filled the air as they lay between two worlds. Heaven's angels were there to free them, but Hell wasn't about to let go easily. This battle for their souls might overtax them to the point their hearts couldn't take it, if something didn't happen soon. Satan wouldn't mind killing them if they weren't useful to him anymore.

"Listen to me." Jethro shouted. "God's light has come to set you free, but Satan wants to take you out. The only way you can escape is to make a better choice. Right now evil has control of you. That don't seem to be workin' out too good."

God are you sure that's what you wanted me to say?

The groveling ones got even louder.

More words burst through Jethro's lips. "You gettin' a good look at Hell? That's where you'll be livin' forever. In a place where there's no life, no love, and no peace. Those things only come from God."

The moans turned to begging. "Help. Save us. Please."

Jethro prayed silently, *Lord, how do ya want us to help them?* He listened to hear the Holy Spirit.

With new boldness he glanced at Charles. "I think we're supposed to set them free. Do you agree?"

Charles nodded. "I hate seeing these young guys suffering so."

"Okay, here we go." He yelled above the moans. "I can't help you. You're too far gone. But, you could give your life to God. He's the only one who can do anything for you."

Strong evil forces held them captive as the curses flew. They twisted and scratched at the street as if something powerful was dragging them into an abyss.

The leader groaned and let the swearwords fly as he fought the strong forces that held him captive. "Yes … yes … Help us. Here." He tossed his knife at their feet. Then pulled a revolver from his boot and slid it over. The others did the same.

Charles grabbed the weapons and placed them in his jacket pockets before the leader could change his mind.

Jethro's compassion took over. "God created you for something much better than the life you've got now. He loves you and wants to set you free from an eternity of hate and tormented loss. If you're sure you want to be free, we will ask God to get these tormentors out of your life. When they're gone, the only way you can stay free is by inviting Jesus to take over your life. He will fill the empty places the evil ones leave, so they can't come back and bring others with them.[4]

"Yes, help us."

"Okay, Lord, your Word says you have given us the power to cast out demons, so Charles and I are going to kick these despicable varmints out of these young men you love. We do this by the power of your name[5] and the power of your blood.[6]

Nate cried out, "I'm sorry, God. Forgive me?"

The others yelled, "Yeah, me, too."

They continued writhing on the ground while crying to God for mercy.

Jethro spoke. "Satan, the blood of Jesus paid the price for these warriors who you've tried to destroy. This night they choose Jesus. Tormentors, we demand you to come out of them right now in Jesus' name."

The gang members began to gag. Disgusting goo poured from their mouths. Jethro was sure he heard squeals of frustrated imps as they were expelled from the men's souls, and sent into some unseen vortex. After a while, the spastic pulsing left their bodies and they lay quiet as death.

The light behind Jethro and Charles moved forward revealing the brilliance of a heavenly angelic host within a glowing sphere. It hovered over the bodies. Several reached out from the glorious mist surrounding them, and touched each of the repentant ones with their shining swords. On contact the yielded bodies jerked as electricity-like charges zapped through them.

Jethro and Charles were wide-eyed. Never had they seen such beauty. They watched in wonder.

The gang began to roll back and forth, giggling like little girls. Jethro analyzed what was happening. The Holy Spirit was taking ownership of their lives. *I know that feeling. Joy is bubbling up inside them.* He smiled as laughter consume the group on the ground. The whole situation was contagious so Jethro and Charles couldn't keep from joining the laughter. They, too, felt a fresh infilling of the out-of-this-world elixir, all through their bodies. Jethro wiggled his toes noticing they even felt tingly and alive.

Back to business, he announced, "Guys, the Holy Spirit is here to fill all the empty places the demons left. Open your eyes and see a little bit of what heaven looks like."

In the midst of all the giggling, those on the ground watched in awe as heaven manifested.

Too soon, the light faded and everything was quiet. Smiling, Jethro and Charles dried the tears from their faces and slapped hand with a high-five.

Charles moved forward to gather the rest of the weapons. Then he turned to Jethro and whispered, "Now what?"

Jethro only shrugged. Good sense would tell them to run. But something else compelled them to stay.

Charles's pockets, usually filled with things to help people, dragged to his knees. He stepped back to lean against a tree. The two men waited until the Gladiators began to move. When the first one sat up, Jethro's heart melted. *Five new brothers.*

He walked over and held out a hand to help the guy to his feet. "I told you God was taking over this city." He looked across the others as they began to move. "And yes, you are all warriors. But now you can serve in the army of God's kingdom, not Hells."

The leader sat up in a daze. "That sounds good, man. I've never felt so clean. My mind is so … quiet."

Jethro reached out to Nate, and he popped up laughing. The tall man bent a bit to give the leader a shoulder bump hug and said, "God loves ya, man. He has a great future planned for you. Tomorrow's going to be a brand new day. Do you have a place to stay?"

"Yeah. I can sleep at Ma's."

Jethro nodded. "Okay." He checked the others who didn't look very steady on their feet. "How about the rest of ya?"

"We'll go home." They looked at each other in agreement.

The youngest of the five said through his laughter, "My Ma ain't gonna believe what's happened to me."

Jethro felt hopeful hearing the same man who pointed a blade at his heart, was now talking about his mom. "All right. We're at Maggie's Café Tuesday nights at eight. Come, and you can learn more about God's love."

The whole group could barely stand up as they continued to laugh like fools. The hardness in Nate's face was gone. He looked like a different man as he cracked jokes with the others. "Thanks. We'll be there." He waved his followers forward. The ex-rebels looked like a bunch of drunks as they staggered past Jethro and Charles and nodded respectfully.

Nate looked up at the men he threatened before. "What is this. I've never felt this high before."

Charles announced, "We call it being drunk in God's spirit."

Nate sighed. "Whoa. This is better than anything we're sellin'."

Compassion filled Jethro, "Nate, you may not remember what I'm telling you tomorrow, but try to listen. You're a born leader. Those guys would follow you to their grave. Give them something good to live for, man."

Nate looked at the little group laughing and sharing as they bumped into each other while staggered along the street.

Charles reached in his breast pocket and pulled out a New Testament Bible. "Here, take this. Read it and learn how to be the leader God created you to be. The words sound kind of crazy at first, but when you believe what it says and just go with it, you'll love what happens."

"Thanks, man." Nate gave Charles a hug. "I love what I'm feelin'. Looking at the book he said. "These were in the prison, but I never picked one up. I figured it couldn't do nothin' for me." While weaving, he looked at the sky. "Now I think it might." He held the book close.

Charles stretched his hand out to shake Nates. "My name is Charles and this is Jethro."

Nate grabbed his hand and shook it hard. "I'm Nate Grady. Thanks for being here tonight. We've watched you, and wondered what you were up to." His head bobbed up and down as he thought about the experience. "Nice." He turned to shake Jethro's hand. "I wanta learn that stuff you know."

"You'll be great at it." Jethro slapped his back affectionately.

Nate sauntered toward his men, then looked back and gave them a quick wave. He put his arms around the first two he reached. They all talked at once as they disappeared into the darkness.

Jethro and Charles stood silently. Charles was the first to utter a word. "Wow." He took a deep breath revealing tension he would never admit.

Jethro put his hand on the man's shoulder. "You are so right. We better go."

As the two men moved on toward the police department Charles asked, "How did all those things happen. I've never seen anything like it before. Do you do deliverances like that all the time?"

Jethro shook his head. "No, of course not. But we need ta always be ready for whatever God wants to do through us. You didn't know you were gonna bring a dead man back to life, did you?"

"No. but when I saw him I knew. I could hear his parents praying for him."

"Right. When I looked at those miserable young men I could see who they were created to be. I knew God wanted them free. I didn't know how he was gonna bring the change so I prayed for him to lead us.

"It was obvious to me they were under the influence of murderous, hateful spirits, but the Holy Spirit said it was an arrogant spirit. I wasn't considering that one, but that evil thing must have been in control, hiding behind what was obvious."

Charles asked. "So … is what you did tonight a pattern for us to follow next time we see that sort of thing."

Jethro laughed. "Oh, Charles, you should know by now, there ain't no patterns. We are totally dependent on hearing the Spirit's voice and obeying. We can't go by what we think needs to be done or we'll get ourselves in a fix. No … our only pattern is to follow the Holy Spirit's led. That's all we've got.

"Now, the angels, I've never experienced anything like that before. Sometimes I've felt their presence. Ya know, I think maybe heaven has come to open our eyes so we can see the things that are not as though they were."[8]

Charles' head jerked and he stopped walking. "That's what Beth was describing to me when she saw heaven open. I thought she was hallucinating, or dreaming, but now I think she really did see heaven and Jesus."

Jethro nodded. "And just think, we've only started to understand that there's a whole lot more going on around us than we can see."

The men walked the rest of the way in silence.

***

When they entered the police department, the Sergeant on duty greeted Jethro as he would a good friend.

"Evening, Sergeant. This is Charles Morgan. He goes with me some nights. He has some stuff for ya."

Charles emptied his pockets of two large switchblades, three revolvers and a hunting knife.

The officer shook his head as he gathered up the cache. "You guys. We ought to put you on the payroll."

They grinned. Jethro knew the police would want an explanation. "These came from some fellas who said they were the Gladiators. The leader's Nate Grady."

The Sergeant nodded. "We heard rumbles of two gangs trying to get a foothold in town. Nate. Is he looking for trouble? He just got out of jail in January."

Excited, Charles responded. "Well, he and four others met God tonight. Don't think they'll be causing any more trouble. Hope they use their energy and talents for something good now." He turned to Jethro. "I'm exhausted. It's time for me to go home."

Jethro nodded. "Thanks for going with me, man. What a night. Those angels were so cool. See, we don't need to be afraid."

Charles scratched his head. "True, they just stepped right out of heaven, became visible, and took care of everything."

Looking puzzled, the officer listened with interest.

(1) Proverb 16:18, (2) Philippians 2:10, (3) II Samuel 22:4, (4) Luke 11:26, (5) Mark 16:17-18, (6) Hebrews 10:19-23, (7) Acts 2:14-18, (8) Romans 4:17

Chapter 25

Randy burst into the sanctuary in hopes Cassius might be there. His heavenly companion hadn't shown himself in several weeks so he yelled, "Cassius are you in here? I need to talk to you."

Silence reigned.

"Oh, Father, I need to make things right. Please."

"Please what?" a voice bellowed.

The young man whirled around. "Cassius, it's so good to see you."

"Really? Why? I don't have any new messages from the Master for you."

"That's okay. I just want to tell you I'm sorry for being such a jerk. I've always been that way with the people closest to me. Isn't that sick? My poor parents, I was so hateful to them.

"It's as if I'm two different people. I put on a good face at church, but ... well, like last night. When I got home, Sherry had the kitchen all torn up. She was painting the walls with some new color she was excited about, and she was covered with paint. It was even in her hair. The place was a mess. There was no dinner in sight. I blew up. The least a man can expect after work is a meal on the table."

He looked up at Cassius who nodded, "Go on."

"I was steaming. But eating wasn't going to happen for a while. I chewed her out about the foolishness. I could hear the girls in another room so I stomped out to check on them. When I called Sherry out for neglecting them, because she had no idea what they were doing, she started crying.

"Those kids made a mess all over the living room. Sofa pillows covered the floor and blankets were hung across everything. When I asked ... okay, I yelled, at them about destroying the room, there was fear on their faces that still haunts me. I went to the garage to get myself under control. After I quit fuming I realized I really am causing damage to the most precious people in my life with my anger and bad temper, just like you said.

"Sherry didn't speak to me this morning. I only got dinner because I made a sandwich after they all went to bed. She usually just lets my outburst slide, but I think I've screwed up too many times. The damage may not be repairable.

"The pressure from all the activity at the church is too much for me." He shook his head and looked at the floor, "If I don't change I'll need to quit this job. I can't stand the turmoil."

Cassius crossed his legs and settled in the air with a puzzled look on his face as he listened.

Randy continued. "I think I only became a minister to prove I wasn't a hot head. But I'm still the same. I hide it better around other people, but my family sees the real me, just as you have. I need your help. How do I move on? How do I change?"

"Love," Cassius responded.

Old anger began to erupt inside Randy. He took a deep breath before he said harshly. "I know. That's always your answer." He began to pace. When he stood just below Cassius he looked up. "But how?"

"It's not how. When the Holy Spirit fully lives inside of you, love will become natural. You don't have to work for it, or pretend. He gives you the love you need for others."

"How can that be?"

"Again, Randal, it's all in the Word." Cassius leaned back and put his hands behind his head. "In fact, if you knew nothing else from the Bible but the two commands about love, you could be successful. Do you remember them? Love the Lord your God with all your heart, soul, and mind, and love your neighbor as yourself.[1]"

"The two New Testament commands. Yes." Randy took a breath. "God does keep things simple enough for a child to understand." He looked at the carpet and took a few steps. "But I don't live those commands. I'm not sure I even like people."

"I know."

The pastor looked up. "Yes, I know you do. I'm sorry. You were sent to me as a gift from God, and I treated you with disrespect from the beginning. I can't believe I've been so stupid."

Cassius dismissed him with a wave of his hand. "Don't worry. I've dealt with more controlling, angry, stubborn people than you. I'm actually surprised you've come around so quickly."

Randy stared at the amazing example of heaven's kingdom. He hadn't considered Cassius might have helped others before. Thoughts of Israel's history, world wars, and the angels who interrupted peoples' lives all through the Bible, flipped through his mind. "I'd love to hear some of your stories."

"Randal, you too, were created to be a history maker. What are you going to do about that?"

The question burned through his heart like fire. "I guess love is the only answer?"

"Yes."

The pastor contemplated Cassius' words, and then he responded, "History maker. I don't understand."

"The answer is always the same Randal. You could preach it every week. Ask the Father to forgive you and fill you with himself. Remember, God is love. He wants to love through you." Cassius opened his palms. "And forgive yourself, too."

Randy nodded, but continued to remember all the times he tried to love, and failed.

As if an afterthought, Cassius added, "Just give him your anger and pride. You don't have to be in control of every situation. You're trying to take care of things the Father wants to fix in a much more powerful way than you can."

The pastor felt helpless as he wondered about the possibility of being free from his old character traits.

The mighty angel continued. "Judgement is a stronghold in your life too, Randal. You can't love people when you judge them. Your expectations of others, and yourself, are unrealistic. You must accept people just as they are to be able to love them as Jesus does. No one's perfect. Perfection is an illusion.

"Our Father loves unconditionally. He accepts us with no strings attached."

Randy sat down on the altar stairs and put his head in his hands. "Oh, Father God, forgive me. I love you with all my heart, soul, and mind. You know that isn't the truth right now, but I'm asking you to make it true. Cleanse me from anger, judgment, pride and feeling I need to be in control. As you take those things out of me, please replace them with a love that brings you pleasure."

Cassius vanished as the pastor continued.

"Father, forgive me. I gave you my life a long time ago, but I didn't realize you wanted me to surrender everything. I've been handling this ministry as if it were mine to make successful. I've taken pride in my articulate sermons, and my skills as a counselor. I surrender those things to you as well."

Peace beyond his ability to understand flowed within him.

***

When Randy heard someone call his name, he sat up in bed. The room was dark. Sherry slept quietly at his side. Throwing the blankets off, he walked into the living room. The presence of something indescribable filled the quiet atmosphere. He stood in the silence as an out-of-this-world presence flowed around him that tickled with energy.

As if a floodlight turned on, the room filled with light. When he opened his eyes to the brightness, a glowing man stood in its center. He had shoulder length hair and wore a white robe. Currents of love, that felt alive, radiated from him.

"Lord." Randy dropped to his knees and stared in awe.

Pulsating light surrounded the glorious manifestation. Without speaking verbally, he communed with Randy. "Son, receive my love."

Powerful heat moved through him. Feelings of ecstasy surged through his body. His muscles weakened, and what felt like a puddle of human flesh wilted to the floor. *Oh, Lord. This hurts but it's too wonderful to ask you to stop.* He collapsed in rapturous fulfillment as the room went dark.

After some time, he stretched out on the floor. "Jesus. I didn't know. You are more than anything I can ever comprehend. Love. I received your love. It's true, I can only know how to love by knowing your all-consuming, unconditional love." Overwhelmed by emotion he whispered. "Thank you."

He pondered the amazement of the experience for some time. When he finally felt his strength return, he headed back to bed. On the way, he stopped at the girls' bedroom door and peeked in. "I love you girls," he whispered. Back to his bed, he looked at his wife with more affection than he knew was possible. "I love you my precious wife." *I must tell her when she's awake.*

He laid down. *I love this bed. It's so comfortable. I love the silence of night. I love your Word, Father. I love my job. I love the people in my church. I love feeling this love.*

Excitement filled him so completely he couldn't sleep. Heaven's love had come down and kissed him. He lay awake until dawn enjoying the overflow of a love he hadn't known existed. The word "impossible" lost all power as possibilities for the days ahead inspired his thoughts.

***

Sherry rolled over. "You're still in bed. Are you okay?"

Randy took his wife in his arms, hoping she would enjoy the warmth of his embrace. He kissed her, and kissed her again and again.

"Oh, nice," she responded with a smile.

"I love you Sherry. Can you forgive me for all the stupid things I've said and done? You are so precious to me. I want to be a better husband and father. Will you help me? I probably need some training. I've been so selfish."

"Of course, sweetheart. Is everything all right?"

"I had an encounter with Jesus last night. It was the most unbelievable experience in my life. I never understood that God *is* love.[2] It's true Sherry, and he put his love in me."

The girls knocked on the bedroom door.

Sherry said, "Shall we let them come in, or have them play a bit and come back later?"

"Yes, let's have them come in. Come in my beautiful daughters. I want to hug you and kiss your faces."

The girls invaded and jumped into the bed to lots of giggles, wiggles and kisses.

(1) Mark 12:30-31, (2) I John 4:8

Chapter 26

Sherry sat curled up in her bedroom chair looking out the window as squirrels made loops around the big oak tree in the back yard. The sunny summer morning added to the warmth she felt from Randy's affection earlier. *What a way to start the day*. Her fingers routinely opened the Bible in her lap. She put the bookmark on her journal pad lying on the little table beside her.

Before she started to read she decided to wait and see if God wanted to say something to her in the quietness of the morning. "Father, what do you have for me today?"

Her mind flipped back to the years when she, as a child, first experienced the peace of a quiet house. She saw herself moving silently around the rooms of their tiny home so her mother didn't get upset. Because, when Mommy brooded, it felt like a black cloud covered everything.

Those memories brought sorrow to her heart. To brush them off she looked down to read. However, they invaded again. There she was, as a little girl, hiding in the closet so her mother couldn't find her. She could feel the fear and utter helplessness of being dragged out and beaten with whatever the raging woman grabbed while on her search. Sherry watched the memory as if it were a video in her head. She always tried to push thoughts of those years of her childhood away, but today they wouldn't leave. As an adult observing the scene, she realized the sick woman controlled herself enough to make sure she only hit her where the abuse wouldn't show. Sherry shook her head to get the picture out of her mind. *Even while she was angry, she knew what she was doing.*

More thoughts flew in. She was twelve when she went to the school nurse and showed her the oozing sores on her legs and back. Sherry remembered that was the day the authorities took her to live with the McDonalds. *They were so kind.*

Anger surfaced at the thought of her mother's alcoholic self-destruction. Sherry felt relieved to be far away from her. *I wonder if she still lives in the same place.*

Again, she refused to follow that line of thought. "No. Sorry, Father, this morning is too lovely to think about the past or my mother." She tried to focus on reading, but another vision came. There she was at sixteen, crying beside her bed, begging God to let her know who her father was. Watching, she knew what the vision of her young self was saying. She joined the girl as she spoke. "I just want to feel loved."

Quickly, the picture changed. She was with Randy in the garage. He was ranting about who-knew-what. She watched herself try to avoid his line of fire. Fearful his harsh voice tones would turn toward her.

Again her mother appeared. The child was trying to survive by using soothing praises to defuse the woman's hot-tempered anger.

Back to Randy. In the garage her soft words didn't work with him either. He wanted to express his fury. After the blow-up, he seemed fine.

But she wasn't fine. Fear gripped her at the thought she had married into the same situation as her childhood. That's why she stayed away when he went to the garage to let off steam. She knew she could never fully trust someone with that kind of temper.

The Holy Spirit's voice interrupted her thoughts. **"So how have you solved the problem?"**

She thought about the question. In her mind, the problem wouldn't be solved. Instead, she chose to never confront him, or anyone else. Any sort of disapproval triggered the voice of her mother's screams.

"Lord," she whispered, "This isn't the person I want to be."

"My precious bride, I brought these things to your mind today so you can be free to move forward in the great days ahead. Your husband has chosen to change. He needs you as his brave and bold partner. My love will wash your memories of those hard days. The experiences will now help you, instead of hold you back. You didn't recognize that during your childhood you learned to be sensitive to other's emotional moods, which is an important virtue. Because of the abusive pain, you recognize the hearts of women in bondage. You can almost see their captivity, whether physical or emotional. Reach out and love them to health.

"You also quickly recognize if a child is in danger and take action to protect them.

"Today, I am going to free you from a spirit of intimidation. We will replace it with a spirit of boldness, wisdom, and freedom. You were created to set many free so they can live life fully."

Sherry wrote in her journal as fast as the pen would fly. "Was that really you, Lord? It's so hard to know if I'm making the words up in my head, or if I'm really hearing your voice. It sounds like my own voice, but I would never say those words to myself."

Faith believes. She reread what was scribbled on the page. *This is who I am, isn't it. I hated being reminded of my past, but you are the only one who can make all my pain purposeful."*

"Lord, I squelched all those memories, and buried them so deeply I hardly remembered them, but they really do define my life, don't they? I hated to look back. Now I see. You take all our pain and loss, and turn it into something we can use to help others."

She considered what change would mean. *"If I'm free, I won't even know how to be with Randy. Father, I've never been able to trust him knowing if I say or do anything he doesn't like he gets angry. Lord, free me to trust him because you do, not because he never messes up."*

Feeling relieved, she took a deep breath. Skimming the words in her Bible, she noticed that Romans 8:28 seemed to jump off the page. *And we know that God causes all things to work together for good to those who love God, to those who are called according to his purposes.*

She smiled. *My new favorite verse.*

Two little girls burst in. Olivia announced, "Mommy, we want to go outside and play. Are you finished praying yet?"

"Yes," she responded as she uncurled, then wrapped her arms around her little darlings. "It is too beautiful to be inside today. Thank you for being quiet so I could talk with Jesus."

They chattered while tugging on her hands to help her get up.

Chapter 27

Glenda peeked her head around the pastor's office door, and announced, "You have a call. It sounds like an emergency."

"Thanks, Glenda." Puzzled, Randy picked up the receiver. "Hello, this is Pastor Wright. How can I help you?"

"Pastor, my name is Sam Moore. My girlfriend and I were driving through town, and she started acting very strange. I stopped at the auto shop and asked a guy named Spencer if he knew anyone who could help us. He gave me your name and number."

Spencer? I don't know anyone there named Spencer. "Is she ill?"

"I don't think so. This is different."

"How different?"

"She's growling, hissing, and swearing, using words so vile I've never heard them before, and I was in the Navy."

Randy froze. *What am I supposed to do with this?*

"Please, sir. Help us."

"Do you know where my church is?"

"I can find it. Spencer said it's on the hill just out of town."

"Yes. Millbrook Road. I'll meet you in the sanctuary. The church will be open."

"Thank you, sir. Thank you."

Randy took a deep breath. *What now?* He got up from his desk, tucked his Bible under his arm, and told Glenda he would be in the sanctuary. As he started to leave her office, he paused. "Will you keep your cell phone handy in case you're on the land line and I need you? Something is wrong with a woman. I have no idea what to expect."

"Sure." She pulled her phone out of her purse and set it on her desk. "I'm right here if you need me. I'll be praying."

"Good … good." He scurried out.

***

Twenty minutes later a young couple entered the church and found Randy. "Hi, Pastor Wright. I'm Sam and this is my girlfriend, Amy."

They shook hands. Randy thought the woman looked fine. Normal. Sane.

After some small talk, Randy questioned the couple. "Tell me what I can do for you."

"Well, we have some issues," Amy responded.

Sam nodded. His eyes looked fearful.

"Tell me about it." Randy knew his best strength was his counseling skills.

Amy looked at Sam. "Sometimes … without any reason, I flip out."

"Flip out. What do you mean?"

"I switch personalities."

"Oh." *Good grief. Really?*

"You see me now. See anything wrong?"

"No, not that I can tell so far. Please, let's sit here." He motioned to the chairs he placed at the back of the room before they arrived.

She continued as they got comfortable. "Well, often, even more often now than before, it feels like something takes over my body, or mind, or soul. I don't know what happens."

Randy responded, "I see. Are you aware of anything that might trigger the attacks? I'll call them that for lack of a better word right now."

"No, not most of the time. All I've been able to catch is I start swearing. I use words I've never heard anybody say. The next thing I know, I'm on the floor exhausted and sweaty. What could be going on?"

Oh, Lord. Why did you send her to me? I don't know anyone who knows about deliverance? What is it the scriptures say about demons? I can't remember. This poor girl needs help.

He looked at Sam. *I wonder why he hasn't run away.* "Do you love this woman?"

"I do."

"Are you willing to stick with her and see her through this thing?"

Sam thought a moment. "I won't kid you. I was scared to death when she started acting out. I felt like she could kill me if she wanted to, and I'm not sure she didn't want to. But something's wrong. She's sick. Just like if she had a disease, she needs to be healed."

The petite young woman stretched tall. "How dare you. Who do you think you are? You men think you can do anything and get away with it. You should all be hanged publicly so we could scoff at you the way you have us."

Randy looked at the seething temptress. *Dear God, what am I supposed to do with this?*

"My son, it is time to grow up and take your authority over the enemy of souls. Amy needs to be set free."

Was that really God speaking? It must have been. I wouldn't say that to myself, and the enemy wouldn't tell me such a thing either.

During his short pause, the gal began to convulse as if she were having a seizure. Her head fell back against the back of the chair as her body stiffened and shook violently.

The men jumped up, and Randy asked, "Does she have health issues?"

"No. Really, she's healthy." He shook his head looking fearful as he stared down at her. "Should I hold her or something?"

"Has she done this before?" The pastor questioned.

"She was different in the car. Honestly she looked like a vicious animal wanting to kill. I've never been so scared in my life. After I talked to you she quieted down."

Randy felt desperate. *Lord, what should I do?*

"Today you will learn how to deal with demons. I'll walk you through it. Now, look at her."

The pastor moved over and stared down. Her friend came long side him.

"See how her eyes are rolled back."

Yes. That could be convulsions. Should I call 9-1-1?

"That's a demon. Touch her."

The pastor put his hand on her arm. She felt like stone.

"A demon has taken over her body. It wants to kill her. What are you going to do about it?"

Me? I don't know.

"Think," the Spirit challenged.

Looking at Amy he said, "The blood of Jesus covers all evil. The name of Jesus has all power. The Word of God delivers and sets free."

"Good. Now use your tools and tell the demon to go."

Randy watched the poor woman a few seconds longer. *If she's conscious she must be scared to death.*

Very gently he said, "Jesus says you have to leave now."

Amy's body immediately relaxed, and then she opened her eyes.

"Ah, thank, God," Sam shouted.

She sat up and smiled. "What happened? When I opened my eyes you were smiling, Pastor. Am I alright now?"

"Well, at least we know what we're dealing with, don't we?" He breathed a sigh of relief. *Really. That actually worked. How could it. Does Jesus's name have that much power? Oh, dear God, what have we been missing?*

Sam embraced Amy.

After a few moments of wondering how such a thing could

176

happen, Randy felt he should continue to council the couple. "Tell me Amy, has anything happened in your life that could have made an opening in your soul for demons to enter. Do you remember anything?"

"Demons? Do you think there's more?"

"Oh, I imagine there are. Think carefully. Anything from your past?"

"I don't have to think hard. I know." She looked at Sam, "This is going to be hard for you to hear. I might even lose you. But I can't stand these bouts any longer."

She looked at Randy, "I'm going to tell you something I've never told another soul." She scanned the room and looked at Sam.

He dropped back into the chair beside her and put his arm around her.

Quietly, Amy began. "When I was very young, before school age, my father was into witchcraft. Satanism. He took me to their rituals. They did all kinds of horrible things to me."

She trembled, and the pastor wondered if she would be able to continue. "Can you tell us what happened?"

Choked up, she began to cry as she gave Sam a pleading look. After taking a deep breath she burst out, "They used me as part of the rituals. I think sexual things. I had no understanding of why so many covered faces would come at me while I was strapped to a board or something that was hard under me."

She moaned and held her ears. "There were drums and chants. We were in the woods. The only light was a fire. It was so dark." Through sobs she became louder. "The horror of those men coming at me was so scary. I cried out to my Daddy, but he just leaned against a tree smoking a cigarette, and watched. ... I can't. Please, I can't...."

Sam held her close and she wept into his chest. After some time she lifted her head to speak. "Maybe I blocked all that happened to me. I do know I can never have children.

"Lately, some of the memories have been coming back. I

wonder if it's because I've found real love for the first time." She looked at Sam. "This man has been so kind. I've actually hoped that we will share our lives together." She looked adoringly at her troubled companion.

Randy kept focus as he asked, "That's when the episodes started? When you began to hope?"

Child-like sobs filled the quiet room. In a little-girl voice she said, "I have to tell. I have to. ..." Words burst forth, "They made me kill a puppy. A cute little puppy." She hid her face in her hands and sobbed even more.

Randy waited, hoping surely she had shared everything. But, no, a moan, almost a roar, came forth from the very depths of her soul. Then a piercing scream filled the room that sent quivers down his spine. *Such a sound could only come from deep within a tormented soul full of great pain and loss. Perhaps that was a demon as it left its host home.*

The woman was pale, like someone who just threw-up their lunch. After taking some deep breathes, she grabbed Sam's hand and proceeded. "During one of the rituals, my father told me I had to kill a baby. I stood over that tiny crying child, no bigger than a doll, with a huge knife in my little hands." She paused, as if reflecting on the impossibility of the situation all over again. "I couldn't do it. I just couldn't do it. I remembered how bad I felt about the puppy. I would die before I killed that baby." Uncontrollable sobs mingled with gasps for air. Sam cuddled her in his arms as she wept.

Randy knelt down, and in a kind voice said, "Of course, you couldn't do it. Why are you upset you couldn't kill?"

Amy looked at him. "My father said I was useless. Useless was one of his kinder words. He said I disgraced him before his elders. After that he was even more evil and hateful to me. My bones still show his angry abuse." She held up her arm to show it hadn't healed straight after being broken more than once.

"Where was your mother while all this went on?"

"She always seemed oblivious to everything that happened to me, even when I came home covered with blood. I left as soon as I was old enough to get away."

"How old were you then."

"I don't know. I'm not sure how old I am. I've never seen my birth certificate."

"How did you get in school?"

"I didn't."

Randy paused, overcome by such a devastating story. *Lord, what should I do to help this couple?* "Amy, where were you two going?"

"We were just passing through. We thought we might go to Tucson for a new start."

Randy thought out loud, "So it could be possible for you to stay around here for a while?"

She looked at Sam. "We could."

With a nod, he agreed.

"All right, here is how I see this situation. Your only hope of being free from your past is to give your life to God. He is the only one who can heal all the damaged places in your soul. The demon we sent away today will be back to see if you still have openings in your heart. When he comes, he will bring others with him.[1] Then you might be worse off. What do you know about Jesus?"

"Who?"

"Jesus, God's son."

"Oh, baby Jesus in the manger. That's all we know." She turned to Sam. "You know. Christmas?"

Sam nodded.

Randy explained. "Yes. Well, the big deal about Jesus in the manger is that he is God's son, born of Mary, who became the Savior of the World. Your Savior and mine.

"We have the privilege of inviting Jesus, who died on a cross for us and rose from the dead, to live in our hearts. When he fills us with his Spirit, the demons can't come back in."

"I want to invite him into me," Amy said quickly.

"Okay. Go ahead. Just tell him," Randy directed.

"Should I bow my head?"

"If you want to."

Amy folded her hands in her lap and bowed her head. "God, thank you for sending Jesus to free me from my past. Please come in and own every place in me that was given over to evil when I was little."

Randy put his hand on hers, and laid his other hand on Sam's shoulder. "Excellent Amy. Father, you have brought this couple to us. I ask your protection and direction over their lives as they begin again."

Amy looked at Sam. "Do you want to pray, too?"

"I already prayed to receive Jesus when you did. This might be the missing piece for us and our future."

Randy patted his shoulder. "Good, Sam. I believe you're right."

"Amy this is only the start." He reached over into the back of a pew and pulled out a Bible. "Here, you'll need this. Can you read?"

"Yes." She ran her hand over the cover as if he gave her something she would treasure.

"My mother taught me when my father wasn't around. We kept my books a secret. When I ran away I spent hours in libraries. They were a good place to hide, and I love learning. Maybe I can be a Librarian someday."

"Wonderful, then you will really enjoy this book. Let me show you." Randy flipped through the pages. "When you start reading go to the back half first." He held a page open. "Start at the book of John and read to the end. You will learn who Jesus is and what he has done for you. When I found the Bible to be the truth, it became a book I always keep close to me. It contradicts a lot of what's being accepted in the world today. You already know what that leads to."

They both nodded in agreement.

Randy pulled out another Bible. "Here Sam, you better have your own."

"Now, Amy, what happened earlier is only the beginning of your journey to freedom from the past. I know you've been through a lot today, but I have one more question. Can you forgive your father?"

The woman looked at him in disbelief. "You're kidding?"

"I'm not. Unforgiveness holds us captive and makes room for the enemy of our soul. I know in yourself you could never forgive those who violated you. But when you're ready, you can tell God you are willing to forgive. He is able to help us accomplish what we can't do ourselves. Also, it's very important to forgive your mother and yourself for your wrongdoings. As we do that we close all the openings where the tormentors can overtake us."

Randy considered what else he should do to help. "I will try to find a good counselor to work with you. Unfortunately, my church people have not been trained in this area."

He looked at Sam. "Do you have a place to stay tonight?"

"We're traveling the country to see where we want to settle when we get married. We can get a hotel room. I think what's happening here is the most important thing right now."

The peaceful young woman nodded in agreement.

Randy raised his hands in excitement. "This is great! I have learned so much today. I didn't have any idea that would really work." They all laughed. "You have some answers, and it appears you also found new hope. I feel you two might be the first of many needing to come here for help. I've got to figure out how we can make that possible."

Amy stood, and the couple wrapped their arms around each other. They looked around the large room. Sam spoke. "So, this is what the inside of a church is like. Nice. I like the way it feels in here, almost as if angels are with us."

Randy smiled as he pulled out his card. "Get in touch with me tomorrow. I'll work on making some helpful contacts for you. Oh,

I know. This is Tuesday. You can go down to Maggie's Café after eight tonight. Jethro, a guy who comes here to church, has a group meeting there tonight."

"Sounds good," Sam responded. "We can go for dinner before they meet."

They all walked out together knowing this was a very good day.

(1) Matthew 12:45

Chapter 28

Barbara met Randy in the hall as he returned to his office. She took hold of his arm. It was obvious she wanted his undivided attention. "Pastor, I was looking for you. I have to tell you what I saw as I drove by the church just now. I'm on my way to pick up my children who are playing at their friend's house." She paused to take a breath. "There were dark, ugly demons flying out of the church. They whizzed past my car window. The sound they made was really strange. It sent chills all through me. I was so shocked I slammed on the brakes to miss hitting them. Then I saw big angels right behind them." She laughed with delight. "What a sight. The angels looked like glowing warriors right out of heaven." She stared into space before she continued. "I thought you might want to know."

"I like the sound of that." Randy took time to look into her face, and felt he really saw her for the first time. "Barbara, maybe you can answer a question that's on my mind. Do you know anything about deliverance from demons, or inner healing?"

Barbara looked a little embarrassed. "Well, I've been trying to learn what I can. When you see all the things I do, it doesn't take long to realize seeing isn't enough. We are shown so we can take our God-given authority and do what the Word says."

"Yes, true. So what have you found to help?"

"Well, Pastor," she seemed hesitant. "There's a little … I guess you would say, ministry. It's called Winds of Life. Have you heard of it?"

"No. 'Winds of Life.' Hmm."

"There are only about twenty people, but they have some understanding of the prophetic, and deliverance. They've even learned to interpret dreams."

"I see. Would it be possible for me to meet the leader, or whoever is in charge? It's time our people know how to live in God's full plans and purposes. Maybe that group could help us."

Barbara stared at him as a huge grin filled her face. "Would they be welcome in our church, Pastor?"

"Perhaps. Maybe I can meet with someone who represents the group and see if that would be something we could all consider. They might want to join us, and we need their wisdom. Those are subjects I didn't study in Bible school."

Laughing, Barbara responded, "No, I don't imagine you did. But it's all in the Bible and sure belongs in church."

"Do you have the phone number for someone I could call?"

"Sure." She pulled out her phone and began to search. "The guy's name is Josh. His wife is Miranda. What is his last name? Oh, right here, Josh Nelson."

Randy pulled out his phone. He leaned over and looked at the numbers, then entered them into his phone. "Thanks, I'll give Josh a call."

Barbara's excitement was obvious. "Great. This will be so wonderful. People really need their help, but some are so afraid of anything they don't understand. Good luck introducing the idea to everybody."

"I know, but God may want us to move forward in this way so we can help people better. He seems to be making that pretty obvious to me."

"Oh, Pastor, you've made my day. I've felt so alone. I know I'm strange. It would be wonderful to have other people around who understand such things." She glanced at her phone. "Well, I've got to go. My children will be waiting for me. See you soon."

***

After dialing his phone, Randy leaned back in his office chair as he heard Dan's voice. "Hi, Dan. … Yes, we're all good. I won't keep you, but I'm wondering if it's possible for you to meet me at my office in the morning around nine. I know its short notice, and you have a busy schedule, but I may have some help with the prophetic thing. I'd also like your input and discernment, as I meet with a guy named Josh Nelson. Any chance you know him? … Me either. But he may have some answers for us. He said he is available tomorrow morning.… Great. Okay. See you then."

***

Randy liked Josh the minute they shook hands. He seemed humble, energetic, and excited to be there.

Dan joined them in Randy's office carrying three coffee cups in a cardboard container and a bag from The Bistro. While he was being introduced to Josh he handed out coffee and breakfast sandwiches.

"Thanks Dan." Randy said. "The Bistro. I think they've stolen part of my heart by now. Glad I didn't eat breakfast this morning?"

"Me too." Josh replied.

"Who has time to eat?" Dan added as he took the other wingback chair in front of Randy's desk.

They all wolfed down the tasty breakfast, and voiced their appreciation for people who knew how to create good food. As the guests enjoyed their coffee, Randy explained the reason for their meeting. "Josh, God is doing some unusual things around here. It's made us realize prophets and their prophecies, and dreams and visions are often from the Lord. We believe we need to learn and teach about those things along with the fact angels and demons do exist. Deliverance from demonic influence is clearly taught in scripture, yet we've avoided the subject."

He continued by sharing his experience with Amy and Sam without using their names. Then he described how he was completely dependent on God to lead him through the deliverance. "Of course, that was an amazing experience, but it made me realize we need input, help, and wisdom about such things."

Dan took a swig of coffee before saying, "So true. This stuff is way over our heads. I'm reading my Bible as much as possible, but I find my void of understanding feels more like a vortex of stupidity."

"I doubt that," Randy commented.

Josh was on the edge of his chair. His knees bounced up and down. "Really. So you're thinking you'd like to have some help with the supernatural ways of God?"

Randy thought he had already made that clear so he looked at his guest puzzled. "I'd like to hear what you think, Josh. I understand you know about such things. Would you be interested in working with us? What you already know could help us process what we're trying to learn more quickly. And, I wonder if your group might want to try us out to see if we want to work together. We probably have resources you could use, and we have a great group of people. What do you think?"

"Well," Josh smiled and jumped up. "Well, I would say, it's about time." He laughed before he continued. "It would be wonderful to have a home church where other people understand what we're about." He walked back and forth, then took his seat again and leaned forward. "Here's the deal. We go wherever God leads us to share his love with people. If someone's sick, we pray for them to be healed. We speak to others about the destiny God shows us he has for them. We love doing those things, but sometimes it feels we're out there all alone. No one should be without a support system."

Josh paused and looked at the two men. "The down side is, Pastor, we've been kicked out of any church we've tried to connect with. Leaders seem to fear us. They don't like change. After all, status quo is comfortable. I don't see anywhere in the Word where people were told to get comfortable."

Randy watched Dan listening to Josh, and knew he was discerning the visitor's intentions. He relaxed a little when the man finally asked a question. "Josh, what are your hopes for the future?"

Josh turned to Dan, whose countenance always made people feel honored when he asked them a question. "Miranda and I have degrees in psychology and sociology. We wanted to help people through counseling, but our first practice was a disappointment. The people had such deep problems it took years to work through them the way we were trained. We were devastated so we closed our practice and began to search for better answers. The bottom line finally revealed itself. There is an invisible evil force the world evidently chooses to ignore. The thing wraps people in deception, sickness, and bondage of every form. When we realized that truth, we felt even worse. How could we, or anyone, move into the inner-man and free people from forces beyond their control?" He looked at his audience, who seemed to be waiting for the answer.

Josh sat up straighter. "I'll make a long story short. Our search led us to the Bible. It was probably the last book we picked up. Isn't that always the way?"

Everyone laughed and nodded.

"Scripture filled all the holes left after our educational training. God's plan was there all the time. When God puts good inside someone, the bad can be expelled. Only God is good." He sat back in his chair. "Of course, it's not really that easy, but it is the place to start. So we've been practicing, and trying out what we've learned, calling it God's keys for success. As we continue, we see more positive results."

"So this is new for you, too?" Randy asked.

"No. We've been at it for ten years. We've talked to people about the need for a church that will teach what we've learned, but so far we've always been escorted out, or invited to go elsewhere. You are the first person to ever call and suggest you might need us."

Dan reached over and bumped Josh's arm. "Sir, this is more than a need. We feel we're being driven to learn all we can so we can prepare a community of people to live totally free from the things that destroy their lives."

Randy got up, walked around, and leaned against his desk in front of Josh. "Josh, if you like, invite your people to be with us next Sunday. Let's shake things up around here. Actually, there's so much going on, people may not even notice."

Josh humbly answered. "Thank you. We need a family. Our people have left everything familiar to follow a call we can't explain. To have others accept us, would be healing to our souls. Does that make any sense to you?"

"Yes, of course," Randy responded. "Josh, you seem to be a man willing to take advice. I don't feel you would want to hinder what I see as God's plan here. Do you agree, Dan?"

His friend nodded, so the pastor continued. "Josh, can you take it if I feel the need to call you out about something?"

"Of course. Hopefully, that won't be necessary, but I'm open to any training you have for me, too."

"Okay." Randy turned to Dan. "Will you spend some time with Josh and get a plan?"

"Sure. I'm home a few days next week."

"Great." The pastor shifted his focus on Josh again. "Josh, Dan and Barbara, she tells me she comes to your group, can be the first students you teach about their prophetic gifts. Also, could you meet with me from time to time to tell me what you know about deliverance? There may be others that want to learn, too. I really have no idea at this point."

Josh nodded, "Of course. I'm excited to help you all. But you know from your experience that following the lead of the Holy Spirit is what always brings success. Everything else is just part of the process." He paused, as if just realizing what the pastor said. "So you mean all of us can come here for church next Sunday."

"Yes, please. We need you."

"Thank you so much." Josh stood and shook the pastor's hand. He turned to Dan as he pulled out his card and handed it to him. "I'll make myself available whenever you have time, sir."

Dan shuffled in his pocket and handed Josh his card. "I really appreciate that. I also need help interpreting dreams. I've been having some doozies."

Josh nodded as they shook hands.

"This is a great start," Randy announced.

The others agreed.

Chapter 29

Mrs. Anderson, Agnes to her close friends, parked her car several rows back from the grocery store doors. Now that her pain was gone, she enjoyed taking the few extra steps on a nice summer day. When finished with her shopping, she scurried back to the car and put the groceries in the trunk. As she turned the key in the car door she felt a sharp object press into her side. A man's low voice caused a surge of fear.

"Don't say a word. Get in and unlock the other door."

Shocked, she did exactly as commanded. Once under the steering wheel she stared at the unkempt man who jumped in beside her. Taking a deep breath to bolster her courage she prayed. *Oh, Father, do you see what's happening here? What should I do?*

"Fear not. I am with you.[1]"

His gun was pointed at her, low enough it couldn't be seen by anyone who passed. Not wanting to show fear, she squinted at the man, and with an indignant voice demanded, "What do you want?"

"Give me your money." His eyes darted nervously as his hands trembled.

"Okay." A shiver ran through her. She wondered if he might be possessed by something she shouldn't enrage.

"I'll give you all I have. You don't really need to point that gun at me." She fumbled to open her purse as she stared at the weapon. Her hands trembled while she dug for her wallet. *Perfect love casts out all fear.[2] Fear and faith are opposites.*

"I think there's only twenty dollars in here."

The man shook the weapon back and forth. "Twenty dollars? That's not enough." He fidgeted and talked to himself. She didn't hear most of his words. Those that were audible couldn't be understood.

Opposite spirit. Opposite spirit. Calm down, Agnes, think calm.

She took a deep breath. "You sound like you have a problem. How much do you need? I have my check book here. I could write a check. There's around three hundred dollars in my account."

His head dropped in despair as he mumbled, "Three hundred ain't enough. "I don't know what to do. I need three thousand just to save my house."

Ah, that hateful thing's quiet. Poor man. He's like a little lost boy. "Honey, what's your name?"

Looking hopeless, the man yielded to her question. "James."

"James, whatever you're planning, I don't think you'll fix your problems by using that pistol. How about putting it down so we can talk?"

He jerked his head back as hatred filled his eyes. "No, no, I'm going to kill you if you don't give me all your money. I'll take your car, too."

"I've already offered you all my money. I'll give it to you freely. Obviously, you need it a lot more than I do. You can have my car, too." She held her keys out to him. "But I'd better warn you, it's no prize. We've put a hundred and eighty thousand miles on it. My husband and I like to travel."

The offer seemed to dissolve the man's efforts.

"Now. He is ready to hear."

Agnes sat up boldly. "James, I need to tell you something. If you kill me, I'm going straight to heaven to be with Jesus. I'm looking forward to it whenever he's ready for me." She focused on him eye-to-eye. "Jesus had you come to me today because he wants you to know he loves you. He knows all about your problems and he wants to help you."

James dropped his head. "Jesus don't love me. Nobody loves me. I lost my job. My wife left and took the kids. They're takin' the house. I ain't got no hope no more."

"That is a tough situation. I'm sorry you're having such a hard time." *Now what? A little help, please.* Her next words popped out without thought. "Sounds like you're at the end of your rope."

She saw a glimmer of hope in James' eyes. Maybe, he realized someone actually understood his situation. "That's for sure."

Ah, somethings happened. "You know, I've found when I come to the end of myself, God is always standing there ready to pick me up. If you would like to give your situation to Jesus, he would be happy to help you." She waited for the man to consider his options.

More relaxed now, his gun pointed at the seat instead of her. "I knew about Jesus as a kid. But I never thought I needed him when I grew up."

"Sounds to me like you do." *I'll just let the boy think about that for a minute.* She looked out the window wondering if she might see anyone she knew. Still waiting, she pressed her hand across the wrinkles in her skirt. *Okay, Lord here we go.* "Would you let me pray with you?"

James looked too tired to refuse. "I guess."

"Can I have the revolver first? It makes me nervous."

With the gun still pointed her direction, he gave up possession. Agnes took it by the barrel and dropped it on the floor behind her seat. Then gently taking James's hand, she bowed her head, but didn't shut her eyes. *I've heard in these situations it's better to pray with your eyes open.* "Father, you see what the tormentors are doing to this young man. In Jesus's name I command them to release him right now. Lord, I ask you to fill him with your love and hope."

They sat in silence as her prayer was answered. The car overflowed with God's glorious presence. Tears flowed as a holy reverence engulfed them. Agnes heard James sigh.

He sounds like the heaviness of the world just lifted off his shoulders.

"What is that?" he asked with awe in his voice.

Obviously the tormentors were gone, making room in his heart to receive divine hope. Smiling at the man, she bent closer. "James, you just experienced what it's like when heaven and earth kiss. God came into this car to confirm his love to you. He wants you to know he's real, and always with you. You can invite him to have control of your life and all that concerns you, and he'll help you get back on your feet. What we feel is Heaven's atmosphere. It's made up of love, peace, and joy. Isn't it wonderful?"

A bit overcome, he nodded.

She stared into space. "There's an old song I'm always reminded of when this happens." It says, "Heaven came down and glory filled my soul." She held up her finger as if leading a choir. "It goes like this." She sang him the chorus.

Focusing back on the moment, she said, "James, God wants to help you. He's trustworthy. You'll be fine." She pulled a card from her purse and invited him to join her at church. Then she opened her wallet and drew out her only twenty dollar bill and handed it to him.

"Here, James, let me give you this money. Today is a new day. God's going to give back everything that's been stolen from you. Only this time it will be better because you'll recognize his love as he blesses you."

James drew back, "No, no, I can't take that."

"I insist. I'm blessed to have this opportunity to meet you."

With a sigh of relief, James received her offer. "Thank you, Ma'am. Really. Thank you."

"You're very welcome. You do know God had you approach me today so you could find your solutions are always in his love."

He nodded and opened the car door to leave. She watched the man, no longer in despair, pick up his pace. *Is he singing?* She smiled. *I think he's singing heaven came down and glory filled my soul.*

Ready to start the car, she paused. "My goodness, he forgot

his gun. Oh, well, I can take care of it."

After a drive downtown, and finding a place to park at the police station, Agnes opened the back door and dropped the gun into her purse. Once inside the building, she marched past several officers who glanced at her and nodded. She moved quickly to a man in uniform at the front desk. When he finally looked up, she spoke. "Sir, I have a pistol in my purse to give you."

He looked both ways as if he thought the guys were playing a joke on him.

Agnes began to rustle through her purse. "Here it is." She pulled the thing out with the same disgust she would give a dead rat. Everyone in the area came to attention as she laid the weapon before the officer.

"This gun was in my car. I need to turn it in. If you find it's been used in any crimes let me know. I'll be happy to help. Here's my card with my name, address, and phone number. Otherwise, please do whatever you do with these things."

"Ah, ma'am. I can't let you go before we get some more information."

"Oh, no. I can't stay. My groceries will spoil. Is Dean here? He knows me."

"Who?"

"Dean Dennison. Oh, you probably call him Captain. Is he here?"

The officer yelled across the room. "Hey, Rick. See if the Captain can come out here."

Soon Captain Dennison smiled at Agnes. "Mrs. Anderson, it's such a nice surprise to see you, but what are you doing down here, dear lady?"

"Captain Dean, you look so handsome in your uniform. This gun was in my car. I just need to turn it in so someone doesn't get hurt. I must go now. My frozen food will ruin. I gave the man my card, if you have any questions for me later."

Dean studied Agnes. "You don't want to tell me how it got

there?"

She looked up at him like a child trying to get out of a lie. "No. I gave him my card, in case you need anything later."

The Captain smiled down at one of his favorite church ladies. With a wave of his hand he said. "Let her go on home. I don't think she's a flight risk, are you Mrs. Anderson?"

"Oh, Dean, for goodness sakes."

"You're sure you don't want to tell me anything?"

Sticking her purse under her arm as an announcement to her leaving, she added. "Only if there's been a crime to be solved later. I need to get home now."

"Okay. Tell Gerald hello for me, will you?"

"Of course." All the others in the room were watching so she greeted them as she left. "Good-day everyone. Thank you for your service to our community."

***

Next day, Agnus shared her experience with Hillary while they were having tea. Just as she expected, Hillary puffed up ready to reprimand her for being foolish. "Agnes, you should never have let that man in your car."

"I know. I was afraid, but then I remembered the kingdom of God lives in me, so I knew I didn't need to fear." Not wanting to have a long heated discussion she added. "Let's face it, Hillary, by doing what I did, a man is free, and he knows he is loved by God."

Her friend's expression hadn't changed much. She needed more convincing. "And just think, if everything works out, his whole family will be restored. Sure, it didn't look like a good situation, but actually it's all quite wonderful, don't you think?"

Hillary huffed, and gave into silence.

(1) Isaiah 41:10, (2) I John 4:18

Chapter 30

While on a business trip, Dan rested in a hotel room. He wanted to be obedient to God in his call to be a prophet, but questioned how to prepare for something he knew so little about. As he sat in silence, hoping God would give him insight, a vision opened before him.

He saw himself standing in a field watching an atomic bomb's blast. Even though he was a long distance away, he felt the ground shake as blinding light flashed into the sky. A mushroom-shaped cloud formed and spread across the area as far as he could see. Even with the scene a long way off in the vision, the shockwaves and winds it created knocked him to the ground.

"What are you showing me, Lord? Is an attack coming on our country? Should I pray against this happening in the physical world? I don't feel fear, as if it's bringing disaster. How would you have me pray?"

He heard the inner voice. "What I am showing you will be *like* an atomic blast, but any destruction that comes will be from the bright glory of my kingdom. As I come, those who don't know me will feel devastated because I will remove everything that is not pure and holy."

Dan laid down on the floor in the same position he saw himself in the vision. "Lord, get anything out of me that doesn't please you. I saw myself being blown down by the great wind as it moved. Can you make me pure enough so when your glory flows through me, I will be able to stand?"

The voice replied, "Look. A few are standing."

Still seeing the vision, he looked across a vast space of

nations. Millions were lying, as if dead, on the ground. But, he noticed that where each group of about a thousand people lay, one person was standing. Those few were already reaching down helping others to their feet.

Dan listened as the inner words continued, "Those standing will need to help all the others. As evil's bondage leaves people, the shocking change will cause them to feel confused and disoriented. Their minds will seem blank because the power that darkened men's souls, and sickened their minds, will be destroyed. They have never functioned in wholeness and purity. But don't worry I have put a desire for me in everyone. They will be drawn to my love and freedom now.

What you see is the glory of God coming on the earth in its great power. When purity comes, souls are filled with God's love, which has the power that changes the world. Dan, my people have prayed the way I taught them. You are looking at the answer to your prayers asking for my kingdom to come and will to be done on earth as it is in heaven.[1] This is a view of what it will look like.

"Those scattered about have spirits that will awaken as if from a deep sleep. My glory will help them understand who they were created to be. Evil's hindrances won't hold them back anymore. Look, they are awakening to this new day."

The prophet watched as the standing ones continued to help those who looked desperate to know what was happening, stand up.

In awe, Dan wondered how anyone could help so many.

The Teacher continued. "See those who get up quickly? They knew me once, but through life's challenges, they wondered off the paths to the fulfillment of their divine destiny. They have my Word in their heart and will no longer be polluted by pride, lust, deception, or religion. The power of the tormentors is going to be squelched by my glory, and those who once knew me will be free to join you to serve others."

"Thank you, Lord, for setting them free."

"Watch what's happening around you, Daniel. There will be great economic shifting as lust and pride leave people. Business won't go on as usual. In the glory realm of God, people only want me, so some companies will falter, others will thrive. In my glory sickness is destroyed so there will be no need for medicine, which will also cause economic upheaval."

As a businessman, Dan wanted to consider such possibilities, but the Holy One continued, "Truth will rise from the earth.[2] I will see to it. The evil one will still try to entice the weak, but he will be crushed beneath my feet.[3]

"Now is the time I will change governments and climates as I bring a new day of holiness upon the land, so be alert.

"No building will be big enough to hold the people of God. There will be a shortage of printed Bibles in the same way American's couldn't buy American flags after the 9/11 tragedy."

The awesome vision disappeared. Dan rose to his feet. "Dear God, does your Word say anything about what you showed me?"

In desperation he grabbed his Bible, which fell open to Isaiah 30:26. He read aloud. … *The light of the sun will be seven times brighter, like the light of seven days, on the day the Lord binds up the fracture of his people and heals the bruise he has inflicted.*

He flipped the pages further to chapter thirty-three. *Who among us can live with the consuming fire? … He who walks righteously … He will dwell on the heights.*[4]

Dan scanned down the chapter and noticed he had underlined verse twenty-four. *And no resident will say, "I am sick." The people who dwell there will be forgiven their iniquity.*[5]

Stunned, the prophet asked. "Can these verses be describing something coming now?"

He heard the Lord one more time. *As I live, all the earth shall be filled with the glory of the Lord.*[6]

Dan found the recording app on his phone and entered what he saw and heard as best he could. Then he added his own thoughts and questions.

By the time he finished, he felt exhausted. "Such a great disaster," he mumbled. "But, the Father didn't call it that. He made it sound more like rearranging. What am I supposed to do with this vision? Do I tell anyone what I've seen? I'm beginning to know how the Old Testament prophets must have felt."

(1) Matthew 6:10, (2) Psalm 85:11, (3) Romans 16:20, (4) Isaiah 33:14-15, (5) Isaiah 33:24, (6) Numbers 14:21

Chapter 31

Micah sat quietly on the bank of Millbrook Stream with his fishing line in the water. He stared across the sparkling ripples while he pondered. *I know You're real God. You're the only one who could heal my Mom.* A shadow of sadness crossed his mind as he remembered the fear that gripped the whole family while she was ill. Relieved, he continued his thoughts. *Thank You, for bringing Kevin back to life, and having us there so we could pray for him.* The memory of their victory rested sweetly as he thought about the experience.

A pair of ducks distracted him as they quacked and waddled into the water creating ripples. He smiled and relaxed while he listened to the movement of the stream as it flowed past.

This feels much better than being strung out on something. Why did I think that was fun? I'm glad I got caught. He took a deep breath and looked around. *God must have made fishing for guys like me. I get to be all alone, and no one is pressuring me about anything.*

He wound in the line and cast again. *I didn't know how bad off I was 'til I got to rehab. Don't ever want to go through that again.*

His thoughts continued. *I wonder how David is doing. God, no one else could have brought him back to life, and set both of us free from those addictions. I know these stories are true because I was there. I'm glad I got to tell him good-bye before I left. He really looked different. I wouldn't have recognized him somewhere else.*

A tug on his line distracted his thoughts. He stood and reeled it in until the tension released. "Lost it." He slid a new worm on the hook and cast again. *David's going home to Colorado when he finishes counseling. Dad and I should go by and see him again before he leaves.*

The water moved swiftly, his line tried to follow. *Wonder what I should do when I finish school. I don't really want to go to college ... but I do like playing football.*

Andrew says knowing God is more important than raising the dead. I don't know. That was pretty awesome. How does anyone know God?

He settled on the bank again. *Maybe we're not going to have fish for dinner tonight.*

The voice of a man standing close by surprised him. "How's the fishing?"

Micah looked up, "Nothing so far." The guy had a familiar face, and carried what looked to be a brand new rod and reel. "That's nice gear you've got there."

The guest held his equipment up and looked it over. "I haven't tried it yet. Your tackle is probably better though. There's nothing like things that have been tried and proven to be good. You mind if I join you?"

Micah considered his question. He liked fishing alone. Would they get their lines crossed? He looked the guy over, trying to remember where he saw him before. "Sure."

"Thanks. This is a great spot."

The man prepared his line and cast it in. When he was settled on the grass a comfortable distance away, he spoke again. "I've always loved fishing. I've done it for years."

Micah nodded and remained silent as he brought his line in to make sure his bait was still secure, and recast.

After a bit, the stranger attempted conversation. "You're a student at the high school?"

"Yes sir."

"You like sports?"

"Yes sir."

"Go to church somewhere?"

"Yes sir. Millbrook Community Church." *How do I know him? I haven't seen him at church.*

"Like it?"

"Sure. We've got a great youth pastor."

"That's good." The man switched bait and cast again. "What's your plans after graduation?"

"Interesting, I was wondering the same thing. I don't know. College. Military. Get a job. Hard to know which way to go."

"Yes, it is a big decision."

Silence reigned until a tug hit the shiny new rod. The man jumped up and made quick work of bringing in a big one. He held the fish in his hands and studied it as if it were a work of art. "What a fine specimen. Do you think I should keep him or put it back?"

Micah shrugged, while thinking his luck might be better if he had a new rod and reel. "It's your fish. Do whatever you want, but it's a nice one. I'm thinking twenty-two inches."

"Good eye, young man."

Pretty sure he was correct, Micah responded, "I've been doing this a long time, too."

The man smiled and nodded. "I think I'll put him back so someone else can enjoy catching him." He let the fish slide back into the water.

Micah smiled too. "Sounds good. I'm trying to catch fish for dinner. It's fun to bring food home for my family. There are seven of us." He looked at his empty canvas bag. "That may not happen today."

"Seven, that's quite a family."

"Yes, my mom was real sick for a while, but God healed her."

"I know."

"Oh, do you know my parents, Beth and Charles Morgan?"

"Yes." The gentle speaking man ignored his rod, and squatted closer to Micah. He picked up a rock, turned it over several time as he admired it like someone would a precious jewel. "I also know God, the Father, is pleased with you."

With complete assurance that pleasing God was an impossibility for him, Micah looked at the man. "I don't think so, and how could you know such a thing anyway?"

Suddenly, he forgot fishing and starred at the man who was dressed like anyone else who strolled along the water banks. He was mesmerized by an aura of light glowing around the fisherman who said. "You don't believe me?"

The man fiddled with three more rocks as he held them toward the sun. "I know you and your dad prayed for David, who was dead and he came back to life." He skipped the rocks across the water.

Then he picked a dandelion and examined it as someone would look at a scientific wonder. "I saw you pray for your friend, Kevin, and he survived a car accident."

"You saw us?" Confused, Micah's mind raced.

"Yes. I also know you are going to protect a young lady when something dangerous is about to happen to her, Micah."

The boy's head jerked. "How do you know my name? I've been trying to remember where I've seen you before."

"I knew you before you were born.[1] Father God wants you to know he has plans for your life that are bigger than college, the military, or getting a job. But first you must know who you are. You will learn that as you get acquainted with Jesus. This is what's important for you right now. Even if you raise the dead, but don't know Jesus, you fail. You are one of the young kingdom warriors who have been chosen and protected for great exploits in the future."

"How can I know him?"

"I am He."

Micah stared at the ordinary-looking man whose eyes seemed to pierce his soul. "You are who."

"Jesus."

Trying to grasp the reality of Jesus' visible presence, the young man starred.

"It is true, son. The days ahead will be like no other. I am walking the earth ready to bring unbelievable events and changes. If you choose me above all else, you can join me in the greatest adventure of your life. You were created to do great exploits through God's power. You have already experienced the fulfillment found in being a usable vessel for my purposes, and found nothing else satisfies like having that privilege."

Speechless, Micah nodded.

Jesus picked up his fishing gear and said, "Move over about ten feet and throw in your line there."

Micah shook his head as if coming out of a daze. He looked over. The man was gone. For a moment he felt sad, but the excitement of what just happened washed the feeling away. He glanced at his phone to check the time. *I only have about twenty minutes left. He said to take ten steps over.* With his twelve inch feet he moved ten steps downstream and cast. *Zing.* The line tightened immediately. He clung to the rod and turned the reel. Thrill surged through him at the thought of the size of whatever was bending his rod. Finally, a huge fish flopped on shore. "Woo Hoo," he shouted, and heard his voice echo off the hills across the water. He unhooked the beauty and put it in his bag. Then cast again. *Zing.* The line tightened. He reeled it in. Another big one hit dry land. He jumped around hoping to find someone who could share his excitement.

Okay, I've got to go or I won't have time to clean these so Mom can fix them for dinner. He pulled his phone out of his pocket to call her. The water beckoned him so powerfully he could almost hear it calling. "Oh, I've got to try this one more time." Out went the line. The bait flew off before it entered the water, but still he heard that perfect sound. *Zing.* The rod bent to the water. He pulled and wound, and pulled and wound. One more prize fish was coming home for dinner.

He gathered up his trophies as he yelled to the sky, "Thank you, Jesus. That was the most fun I've ever had." This time the hills across the water echo back, **"I will make you a fisher of men.**[2]**"**

"I know that scripture. Jesus said it to his disciples." He looked around as he gathered his gear. "Jesus was really here."

A Voice in the sky said, **"I am with you always. Even to the ends of the earth.**[3]**"**

(1) Hebrews 13:5, (2) Matthew 4:19, (3) Matthew 28:20

Chapter 32

Micah stood beside his mother at the kitchen counter. The fish he caught were cleaned, and Beth was showing him how to prepare the fillets with spices and lemon for baking.

"Son, you did a good job cleaning these fish. They must have been fun to catch. The pieces are huge."

He admired his contribution to dinner. "Yeah, it was like magic. I sent the line out and they almost jumped on the hook. Seemed unbelievable." He watched closely as she continued to season, and then place the main course on foil in a large pan.

His mom continued. "See how easy it is." She smiled up at him. "You can make this when you're on your own and go fishing."

Micah was pleased his mother recognized he was almost a grown-up, and he felt relieved she was her heathy, normal self again.

She continued. "Son, I haven't had a chance to tell you how impressed I am with the way you're keeping your room clean and organized. Your efforts challenged the other children and they've started trying to keep their's clean, too."

"Oh, it's nothing, Mom." He was a little embarrassed with the partial truth, but it was nothing he did. Anyway, he liked the way it looked too, so he was trying to keep it picked up.

They worked silently together cutting the vegetables. Beth looked over. "Yes, that's a good size. That way everything will finish cooking at the same time."

As they continued to work, Micah said, "Mom, I saw Jesus while I was fishing."

Beth stopped and looked at her son in surprise. Not wanting to ruin the moment she spoke carefully. "Really?"

"I did. He looked like any other fisherman, but he knew me."

"Did he say anything?"

Micah continued to slice zucchini with the procession of a surgeon. "He told me not to doubt, that he is always with me. He said I am a warrior with a destiny, and I'm to help my generation find him."

Tears filled Beth's eyes. She didn't say a word.

Her son added, "Before he disappeared he told me to move over ten steps to fish. When I did all these fish practically jumped out of the water." He laughed and she joined in.

Twelve-year-old Sarah rushed into the kitchen. "Micah, Becky told me her sister likes you." She got into his face as best she could by standing on her toes. "Do you like her?"

Looking down at her, he tried to hide the excitement he felt. "Who, Anna?" He gave her a little push. "You know I don't have time for girls. Get out of here. We're busy."

Sarah left the room chanting. "Micah likes Anna, Micah likes Anna."

Beth continued her cooking lesson. "Now we'll seal everything in this foil. See." She demonstrated. "Pinch the edges to keep the steam in."

She looked up at Micah. The grin on his face revealed all the woman needed to know. "So who's Anna? Do I know her family?"

"She's a new girl who started coming to youth group. Her parents bought the Wilson's house."

"Tell me about her."

"Oh, she's pretty and friendly. She'll be a junior this year." He shook his head. "There's no way she would be interested in me." He wiped his hands. "Are we finished?"

"That's all there is to it. I'm glad I can teach you a little about cooking before you leave home."

"Me too, Mom. I'm so thankful you're still here with us. We

missed you, and we were so scared when you were in the hospital."

"I know, but now I'm healthy, and I'll be around to keep my eye on the girls who chase you. I know I'm biased, but you're wrong to think a nice girl wouldn't like you, Micah. You're an amazing young man with an exciting future ahead. Jesus even said he has plans for your life."

"So what am I supposed to do now?"

"Don't worry. And don't get in a hurry." She looked up. "God is already leading you. Just do whatever is before you at the moment. It's not hard to follow God. You just keep your heart open and listen for his voice. He will make your future clear, including the woman he has for you. Of course, that won't happen for a long time." She bumped against him.

Micah laughed, "Yeah, yeah, I know. Just friends. Just friends."

"Exactly. No need to have more broken hearts than necessary."

Micah looked at her as if she said the wisest words he ever heard. "Wow, Mom. That's so true. Teenagers are looking for love and they don't even know what it is. They get hurt, and used, and heart-broken. Who came up with the idea we're supposed to choose a partner for life at our age?"

She picked up the pan and slid it into the oven, then turned and took her son's hand. Looking into his eyes she said, "You're right. Now don't forget what you just said." She put her arm around his waist and gave him a hug. When she stepped back she wiped away the grateful tear that escaped, and announced, "Okay, dinner will be ready in twenty minutes."

***

Sam and Amy asked Pastor Randy to marry them as they began their new life together. Needing a place to stay for a while, Hillary offered them her rental apartment.

As they arrived she rushed out to greet them in her driveway. "I'm so pleased you plan to stay in the area. Come around to the back and I'll show you the apartment. You can stay as long as you want." When they got to the door she unlocked it and stepped away.

The couple timidly entered. Amy looked up at Sam and cooed, "Our first home."

"Yes," Hillary folded her hands, "Your honeymoon suite. That was the sweetest wedding ceremony I've ever seen."

Sam was quiet while Amy moved slowly through the small rooms. When she returned, she announced. "This is lovely, Mrs. Hunter. You've made everything so cozy. Thank you." She looked up at her new husband. "Sam, this is perfect for us."

"Good," he responded as he turned to Hillary. "Mrs. Hunter, I know you said we could stay here without paying rent until we get jobs. That's so nice of you. Charles Morgan heard I have construction experience, so he hired me. I'll start working the first of the week. Amy got a job at Maggie's helping through their rush hours, and she'll have counseling with Miranda in the afternoons, so we want to give you the money we saved for hotels."

Hillary patted his outstretched hand. "You keep it for now. I want to make sure you have the things you need until you get your paychecks. I trust you." She opened the closet door behind her and pulled out a basket filled with food, household supplies, and small wrapped gifts, then handed it to Sam. "Here, take this, it's really heavy." Sam quickly took the basket and set it on a table nearby, as Hillary explained. "It's a little housewarming gift from all the people at church to help you get started."

A questioning look crossed his face. "I've never met such caring people. Thank you, Ma'am." He gave her a hug.

She smiled, "It's our pleasure. Please, call me Hillary."

"Thank you, Hillary. I can help you with anything you need done around here."

"That would be lovely. There's always something waiting to

be fixed."

Sam nodded, "Any time." He turned to Amy. "Well, Mrs. Moore, shall we get our bags and move in?"

Amy stepped over and laid her head against him. "Oh, Sam what a beautiful beginning. Thank you, Hillary, for making this possible for us."

Pleased, she responded. "The Bible says God sets the lonely in families.[1] You are part of my family now, my dear."

***

Randy stood at the door of the Prayer Room knowing the women were gathering inside. "God, why do you make me do this stuff?"

"Remember my words, 'Humble yourself before God and he will lift you up.[2]'"

With a sigh, he opened the door. Hillary, June, Mrs. Anderson, and three others were pushing comfortable chairs into a circle.

"Good morning, ladies. God has blessed us with another beautiful day."

Surprise covered the women's faces as Randy pulled another chair into the group's gathering. "Yes, he has," they agreed, as each glanced at the other.

The pastor felt humbled by his need for the women's help, but he knew the Holy Spirit wouldn't give him any peace until he spoke to them. "Please sit. I hope you don't mind if I join you? I know it isn't normal for me to show up here, but I must take some of your time today."

"We feel honored to have you with us," Mrs. Anderson responded.

Randy joined in the circle as he took a typed sheet of paper out of his pocket.

"Thank you. I also want to thank each of you for your faithfulness to pray. Many of the good things that are happening come from your sacrifice to set this time aside and talk with God."

Hillary nodded. "It's our pleasure, Pastor. We love to come together and spend time in his presence. This is not a sacrifice for us. It's the greatest joy of our week."

Randy never considered prayer to be a joy, but felt relieved they did. The long lists of the needs of the people exhausted him. Rarely seeing any answers made it worse. Sure, now things were changing, but when the answers did come they usually didn't look like he expected.

"Good. As you know, many of your prayers are being answered. Isn't that exciting?"

"Yes," they all chimed in.

"Much is happening. My job has expanded so I rarely see any of you during the week, but you come to my mind regularly. He paused and took time to look into each lady's eyes, and in respect, nodded. *Do I really confide in them, Lord? Women gossip you know.*"

The inner voice spoke. **"Go for it. What have you got to lose? You know the whole thing's impossible."**

June spoke in a soft voice. "Pastor, we're listening."

"You must keep what I share confidential for now."

Conviction seemed to jolt the women.

Think about it ladies. Remember when you didn't guard your tongues? Randy watched Hillary eye each woman like a mother making sure her children understood the seriousness of their responsibility.

"We'll do our best, Pastor. The Word says, 'death and life is in our tongues.'[3] We will honor your confidence in us."

Nodding, he took a deep breath, then burst out, "I think God is giving us this city."

The women gasped and sat up straighter in their chairs. Some even moved closer to hear every word clearly.

Randy drew back and shook his head. "I don't know how. Or why. I know it sounds impossible, but ..." with a quick glance at the ladies, he added. "What if it's true? And why not?" The women didn't move. "Can you stretch your prayers for something bigger?"

June looked around when no one responded. She said, "I love it. We get excited by impossible challenges. Our God loves to show up when things are impossible."

The other's voices filled the room with chatter. Randy sat silent, elbows on his knees, paper in hand until the women quieted.

"I have compiled a list of ideas that may be in God's plan. For starters, you know the Grand Hotel downtown?" He didn't wait for a response. "I think God wants us to acquire it. I'm not sure why, so if you get some direction in your prayers, I'd like to hear about it. Our community already has many services. What should be our part? United we can make the whole town healthier in every way.

"You've probably noticed the closed businesses downtown. People have lost their jobs and some have to sell their homes and move someplace else to find work. Let's pray for new businesses to come here. Until that happens, how can we help the hurting people through their transition?

"Also, pray for wisdom for our local politicians so they can be successful leaders."

He took a deep breath. "Many in our community are hurting. Did you know there are people living under the railroad bridges? They need help."

Randy checked his sheet of paper. "Let's talk about our church situation. God is drawing people to himself, and they are coming here to find him. We're going to need more space, more workers, more … everything. How does that all happen? Assuming many others come to us, how do we disciple huge numbers of people wanting to know the truth of the Bible?"

The women nodded, seeming to fully understand the situation.

"Five young gang members recently chose to live for God. We need to make a place for them in our church. If we love and train them properly, the whole community will be safer, and they will be good citizens.

"That brings up another concern. Our people may need a heart change to receive them, and their challenges."

The pastor's finger moved to the next item. "The young people in the church are being called to something great, but they face the mounting challenges of today's world. We need wisdom to help them. Andrew is doing a fine job, but I think God has even more for him."

He looked up and smiled at the older ladies as he presented his next thought. "The retired folks have fire burning inside. They're poised to be unleashed to do greater things than any generation before them. How do we help them fulfill their dreams and God's call on their lives?"

The ladies laughed.

"The hippies, I've got to quit calling them that. The new men, who come here for church, have gathered a group of people who haven't been welcome in churches. They are teaching them to know God at Maggie's Café. Could we make a place for them here? Or, maybe we should work more with Jethro downtown, if they need us."

Hoping the women weren't already on overload, he gave them some time to digest the thoughts. Then said, "Is that enough for today, or would you like to hear a few of my wild ideas?"

They seemed a little slower to respond this time, but couldn't resist hearing.

"I've been challenged with the realization that we believers haven't addressed many of the topics which clearly should be part of the church. Ephesians 4:11 mentions apostles, prophets, evangelists, pastors, and teachers as the leadership of the church. Prophets have been ignored. That's not hard to understand. The Bible prophets were strange characters. They didn't act like normal people. Are we willing to welcome today's prophets here, even when they are unusual?"

Putting his pen on the next topic he paused. The women seemed to have meltfrustrationed a bit in their chairs. He swallowed and searched for boldness. *Sorry ladies, but I'm on a roll now. I've got to get this off my chest.*

"It has become evident some people need to be delivered from demonic bondage. Our mandate, as God's people, is to heal the sick, raise the dead, and cast out demons.[4] How is it we've ignored these things in our church so long?

"And what if angels want to join us? Would they be welcome, or do we just want church as usual? "

The women smiled at each other while Randy took a second to make sure everything on the list had been mentioned. Looking around the circle of prayer warriors he fought back tears. "And, pray for me. I am totally inadequate for what's ahead. All I know to do is hang onto God and follow his lead. Please keep me covered in prayer. Please, keep me covered."

Randy got up and laid the neatly typed paper in his chair, He said, "Thank you," and left the room.

Heaven's host peered at the page just as the women did. Hillary took charge. "My goodness, Pastor left so fast we didn't get a chance to pray with him. That's too bad." She took a breath before she barked out, "Okay, gals. You heard the man. Let's go to work. We know heaven is open over us and ministering angels are here to assist. I will read the first request, and we'll pray as the Holy Spirit leads."

Everyone agreed and verbal prayers began. As each request was completed a host of angelic servants moved out to bring the Father's solutions.

***

Four hours later the women exited the prayer room. During their time of intercession, the Holy Spirit filled their hearts with joy, hope, and a special surprise, the excitement and energy of youth. They realized the truth found in Isaiah 40:31 that says *Those who wait upon the Lord will renew their strength, they will mount up as wings of eagles, and they will run and not be weary, they will walk and not faint.*[5]

(1) Psalm 68:6, (2) James 4:10, (3) Proverbs 18:21, (4) Matthew 10:8, (5) Isaiah 40:31

Chapter 33

Still dressed, Dan lay sprawled across the middle of the hotel's king-size bed. The rumpled spread and blanket, and the lopsided glasses on his nose revealed a fitful sleep. His sudden jerk sent the open Bible on his chest onto the soft bedding. When his hand hit the touch reading lamp, it went dark. He grunted and breathed deep in hope of going back to sleep, but he couldn't get settled. *Where am I tonight? Oh yes, Atlanta. Home tomorrow. Need to catch the flight at eight.* He flipped to his side. *Wonder what time it is.* Peeking through an open eyelid he saw glowing numbers. *Two o'clock. What was I dreaming that woke me?*

He still felt the frustration of his dream. "What was it about? I know it's important to learn to interpret dreams." Turning on the pillow, he put his hands behind his head. *What was it?*

Lying there, he sensed a change in the room. Was someone in there? Alert to an intrusion he jerked to get up, but felt bound. "Who's there?"

A large form revealed itself slightly. Dan's logical mind whirled. *Is this a dream? Is he a spirit?*

"I have come from the throne of Almighty to give you a message." With those words, the room lit with blinding light.

Dan couldn't look into the brilliance. However, this wasn't his first experience with supernatural things. Squinting, he tried to see someone who looked like an angel, but appeared to be a man. "Who are you?"

The man-form paused as if checking to make sure he could reveal the information.

"I am Excelsior, one of the King's warriors. I have been prepared since the beginning to assist you in these great final days as the Son establishes the manifest glory of his kingdom on earth. It's an honor to finally be in your presence."

Humility washed over Dan. Fear and fight left at the thought of someone so magnificent and powerful wanting to be with him. "I'm not dreaming, am I?"

"No, sir. The kingdom of God is manifesting on earth and you were chosen before you were born to be a voice to the nations."

Dan was now free to move so he dropped his legs over the side of the bed and heaved a long sigh. "A prophet?"

"Yes, sir." Excelsior smiled. "I'm pleased you're not stubborn and need to be convinced of the Lord's plans."

Dan fidgeted. "I already had a dream telling me about this. I've been trying to accept the idea. Of course, the whole concept is impossible, but so are many of the other things that happen in my life."

The angel nodded and continued. "Everything has been in preparation for now. It is very hard to convince humans that they are amazing and powerful. Deception has really done its work on them. But you, Dan." He paused, evidently listening to someone unseen. "You will pull them into the mighty truth of who they are as kingdom warriors. United, even in their weakness, they have the ability to bring righteousness to a nation in a day."

"A nation in a day." Those words excited him. He remembered how Isaiah prophesied Israel would become a nation in a day and it really happened.[1] Dan smacked his hands and rubbed them together. "Yes. Thank you, God, for having me born at this time in history so I can be part of your great plans."

Excelsior smiled. "It's nice to know my protégé is willing. Right now, as we are together here in the glory realm, anything seems possible. You may not feel this way when I'm not visible, but I'm assigned to help you. Don't forget, I've got your back."

Dan beamed like a little boy being told a super hero was his big brother.

Excelsior continued. "The enemy knows his days are numbered. He is doing everything he can to hold the ground he took. But the earth is the Lords.[2] Father has chosen this time to unite his Son with his bride."

Dan sprang from the bed. "All right. What do we do first?"

The angelic being held out a hand to calm Dan's excitement. "Just keep believing this is real and follow the Spirit's leading as you always do. For now, you can get your rest. Sleep well, Prophet Daniel."

The room went dark. Dan flung across the bed and tapped the touch lamp. He picked up his phone and typed Excelsior. "There it is. Excelsior is Latin, meaning 'ever upward.' He let the words, "ever upward," roll off his tongue, and then nodded. "I like that."

(1) Isaiah 66:8, (2) Psalm 24:1

Chapter 34

After practice, Micah walked out of the locker room with his football pads over his shoulder. He decided to take a shortcut across the football field to walk home. The stadium was quiet, but he noticed three guys facing the wall behind the bleachers. Something didn't seem quite right so he decided to walk closer. A girl was against the wall behind them. He recognized one of the guys was Glen, from his English class.

"Hi Glen, what are you guys doing in here this late?"

"Get out of here." the oldest one shouted. "None of your business."

Micah continued to move forward. "Oh, hey Latisha. You okay?"

She looked at him with pleading eyes as she pulled on her blouse, and shook her head.

"Come on, I'll walk you home." He pushed past the other three to take her arm.

The angry one pushed back. "Oh, no you won't. She doesn't want to go with you. She's with me. That's the way it is. Right girl?"

Latisha looked at the ground.

Micah could see the fear on her face. He stepped over and put his arm around her. She pressed close to him. "The 'girl' doesn't seem to want to be here with you. Come on, I'll walk you home." He pushed past the others. "She's coming with me. Get out of our way." He gave Glen's brother a shove.

"You gotta be kidding. Glen, you know this jerk?"

Glen nodded. "We had English together."

"Do you want to clear up his confusion about who she's with? Oh, never mind. I'll do it."

As he walked toward the couple, Micah put Latisha behind him and pushed the troublemaker away.

When the tormentor landed on the ground, he jumped up seething. He ran toward him and plowed his head into Micah's stomach. The impact caused him to let out a gasp and grab his middle. Before he could recover, Glen moved behind him and got low. His brother hit the tall football player again, who fell back, tumbled over Glen and hit the ground.

"Now that's a good tackle," Glen's brother yelled.

Micah looked up and saw Latisha trembling in the background so he yelled, "Latisha, get out of here."

She took out running across the field to the open gate.

"Ignore her," the angry one said. "CJ, get his arms behind his back."

The third young man tried to obey but Micah kicked and twisted, hoping to break free. Then his attacker jumped on his back and hit him over and over as CJ held his arms. "Who do you think you are, interrupting me and my girlfriend?"

Micah seethed. "I'm a person who thinks you're a troublemaker who didn't graduate from high school, and shouldn't be on the property. Let me go!"

"I'm Lenard, Glen's big brother. I watch out for him," the guy yelled in his ear as he sat on his back. He pulled his belt off. "Here Glen, wrap this around his hands good and tight."

Glen obediently did as he was told. The minute he finished, CJ and Lenard continued hitting Micah. "You think you're some hot football star. We'll show you."

Micah curled up in a ball and tucked his head into his chest as they kicked his back and legs.

Soon Glen shouted, "We better get out of here, the girl may have the cops coming."

"Yeah, okay. He's no fun anyway. He can't fight. Get my

belt."

Glen approached Micah to retrieve the belt. He whispered, "I'm sorry, Micah. Are you okay?"

"Just go." He pointed his chin to the exit. "I'll be fine."

***

Next day, Micah stood at the bathroom sink inspecting his injuries. "Thank God my family's out of town." He examined his face. *At least they didn't beat on my face too bad. These bruises just look like football scuffling. I can cover everything else with my clothes. I hope Latisha got home safe. I should check on her. Wonder where she lives.*

If Dad was here, he would have us call the police. They could check on her. I don't know what to do. I just want to forget the whole mess. Maybe I'll talk to Andrew after practice.

A Voice spoke in his mind. **I know you are going to protect a young lady when something dangerous is about to happen to her.**

Micah starred at himself in the mirror. *Wow. I forgot all about Jesus saying that. It really happened.* "Jesus, it would have been helpful if you warned me some guys were going to beat me up."

Though still in pain, he walked around trying to understand why helping a girl had to include getting beat up. "God, I know you could have protected me. I don't get it."

He finished dressing and headed out the door. *I'm sure glad it's Friday and we're going through our new plays today instead of having practice. Gives me the weekend to heal up before everybody gets back home.*

After locking the front door he turned and stopped. Glen was walking back and forth at the end of his yard. Micah ducked his head and moved quickly past him. "Got any family with you today?"

Glen rushed to move along beside him. "No, Micah. My

brother would have my neck if he knew I was here. I wanted to say I'm sorry about yesterday."

"Sure. You're afraid I told the police. Well, I didn't. Get away from me."

"No, Micah, I want to ask you to forgive me. I should have stood up for you. But my brother, I'm powerless around him." Glen speeded up and jogged backwards so he could look Micah in the face. I didn't hit you one time. Do you know that? I didn't hit you."

Micah pushed him aside. "Okay, Glen. I forgive you. I'm not going to tell anyone what happened. Honestly, I'm embarrassed I didn't have my guard up. Okay? Now you can quit running."

"No wait. Will you stop a minute? Please," he pleaded.

Micah could hear the desperation in his voice, so he stopped before they got on school property. "What?"

"I've watched you in school. You were getting in a lot of trouble for a while, and your grades were as lousy as mine. Then suddenly you changed and became the greatest guy ever. How did you do that? I want to quit following my brother around making a mess of things. The way he's goin', I know he's gonna end up in jail. I don't want to go with him."

"Aw, Glen, I don't have time for this right now." Micah paced back and forth arguing with himself about what to do. Finally, he looked at Glen's pleading eyes. "Oh, come on. Let's go sit in the bleachers and we'll talk. You're making me late for practice you know."

"Thanks, Micah."

Settled on the bleachers, Micah shared how his mother almost died, but God healed her. He told Glen how angry he was because she was sick, and how he started sneaking out at night doing all sorts of stupid stuff that seemed like fun at the time. Then he got caught and grounded, but his dad loved him anyway and even gave him a job at one of his worksites.

Glen listened intently. "I don't have a dad. You're lucky."

"Yeah, it would be hard not to have a dad. Before, I thought my dad hated me. He was always on my back. I didn't respect him, and thought he was a big, dumb, bully. But, when I saw how hard he works, I realized he does that so our family has everything we need. He carries all the responsibility of running his own company, and making sure everything is fixed just right for his customers. It had to be so hard on him when he couldn't fix mom.

"I watched him boss his workers around demanding perfection in what they did, just like he does me. Then I realized, really he is making them learn skills that will help them all their lives. 'Do your best, clean up after yourself.' Oh how I get tired of hearing those words.

"Sure, he's been tough on me, but I know it's better than not having a father." He paused wondering why he shared all that with this kid. "Except ..." off he went telling Glen about God, who is everyone's Father, and that he loves him more than any father on earth ever could. He shared about the miracles he had seen. Well, the teen seemed to want to hear it all so he just kept talking.

One of the other football players ran out of the locker room door and yelled, "We're ready to start. Coach said to tell you to get in here."

Micah waved to him. "I've got to go. That's why I changed. My dad and God showed me I am loved and I have value and a purpose here on earth. Now I'm trying to figure out what to do about that. God loves you too, Glen. He has good things planned for your life. You don't have to be like your brother."

"How?"

"How? ... That's a loaded question, especially for a person who's out of time right now. Just tell God you're sorry for what you've done, and tell him you want to know he's your Father. Ask him what to do about your brother. If you want to talk more, we can meet before practice anytime."

Micah jumped up. "Gotta go."

Before entering the building he turned to look across the field.

Glen was still sitting in the same spot. "Jesus, help him know how much you love him."

Chapter 35

Randy asked, "Okay Cassius. What do you have to share with me today?"

Cassius's smile revealed his pleasure. "Father is so pleased you are eager to prepare for his great and glorious days. Today you are to read from Isaiah 48:6-8."

As Randy flipped pages Cassius continued. "You know usually the Holy Spirit prompts people to seek out truth for themselves, but I have been honored to sit with you to help you learn because time, as you know it, is wrapping up. We must proceed quickly."

Although he didn't understand what the angel meant, Randy nodded and began to read. *"You have heard my predictions and seen them fulfilled, but you refuse to admit it. Now I will tell you new things, secrets you have not yet heard. They are brand new, not things from the past. So you cannot say, 'We knew that all the time!' Yes, I will tell you of things that are entirely new, things you never heard of before."* (NLT)

Confused, the man looked up waiting for an explanation.

"Well?" Cassius responded. "What do you think?"

"I don't know. Doesn't make any sense to me."

Cassius huffed. "After all you've experienced and seen you still don't get it."

"Sure, it's saying we are going to know all the things we never understood before."

"Well, if you believe this is all new, why aren't you declaring it?"

"Really?"

"Yes. This is good news. You need to share what you learn. That scripture was written centuries ago for today. Father God has much stored up for his glorious people."

Cassius paused, "I'm trying to find words to explain this in human terms." He rubbed his chin while in thought. "I've seen what is prepared in heaven. Maybe you would compare it to the warehouses that cover huge portions of land. They're full of merchandise and supplies, and surprising new resources." He paused. "Or, it could be as if heaven dumps all the cargo ships in the ocean over a little town like this one to bless, not just these people, but many others.

"Our Father's people are becoming united. Have you considered how powerful the force of unity is in bringing the manifestation of heaven to earth? People are coming to Millbrook for no reason they understand, but when the hurting get here they're finding the help they need. Others are excited to be working on projects to help bring God's love to the community. The assistance of angelic host is helping everything they do excel.

"Open your eyes man. Things are changing. People who understand are declaring the victory that has always been waiting for them to receive. They're not hiding in foxholes waiting for the world to come to an end. No. No. These people are active and vibrant."

Cassius took a breath. "Read Isaiah 33:17."

Randy flipped a few pages and read. *"Your eyes will see the King in his beauty; they will behold a far-distant land."*

Cassius was excited. "You've already seen him, Randal. Right?"

"Yes."

"Now read the last part of Isaiah 35:2."

Randy turned again. *"They will see the glory of the Lord."*

"You've seen his glory, haven't you, Randal?"

The pastor remembered the wonder of the Lord's presence. "I have."

"Tell the people. They need to know it is their privilege to see their King. They don't need to wait until they die. Check out verse eight."

Randy looked down and read, *"And a highway will be there, a roadway. And it will be called the Highway of Holiness."* He looked at his teacher. "Wow!"

"Yes, that's part of the new things. God's kingdom highway has opened. His people can find him. The glory of heaven is here to kiss the earth with all its blessings, beauty and purity. Isn't this the grandest thing you've ever heard?"

Humbled, Randy stared at the words. "Father, I'm so sorry I've missed this. I've failed as the shepherd of the people you gave me to care for." With new reality of the profound treasure of the words he held in his hand, he lifted his Bible in the air in honor to God. "It's all real. Every word of this book is true."

Cassius gave the pastor some time to contemplate, and then asked, "So what does that mean to you?"

"It means I am to declare this truth, and remind people we are winners. We can come out of hiding and be who we were created to be. We are powerful, righteous witnesses of God's reality."

"Bravo!" Cassius shouted, making the word reverberate off the walls.

"Now, here's another key." Cassius looked into the eyes of his student to emphasize its importance. "One word coming from a power-filled saint that aligns with the Word of God causes angelic armies to push through any negative atmosphere that attempts to hold them back. Think about that." He vanished.

Randy did think, and then he shouted. "I can do all things through Christ who strengthens me.[1]"

In the invisible world, the angelic host's cheers of rejoicing were so powerful they shook the heavens, and made hell tremble.

***

Randy was still thinking about Cassius's words as he entered Mr. Lewis's home. "Good afternoon, sir. I'm sorry it's taken us so long to connect. Thank you for inviting me to your home. I've always admired your farm. You have managed it well."

"Thanks Pastor. The rains have been kind to me this year. We're going to have a good harvest of corn, and the wheat gave a record yield." They continued to talk about farming until Mr. Lewis seemed to run down.

Curious why he was asked to visit, the pastor said. "Tell me sir. What can I do for you?"

"Oh, I don't need anything. I have been thinking of doing something for you."

Randy looked at him puzzled. "Really, what would that be? You barely know me, or what goes on at our church. We would love to have you join us any time."

"True, but you may not know that my family goes back to the start of your church. We donated the land where it's built."

"No sir. I had no idea. Thank you. It is a beautiful piece of property. I always enjoy seeing the building at the top of the hill."

"I do too." Mr. Lewis agreed contentedly. "Well, my family is all gone now. I'm the only one left. I have no descendants remaining. My wife died ten years ago. Our son died before that. He was in an accident with Gene Goble's boy."

"Oh, You knew Gene and Dorothy Goble?"

"Yes. We mourned our sons together. I guess when Dorothy died we both found it too painful to be together. I haven't seen him since her funeral. Anyway, I was reviewing my will and I'm going to make some changes. I would like to donate my land to your church. I don't know if you have any need for it. If you do, I could start passing it over in small portions as you need more space to build or whatever. I've been watching the crowds gather. I'm glad to see it active again."

"Mr. Lewis, thank you. That is so kind. Wouldn't you like to join us and be a part of what's happening? I think you would be pleased."

"Maybe." He shook his head. "Maybe. I'll think about it."

"Please do. You are very generous. And we would be honored to have your land when the time comes, but for now we would prefer to have you in our fellowship. I'm sure you would be a huge asset to our body."

"Well, thank you, young man. I figured I was over the hill, but it might be good to get out with young people again."

They talked together for some time. Then Randy noticed it was getting late. "Well, it has been a pleasure getting acquainted with you, sir. I should have come long ago. I know you have a lot of responsibility with your farm right now, but we will be expecting you at church as soon as you can make it. Can I pray with you before I leave?"

Mr. Lewis bowed his head. When Randy finished he saw tears run down the man's face. "I hope you will consider yourself part of our family. If there is anything you need please let us know."

When they shook hands, each knew they had found a new friend.

(1) Philippians 4:13

Chapter 36

For the umpteenth time, when Glenda finally finished her work at the church, she joined Andrew for coffee at Maggie's Café to discuss plans for the youth group.

He was already seated, so she slid in the booth across from him.

"Thanks for coming," he said, looking more serious than usual. "I hope your parents can do without you for a while. I know you help them, too."

Feeling tense from the pressure of her day, and the rush to get there, Glenda tried to relax. As she looked into his eyes a flutter did something in her heart so powerful she knew the shock of it must be visible. Putting a hand on her heart, she responded. "Oh, let me catch my breath. Yes, I'll need to help Dad later."

A waitress came over with her coffee. She, and everyone else in the café, knew this was their usual routine.

Still feeling flustered, and maybe agitated by that new feeling, she asked, "So do you have some new ideas? I've been so busy I haven't given anything new a thought."

Andrew nodded. "I know you have. I stopped by your office the other day and three girls were waiting their turn to talk with you. I'm surprised the pastor hasn't put a stop to that."

"Yes, I have to stay late to get my work done, but isn't this what we've wanted. Young people excited about knowing God?"

"True, and with school starting soon, I won't have much time either."

They drank their coffee and talked about nothing special. Exhausted, Glenda tried to focus. *Pay attention. Can we get our business finished so I can go home and kick off my shoes?*

Suddenly, Andrew looked at the floor as his face turned red. "Here's the deal."

He let out a huge breath as he reached across the table and took her hand. As if he didn't dare look at her, he hurried to say, "Glenda, I don't want to pretend any longer. I can't stand these feelings."

She frowned and pulled back.

Andrew shook his head. "Oh, that didn't come out right. Forgive me. Let me start again." He cleared his throat. "I've always been attracted to you. I thought we could work together and keep our relationship as friends. But I can't do that anymore. My feelings for you are driving me crazy." He shook his head and looked out the window.

Glenda choked back giggles. *Really?* She smiled and waited. This was too good to be true. She didn't think she ever drove a man crazy before. Well, maybe that stupid Brett.

Poor guy, he looks miserable. "I like you too, Andrew."

Relief covered his face. "You do? You've sure been awfully cool about it."

"It's a girl thing."

He smiled for the first time. "Okay, good. So, would you like to go somewhere together on a real date?"

"I'd love to." She looked around and noticed all the others in the café had become quiet and were listening to their conversation. She leaned across the table and whispered, "Shall we walk across to the park so we can talk a little more privately?"

Andrew sounded excited as he slid out of the booth. "Good idea." While Glenda gathered her things, he tossed some cash on the table and waved at the waitress.

***

As the sun began to set, Glenda looked at her watch. "Well,

I'd better get home. I have some things to go over with my dad before he goes to bed."

"I know you need to help him, but I really don't want you to go. I've never felt like this about another woman before. I've always been a self-contented loner. This is so … unsettling."

"You've never had a girlfriend before?"

"I dated a girl in college, but we were just friends. I've been busy with what I'm doing. As I've gotten older, and watched other relationships, they seemed so complicated. The guys were desperate to get married to their girlfriend, and now they're just as desperate to get out of those marriages. Seems to me that creates a lot of scars that will need to heal. I don't think we're supposed to have throwaway marriages like we dispose of everything else we don't want.

"Maybe God kept my heart sealed until I found the right one. I don't exactly know what to do with my feelings for you. If this is his doing, I don't want to mess it up. But Glenda, I can't hold back my feelings anymore. Could you see us together in the future?"

"I'm ready for the right man to come into my life whenever God brings him. He will help us know if we belong together."

He put his arm around her. "Well, with the way I feel, I've got to take a chance this *is* his will. I'm putting my heart into your hands."

Glenda looked into his face. "I will do my best not to cause any damage to something so precious." She kissed him on the cheek.

He responded. Their lips met.

Glenda always wondered if she would see stars or fireworks when she found the right guy. No matter how someone tried to describe a perfect kiss, this one surely surpassed any other. All the physical alarm systems in her body came alive, and she was sure she saw rainbow colored hearts floating everywhere.

When they finally parted and took a breath, Andrew announced, "Finally. I've wanted to do that for months!"

Glenda smiled as love began to dance in her eyes. "I'd better go. Thank you for making my day … week … month ... year."

They laughed and he said, "I'll walk you to your car." He took her hand, making a public display to the community of a new relationship. At her car, they kissed again.

"Glenda, can you imagine the possibilities of us together?"

"It will be my pleasure to think about that."

Although thoughts of something between her and Andrew had surfaced many times before, she refused to allow them to play with her mind. She had been disappointed by such foolishness too many times. But now, perhaps God was the one putting them together.

Chapter 37

Randy woke, shocked to hear something that sounded like a stampede coming into the bedroom. When he focused, a magnificent warrior angel was present with a host of others. He announced, "Randal, you have been chosen by God." Suddenly, Randy felt like a faulty electric blanket covered his body. Shockwaves of electricity violently surged through him, yet Sherry continued to sleep peacefully at his side. When the dominating energy subsided, Randy lay exhausted from the rush of raw power that overtook him.

***

Next morning, Randy woke refreshed, feeling stronger than he could ever remember. When he arrived at church he burst through the sanctuary doors, and rushed into the room. "Here I am God. What do you want to say to me? I'm willing. I'm listening. I won't argue anymore. Let's do this thing."

Cassius appeared. "Who is this guy?" What did you do with Randal?"

They laughed as Randy responded, "You probably know better than I do. He swung his arms as he circled the open space. I feel so … free. Maybe I'll fly like you do today.

"Thank you, God for sending Cassius to me. He has become my friend." Startled by his own words he shouted, "I'm a friend with an alien. Who knew that was possible?"

He ran up the altar stairs to sit in his chair. "You know what happened to me last night?"

Cassius smiled and explained, "You received a new anointing from God that will bless you, and increase your ability to fulfill his destiny for your life."

"Boy, God does strange things. Okay, what have you got for me today?"

"I have messages from Father."

"Messages, hmm." Randy rolled his neck and looked at Cassius. "That sounds good. Do I need to write them down?"

"No. The words will be seared in your heart. You won't forget them."

"Will that hurt?" He seemed to think those words funnier than Cassius did.

The magnificent companion wrapped his robe around his knees and sat cross-legged, like an Indian, on the floor, which helped them have better eye-to-eye contact. "A divine turn-around has come. There will be many new blessings."

Randy held up his hand to stop the speaker. "Blessings I'll like, or more of those blessing that create good character in me?"

"I don't know. I'm only the messenger. Father has broadened the vision of your call as a pastor. He will give you supernatural knowledge, understanding and clarity on how to proceed in ways you've never known before."

"Well, that will be helpful," he laughed. "I've pretty much been working in the dark so far." The bubbly emotions of last night's encounter remained. "I wonder if this is what being high is like." He noticed the angel waited in silence. "Oh, sorry."

Cassius continued. "All of your people will be needed now. They must be fully trained and free from the world's entanglements. Their fear must be destroyed so they can live faith-filled."

"Check." Randy swung his leg over the arm of his chair feeling completely relaxed. *How will I ever get my people ready for ... something I don't know?*

"Father said you are to allow his Word to reveal your course and direct your steps."

The pastor was reminded the angel knew his thoughts so he didn't interrupt again.

"Much will happen in the next few months because Father God's power will flow like waves through the people."

"I think I felt that last night."

Cassius nodded, "Move without hesitation to complete the tasks ahead. In the midst of what appears to be chaos, wisdom will emerge. Know I AM is strengthening you."

"I know. I feel like Superman this morning."

Cassius gave him a questioning look. "I don't know who that is."

Randy waved his hand to dismiss the distraction and leaned forward so Cassius would continue.

"Father says he has recalibrated you, and set you on course so you can prepare the way for others to advance in spiritual maturity."

The pastor pulled his leg down and sat up straight. "And?"

The angel shrugged. "The growth and alignment of his army is his mandate."

"Okay, let's go." Randy stood and held up his arm like a leader charging with his troops. "Forward in power and glory." He looked at Cassius who wasn't smiling. "What's wrong?"

"There's a bit more."

"More?" Randy dropped his arm and stood at attention. "Yes sir."

"God's desire is for his kingdom to break through and destroy the darkness that tries to hold the earth captive. The assignment before you is the reformation of nations."

Feeling like a big wind knocked him over, Randy dropped in his chair. "Nations?"

Cassius quoted, *"Arise. Shine. For your light has come , and the glory of the Lord has risen upon you. For behold, darkness shall cover the earth, and dense darkness the people, but the Lord shall arise upon you and his glory shall be seen on you. And nations shall come to your light, and kings to the brightness of your radiance.*[1]"

"Wow! I never thought Isaiah's words meant me."

Cassius shrugged, "He has no other plan. He chooses to use weak little people like you. In fact, he said since you've lost all your self-confidence, you've gained his spiritual muscle which comes by being totally dependent on him. That is your key to success."

Randy sobered.

Cassius continued, "The time is now. You are ready to experience increase, promotion, and influence.

"Father said to remind you of Isaiah 54:2. *"Enlarge your house; build an addition; spread out your home. For you will soon be bursting at the seams ..."*

"We're doing that as fast as we can."

Cassius shook his head. "This is bigger. These days require action and decisiveness. These are the day of your destiny. You are part of God's great plans. What honor he has given you. So arise, shine for the glory of the Lord has risen upon you."

"I know. Isaiah 60:1. I hope he remembers I'm only human."

Cassius smiled. "To him, that doesn't seem to be a hindrance."

(1) Isaiah 60:1-3 AMP

Chapter 38

Dave Bruner welcomed Randy and Dan into his office. They noticed the plaque sitting on his desk identified him as the mayor of Millbrook, and they congratulated him for winning the election. The mayor offered them chairs in front of his desk. Once seated, they listen as he shared his concerns for the community. Finally, he said, "I suppose you're wondering why I've asked you to come here."

The men nodded.

"The word on the street is you would like to own the Grand Hotel."

Shocked by what he just heard, Randy did everything he could to keep from showing any emotion, but inside he could feel himself jumping with delight. He said soberly, "Really? Who told you that?"

Dave checked the paper on his desk. "This doesn't say. It's on letterhead from the police department." He leaned forward. "Anyway, the city owns the hotel and they've put finding a solution for the place, on my plate. I suggested we just tear it down, but it's an historical landmark. The legalities of fighting the Historical Society aren't worth the battle or expense. So ... I've been doing some research and learned you guys might want it."

Randy was so excited he couldn't keep his foot from tapping. He knew he didn't dare speak.

Instead Dan asked, "You want to give it to us?"

"Yes, I don't want to fool around trying to find a buyer with the economy of this small town. If you want it, it's yours. I've talked with our lawyers and we've developed the conditions required for the exchange. We would need to see plans on how it would be restored and what it would be used for. You would have to show the financials required to complete any restoration needed."

Randy and Dan looked at each other. The pastor had never discussed anything about the Grand Hotel with Dan.

"Randy, do you have any use for the building?"

The pastor looked at the ceiling and took a deep breath. "We were just dreaming. Jethro thinks it would be a great place to help people. All that space is just sitting there unused. We need more room for the church now, too. Maybe it would be good to move some of our activities downtown. Then more customers might use the shops, and help the restaurants stay open. I miss our bookstore.

"I've never been in the building but the possibilities could be endless. Mayor, are you aware the people from our church are helping the homeless under the bridges?"

"Yes, it has come to our attention. They are doing a fine job."

"Would you be open to us using the hotel as a half-way house, or for rehab, or a shelter?"

The mayor pushed his chair back. "Our board agreed you can do whatever you want with it as long as it is restored properly according to historical specifications, and becomes an asset to our community, instead of what it is today."

Dan spoke up. "What about taxes. I suppose the back taxes are enough to buy a better place."

"We wiped past taxes off the books. Our hope is you choose to do something that will reflect on the rest of the community, and make other businesses around here profitable. Just get us a plan and we can all work through it.

Randy and Dan nodded to each other as the mayor continued. "We'll work with you and try to make the process as simple as possible. Is there any chance at all you might come up with enough money for renovation?"

The pastor took over. "Mayor, this is a total surprise. We really weren't considering such an opportunity as a possibility. We will need to go to our church board, get a lawyer to consider what you've offered, and check with some contractors for some sort of plan to have an idea of the cost. Why, we haven't even seen how bad it is inside."

The mayor looked at his clock. "It's almost noon. I have a set of keys. Do you have time for lunch? Then I can take you to see inside."

The men looked at each other, and then checked their phones. Dan said, "I can change my afternoon appointment. How about you, Pastor?"

"I'll call Glenda and have her shuffle things around for me."

"Good, good," the mayor replied. We'll run over to the country club."

*****

The mayor bent their ears for two hours before he unlocked the front door of the Grand Hotel, and stepped back for the men to enter. He followed them in. "The building has electricity but it will need to be brought up to code. The plumbing and heating systems will all need replaced. Those are big expenses."

Sunlight beamed though the foyer. The two men stood in the entrance staring at the beauty of the grand staircase a good distance away. They could almost see men in tuxedos, and women wearing floor length gowns covered with fur shawls gliding up and down the steps in the early 1900s. Exquisite chandeliers remained as they did in their glory days.

The mayor said, "Rather impressive isn't it? There's a theater behind the doors at the top. Let me show you a few of the rooms on this floor."

As they entered the lounge, Dan spoke. "I wish I'd called Gayle to come with us. She would know more about what needs to be done here. These carpets look like they might still be usable. Are you leaving all this furniture?" He looked at the mayor.

"You can keep it or clean it out."

"I'm surprised no one took this stuff." Dan added.

The Mayor agreed, "And no one vandalized the building. The beveled glass in the first floor windows and the stained glass ceiling in the atrium are still in good shape."

They looked at the carvings around the lounge's fireplace, and admired the molding along the ceilings as they moved on down the hall. They stopped and the mayor said, "This was the ballroom, and over here on this side is the dining room."

A large dining area was waiting just as it must have looked the day they locked the doors. Heavy drapes hung beside floor-to-ceiling windows. Ornate, giant mirrors and paintings engulfed the walls as if hoping their beauty would be appreciated again.

Randy stood in awe. "This is too much."

Dan nodded, "It is a lot to take in." He looked at the Mayor. "Where did the spring come in?"

"It's down this hall."

They moved past the atrium. Randy thought the soft light coming through the stained glass would make a nice prayer chapel. As they went down some stairs, the mayor said. "They must have put the pool down here to get the best use of the flow of the springs."

A large room echoed with every step they took. There was majestic art painted on the walls, and in the floor tiles. The large tile pool was empty.

"Do you know what happened to the spring that fed the pool?" Dan inquired.

"I've heard it dried up. Some of the records show the hotel went broke. They might have closed it off.

"I think there are about four hundred large hotel rooms. They would need closets, although many of the wardrobes are still there. This place is large and regal for a town our size. Could it be brought back to life? Are you the guys for the job? I just want what's best for our community. Everyone I've met from your church has impressed me, so I thought I'd give you first shot at this project."

Bewildered by it all, Randy continued looking around. "Thank you, Mayor, for thinking of us. This is an amazing opportunity. We'll need to take some time and pray to know if we are the ones for the privilege."

"I understand, Pastor. But if you have any interest our lawyer gave me this form for you to sign. It says, Intent to Purchase. The purchase amount is listed as one dollar. That will satisfy the board that I am moving forward on the building. It also gives you sixty days to decide if you want it, and another sixty days to get a plan of action and the financing for the remodel. We would appreciate it if you use local labor as much as possible."

Dan looked at the mayor. "Have you made any stipulations about us selling any of it to someone else?"

"No. But we can discuss the possibility, and add whatever we need to the contract."

"I see," Dan said. "Randy, are you interested enough to have our lawyer look this paper over?"

Randy hadn't used a lawyer before. "What do you think, Dan? This feels way over my head, which makes me think it might be something God wants us to do."

"I agree. The timing is interesting with our need to expand." He turned to the mayor. "Okay, Mayor, we'll take the paper and get back to you as soon as we can."

Randy added, "Thanks for bringing us here. I've wanted to see inside this building. I didn't know something so beautiful was in our town. I knew it was a historical landmark but I wasn't aware it was a tourist destination." He looked at Dan. "Think we should make it one again?"

Dan laughed, "I have no idea." He shook the mayor's hand. "Thanks again, for this opportunity, Dave. We'll get back to you soon. Also, we'll need to get inside again, if we have any interest."

The mayor agreed. "Of course. Hopefully, we can work on this together and bring our little town back to life."

***

When Randy and Dan got in their car, they sat inside trying to decompress from what just happened.

Dan spoke first. "This is so much like my last two businesses I told you about. They just handed them over to me. But, man, if we tackle this, it will be a big project."

The men sat silent for a full minute.

"Gayle should see what it's like. She might have ideas about the restoration. I know she has connections with antique dealers. I didn't say anything in front of the mayor, but some of the furniture and the paintings may be valuable. People love antiques like those, if we wanted to sell them. Of course, some of the beautiful things should stay."

More silence.

Randy spoke. "Gene offered the church money for whatever we need. I wonder what he would think of this idea." Suddenly, he looked inspired. "Wouldn't it be fun to restore the first floor for the whole community? We could use the theater for Jethro's church, or other activities. The ballroom would make space for our growing youth group. It would be a wonderful venue for weddings, banquets, or business meetings, too.

Dan agreed. "Maybe we could have a community theater." Finally, Randy shook his head as if coming out of a dream. "Okay, I can't think about this anymore.

Suddenly, Dan looked stunned. "Randy, I just remembered I didn't tell you about the ridiculous vision God gave me. I wonder if it relates to this building in some way?

"I watched an atomic bomb blast blow millions of people down. I heard God say his glory is coming with such power it will be a similar blast as it destroys the lies and deception that holds people captive. I watched as the people began to get up. He said as they awaken to the truth, they will come to him. If what he showed me happens soon, we will need every room in the building to help all the people."

"Dear God." Randy said as he looked at Dan." "That's what he's been telling us for some time. This might be our best solution to quickly help people."

"True. We better take this opportunity more seriously. I know you don't have a lawyer for the church. If you like, I can run the papers by mine."

"Sounds good. Now, can we get back to normal life?"

Dan started the car, "I guess we better. Actually, this is beginning to feel normal, don't you agree?"

Chapter 39

After Sunday lunch with the family, Randy and his dad sat on the patio enjoying their ice tea.

"The weather sure has been beautiful," Randy said as he put his empty glass on the table. On que, Sherry stepped out the door to refill their drinks, and sat a plate of warm sugar cookies on the small table between them. "The girls are baking with Grandma."

"Thank you." The men responded.

Sherry smiled and patted their guest on his shoulder. "We're so glad you've come to be with us. Enjoy the cookies. I'm going to try to put the girls down for a nap as soon as they finish cleaning up."

"Good luck," Randy smiled.

"Exactly," she replied as she headed inside.

When the door shut, Chester asked, "So what's next, son? Where do you need my help? We're ready to get started."

Randy looked at his father. Though he rarely confided in him in the past, he wanted to share everything that was happening now. Maybe he was learning to appreciate the maturity of the man he spent most of his life competing with, or avoiding.

"You are a godsend, Dad. I mean it. God has sent you just in time."

He described the excitement of the people, and told him about the new families coming in. Then he jumped up, "Excuse me a minute. I'll be right back."

Like a flash he was back with a blueprint of the Grand Hotel. He spread the old papers across the patio table.

"Mayor Bruner offered to give us the Grand Hotel downtown.

He loaned me the original plans for the building to give us some perspective of what's there. Have you ever seen it?"

"Is it that old ten story building on Eighth Street?" Chester got up to look at the papers, as Randy smoothed them out.

"Yes, that's it. Were you impressed? I was the first time I saw it."

"Yes, I was. It's the classic architecture of the turn-of-the-century, and looks in pretty good shape. Seems kind of out-of-place for a community this size."

"Yes, it does. The mayor told us if we present a plan showing how we will use it, and how it will be restored," Randy took a breath, "and prove we have the financing to complete the work, they will give it to us."

Chester looked shocked. "Really? What would you use it for?"

"So far only Dan and I have tried to figure out that answer. We agree this might be one of God's miracles, and figure he may be planning something we don't understand yet.

"We know Jethro's church is outgrowing Maggie's Café. Wouldn't that be something, if God wanted them to have room in such a classy place? I'm also aware of the need for apartments to house woman who need some help getting their lives together while also having a safe place for their children. Maybe there could be classes to help them prepare for good jobs."

Randy saw Chester's excitement as the man leaned across the table to examine the blueprints. *Yep, the old man is impressed.*

"Isn't it something, Dad? I didn't know the building is square with a large courtyard in the middle. When it was new, people would go into the hotel pool that was fed by Millbrook Spring. They thought it had healing waters. Then they rested out here." He pointed to the veranda beside the courtyard lawn. His fingers directed his dad's eyes around the plans. "Basically, all ten floors have a view of town or the first floor court yard. They could be sectioned off for different purposes. Fire walls and doors have already been added to keep it divided.

We talked with an architect who thinks the beauty of the lobby can be restored to look like it did in the early 1890's yet have modern conveniences.

"We're doing some research to see if the water from the spring was tapped off. Perhaps it's still viable. Wouldn't that be something? If so, Millbrook might become a tourist destination again."

He ran his fingers around the paper showing entries, the back parking, and the place where the spring once flowed. He continued to share that Gene Goble offered his financial help.

Finding his dad was interested he went on to tell him about the miracles that were currently happening as people were healed, and even raised from the dead. Quietly he shared the devastation he saw under the bridge and in the streets of their community. Then he got right down to it and shared about Cassius and his announcement of the great and glorious day of the Lord.

Chester was so excited he paced the last hour as Randy sat and told his stories. When the young man finally stopped, the wise father turned to look at his son. Randy felt his dad knew he was leaving out a piece of important information. So finally, ever so sheepishly, he revealed words he didn't really want to speak. "God said he is giving me the city."

The father looked at his son, and then to heaven. "Thank you, Lord. Thank you, God."

He sat down across from Randy. "I've always known you have a huge destiny on your life. I'm proud of you son. And I'm so thankful I've lived to see this day." Compassion, pride, and excitement oozed from his words as he continued.

"Randy, God doesn't give us more than we can handle. You're prepared. You may not feel as if you are, but you're ready. He will lead you every step. If you just keep your hands off and follow him, you can't lose. My greatest desire has been to be part of

God's last days harvest. I believe he's answering my prayers. How can I help?"

Randy sighed with relief. "When you said you felt led to come help us, I started thinking of all your experience in accounting and business. I'm hoping you can help ... I guess I would say structurally. What is God planning by giving us a hotel? Dad, it's all so expensive and time consuming to remodel, and there seems to be much better places to spend our resources than with a building.

"I would love to have you and a few guys with business experience get together to plan for our needs as we move forward. Talk around town; get acquainted with the governmental people, and the other churches. Find out what the needs are in our community, and where our people might commit to help.

"I've started going out with Jethro sometimes. Have you met him yet?"

His dad thought, then shook his head. "The one you mentioned has a church and needs more space. I don't think so."

"Well, he introduced me to the devastated lives out there. We need to help them. Once our community is healthy and whole we can move on into our county.

"I don't know how to start on something like the hotel, even if I had the time. I'm thinking if you, Gene, and whoever else you might think would work well with you, could look into what we can do to help the homeless people, and maybe also create a place to train people for jobs. Maybe the hotel is a good place to do that.

"The first floor is still in good shape so there could be a restaurant on the ground floor or a coffee house. The big rooms would be great for many types of activities, and the theater could become a treasure for our community again." He paused. "I guess if God is giving me the city, I'd better start acting like it. Wonder what that even looks like?"

They laughed.

"Dad, there's a harvest of souls coming into the kingdom of God. Many will be hurting and misdirected. Can we prepare a place to mentor them and help them heal? If so, how do we go about it? Who are the people who will work to see it succeed? What do you think?"

His dad sat quietly for a few moments. "Well, I was excited before about being part of what you're doing here, but I had no idea it would be this big."

Randy nodded, "Yes, there's sure plenty to be done. Much of it, I probably don't know about yet."

"In God's time, son. In God's time."

Fresh from their naps, the girls burst through the door, ready to show Grandpa how well they could ride their bikes.

Chapter 40

Cassius sat cross-legged suspended in the air in front of Randy. "We have much to discuss today, Pastor. Now that you believe we really exist and that we've come to assist you, our glorious God, Ruler of the Universe, wants me to enlighten you about the enemies' evil ways."

"Oh, I've already recognized some of them."

"Very good. You must know he exists and he is not with us. His kingdom is also in the invisible realm most of the time. He is powerful, and his goal is to take Father God's throne. Can you imagine?

"Memorize God's Word. You'll need to attack the evil one with Father's truth, when the liar comes to take you out."

Randy gulped. "Take me out?"

"Yes sir." Tears filled Cassius's eyes. "When he comes, you must have faith to stand strong and fight him with the Word just as Jesus did when he was tempted. Remember how he said, 'It is written,'[1] as he quoted scriptures to Satan?"

Randy nodded.

"Have the Word on your tongue at all times."

"Why would he bother me?" Randy asked in a trembling voice.

Cassius tears turned to laughter as he roared, "Oh, my dear young man. Don't you know the heavens have been stirred by what's happening here? Do you think any leader of a church can stand when the evil one sends his destructive forces against the House of God?"

Silence filled the room.

As if trying to be gentle, the mighty angel shook his head and continued. "I cannot help you when he comes. This will be your battle to fight."

A shiver ran through Randy. "I can't do this. I see the concern on your face, Cassius. I know this will be too much for me."

"Yes, but Almighty God has found you worthy. I hope I have prepared you properly. Even in the torrent of wickedness, you take the shield of faith[2] and hang on to Truth. You will survive."

"Survive? I was worried about not failing as a leader. Survive?"

Cassius was gone.

Fear joined Randy like a tormenting bully.

***

Completely exhausted from the challenging day, Randy went home. When he entered the kitchen, Sherry turned from the sink looking as concerned as he felt.

"Randy, I'm so glad you're here. I received a call saying my mother is in the hospital. It's bad. They don't think she's going to make it. I need to go to be with her. I've prepared some meals for you and put them in the freezer. The girls are packing to go with me. I tried to call you, but your phone didn't seem to be working."

Randy plopped in a chair. "You're leaving, too?" Fear held him tight. He didn't want to face what was coming by himself.

"Leaving too?" Sherry responded. "I must. She doesn't have anyone else. I don't want her to die alone."

He shook his head, "Of course not. Maybe I should go with you?"

Sherry looked surprised, "Really? Could you get away?"

"I want to."

His bride quickly stepped over, sat in his lap and put her arms around his neck. "Oh, Randy, thank you for wanting to go." She gave him a kiss.

He didn't dare tell her he was frightened to think of being alone. Fearful of what might happen soon.

Reality hit him like a giant weight. *So many responsibilities. The people have needs. All the changes. Not to mention what's going on in the unseen realm.* "I guess I really have to stay here."

Sherry nodded. "I know you do. But thanks for being willing to go with me as moral support. This won't be easy."

"Are you sure you want to take the girls? They don't really know her. Maybe it would be better for them to be with my mom."

"That's a great idea. Why didn't I think of asking her? I was trying to figure out how I would manage them while I'm at the hospital. I'll call."

Randy sat lost in thought as his wife chatted on the phone. Turning back to him she announced, "Your mom said they would love to have them. The girls will be much happier with that arrangement."

She kissed Randy again. "I'll go pack. Your dinner's in the oven."

Dinner? The thought of dinner makes my stomach hurt even worse.

***

In the days that followed, the house was so quiet with Sherry and the girls gone, Randy didn't even want to go to his man cave for respite. Instead, he longed for the noises of their normal life.

Unaware of the activity in the invisible world, he didn't know the host of heaven had been called away, too. As sure as if their hands had been tied behind their backs, angelic warriors rose above the current atmosphere.

Exhausted, he went to bed.

Late into the night, Randy woke with a gasp. Fear surged through him as he realized he wasn't alone. The moonlight revealed a large man dressed in a black trench coat and hat. He towered over him beside the bed.

By the time he was awake enough to know he wasn't in a dream, the vision disappeared. The same thing happened the second night. Again, Randy felt someone standing by his bed. This time, when he opened his eyes he felt the form wanted to say something to him. The moment he sat up, the black shadow disappeared.

What is that? Are there really ghosts? Oh, the whole thing Cassius warned me about has me imagining things. He lay back, but couldn't get to sleep. *What am I supposed to do if he comes again? The Bible says I have authority over spirits.*[3] *Never thought I'd need to know that.*

On the third night, as Randy slept he felt someone standing by his bed. When he opened his eyes the form was looking down at him again. He asked. "What do you want?"

Moonlight beamed into the room. There was no doubt a tall man was really standing there. His features were hidden in the shadow of the hat's brim. Again, he didn't speak.

Randy felt sadness coming from the illusion or spirit. *This is not the evil one. He is definitely a ghost. I wonder if he died in this house.* "Are you lost?"

No answer came from the dark form.

"Well, I don't know who you are, or what you want, but you are not welcome here. You must go away and never come back."

The form slowly walked around to the end of the bed and out through the wall.

Well, that was easy. I do seem to have the authority to send such things away? Interesting. Maybe that was what Cassius was telling me about." He rolled over and went back to sleep.

***

After an eight hour drive and a nights rest in a hotel bed, Sherry was surprised at the strength she felt as she walked the hospital halls to find a woman she hadn't seen in twenty-one years. She clutched the note in her hand that she received from the front desk. Margaret Smithton, Room 413. *Here it is.* She took a deep breath and pushed the door open.

A tiny woman slept peacefully among wires as machines blinked beside her bed. Sherry knew she was in a coma, so she took the opportunity to move close and search the woman's features hoping she might recognize her. But the patient could have been anyone. At that moment she wished she had a sister or brother who could be there with her. In the past, she was grateful no one else had to survive the abuse she experienced as a child.

Now somewhere around fifty-five years old, her mother's hair had grayed and wrinkles etched the contours of her thin face. Sherry remembered her being a pretty woman, but there was nothing left of that beauty. She assumed her mother continued the abusive lifestyle because over the years she called once or twice begging for Sherry's help. She always hung up on her. *Could I have made a difference? Didn't I have to protect myself and my family?*

The quietness helped Sherry relax. *I have her nose. Oh, she's the one I got my long fingers from. Her hands look just like mine.* She was surprised by the compassion, maybe even love, she suddenly felt for this stranger who once hurt her so badly. Reaching out she took her mother's hand. "Mama, it's Sherry. I'm here to be with you. Do you remember me? I know they said you wouldn't wake up. The stroke has damaged your brain, but I wish I could know if you hear me." Sherry watched her mother's face and was sure she saw a tiny flicker under her eyelids. As she leaned forward she laid her hand on the blanket covering her mother's leg. It began to move. "Oh, you can hear me, can't you, Mama. I'm here for you. I'll stay as long as you need me."

A nurse came in, excused herself, and began to change the bags hanging from a pole beside her bed. She checked the computers and entered updates.

Sherry announced. "She just moved her leg,"

The nurse looked at her. "Probably just reflexes." Out the door she went.

"That wasn't a reflex, was it Mama? I know you were talking to me." Not knowing how much time she had before another intrusion, or how long her mother would live, she hurried on with her reason for coming.

"Mama, I had to come to tell you I forgive you for all the things that happened when I was little. I hope you found someone to love you. God loves you, Mama. God loves you. And because He does, I love you too." She stopped and realized the miracle she was experiencing. *Now, I know why I had to come. This was for me as much as her.*

She pulled a chair closer to the bed, and took her mother's hand again. "I want to tell you about my life, Mama."

Not knowing if she had minutes, hours, or days, she decided she better get started. "First, you are a grandma. Randy, he's the wonderful man I married, and I have two adorable daughters. I know they would make you smile."

She pulled a bottle of water out of her bag and took a drink as the stress she brought with her melted away. Holding the woman's hand again, she began to tell one story after another about the clever things her children said and did. She could imagine her mother laughing, even though she showed no response.

The days passed, Sherry slept in the chair beside her mother's bed and ate in the hospital cafeteria. There were no changes in the woman, but Sherry's heart was full. After talking for hours on end about everything that happened in her life from the time she last saw her mother to today, she realized she was now a free woman. No longer a victim, she felt strong and whole, knowing her past, with its hardships, was finished. Now, her new life defines her as an overcomer who loves people and lived life with purpose.

***

After several days Randy felt hungry, so he dug through the freezer for one of Sherry's home-cooked meals. He pulled out a container with the word lasagna printed on top, and stuck it in the microwave. With the many activities of his days, the conversation with Cassius had been pushed aside. Sherry's mother lingered between life and death, and he only saw his daughters at his parent's house when he was there for Sunday dinner.

The night visions continued. Some illusions tried to challenge him with fearful thoughts. Other left him awake, in wonder of the invisible world he knew so little about.

At three in the morning on the tenth night of tormenting visitors, he sat straight up in bed. "Now what?"

No one was there, but the stench of sulfur filled the air, and something like smoke floated about. Fear, fear like he'd never known, wrapped him and it would not let him go.

"You are mine," demanded a hissing gravelly voice. "I own you. You have failed in everything you've tried to do to make yourself look good. You are nothing."

Randy knew those words were true. Was this the test? Face the truth of who he really was and accept the fact he could never change?

The vial words continued. Each declaration sounded like a hammer banged its truth into the evil self-willed soul he tried so hard to free himself from.

"All your hard work has been for nothing. Thud. … Your imagination created this God you think you serve. Thud. … You don't know how to love. Thud. … You will never amount to anything. Thud. … You're missing out on all the fun you could be having if you weren't so stuffy. Thud. … Don't you know your wife decided to leave you? Thud. … You would be better off dead. Thud. … "

This torrent of evil was so much worse than all those other attempts to steal his sleep or attack him. He knew the words were true. How could he fight the power of truth? He trembled with the cold reality of knowing he would never be good enough to be the man he longed to become.

The evil voice growled. "I know the truth, don't I? Quit. Give up. Run away. No one will miss you. You're hopeless. Just kill yourself and be done with it."

The disgusting smell in the air sent Randy into a coughing fit. Overcome and exhausted he laid back, grabbed the blanket, pulled it over his head, and curled up into a ball hoping to die.

After a bit, somewhere in the innermost depths of his being, words began to form. He mumbled some scriptures into the bed, "Greater is he that is in me than he that is in the world.[3] ... God is love.[4] ... Perfect love casts out all fear."[5] ... *Wow. The suffocating pressure loosened. What else do I know?*

The Word, hidden in his heart, began to come alive. He threw off the blanket. "I can do all things through Christ who strengthens me.[6] ... It is no longer I who lives but Christ who lives in me and the life I now live is in faith in the Son of God who loves me and gave his life for me."[7]

Screeching sounds filled the room with demands. "Don't say that. Don't lie. Those words are lies. No. Stop."

Randy shook off the spirit of deception that had him bound and sat up. Boldness filled every place fear held him before. "I am the righteousness of God in Christ Jesus.[8] ... I will live and not die and see the glory of God on the earth.[9] ... You are a defeated foe."[10]

A whirlwind swept through the room as fear, and the darkness of death, vanished.

"All right, is there anything else around here that's not of God? You are bound from my house forever. Get out. I'm too tired to be bothered. Be gone in Jesus name. I am going to sleep now, and I won't put up with you anymore. Do you understand me?

"Father, put your angels as guards around my house[11] to fight the enemy so I can get on with what you've called me to do."

Heaven's sentries returned to their post and applauded with delight at the man's successful victory.

(1) Matthew 4:4, (2) Ephesians 6:16, (3) Luke 10:19 NKJV, (4) I John 4:8, (5) I John 4:18, (6) Philippians 4:13, (7) Galatians 2:20, (8) II Corinthians 5:21, (9) Psalm 118:17, (10) Romans 16:20, (11) Psalm 34:7

Chapter 41

Gayle hugged Sherry as they met for lunch at Maggie's Café. Dan called their time together their tete-a-tete. She waved at Helen, who always wore her bright pink T-shirt at work, and said, "We'll sit at our table in the corner."

Helen nodded and grabbed menus to bring to the ladies. They quickly ordered their favorite salads and a pot of tea. With a sigh, Gayle relaxed in the pleasure of being with her friend. "I'm so glad we've finally gotten together. Sherry, I was sorry to hear about your mother's death. How did it go while you were with her at the hospital?"

"You know I didn't want to go. I've blamed her for everything wrong that ever happened to me. But I knew I had to be there for her. She was unconscious the whole time. Somehow that made it easier." She leaned forward. "I had no idea God's plan was to help me forgive her, and to heal me from the emotional scars of her abuse so many years ago."

"I'm so happy for you. Forgiving others is such a key to our miracles."

"Yes. Okay, Gayle, tell me everything that's happened while I was gone. I feel like I've missed so much."

"Well, Dan took me into the hotel yesterday to see what I thought."

"And?" Sherry asked.

A smile spread across Gayle's face. "When I stepped inside I knew why they called it The Grand Hotel. Everything is ornate and it looks as if it were held in a time capsule, waiting for us. I'm excited to be part of helping restore the jewel for our community.

We'll need professionals to bring some of the treasures back to life."

"Really? Randy mentioned the church was offered the building, but he didn't tell me what it's like inside. Of course, he has a lot on his mind."

Gayle agreed. "Yes, true. How are things going with his parents being here?"

"Oh, I'm so happy they came. I think of them as my parents, too. They kept the girls while I was gone and seemed to enjoy having them. I hope they decide to stay in Millbrook."

"Yes, that would be nice."

Helen appeared with their lunch. Sherry thanked her as the waitress filled their cups from the teapot and then slipped away. "She knows we prefer to be left alone to visit. Please, go on."

After swallowing a bite of salad, Gayle said, "Well, God's been doing some strange new things in my life."

"Tell me. What's he's up to now?"

She laid her napkin aside. "The whole thing started when I shared with our Bible study group what the Holy Spirit taught me about receiving praise."

Sherry nodded with a questioning look and took a sip of tea.

Gayle continued. "Right, it sounds like a strange subject. I knew all praise belongs to Jesus, but I'd never considered the balance in everything. I shared with you how I've been hearing the Holy Spirit's lovely words. They are so affectionate they're too amazing to believe. Well, I realized because I didn't feel worthy of his praise, I pushed God's words of acceptance away. I had no idea the power of his love could free me from who I thought I was, so I can become the real person he created me to be."

"Gayle. That's profound."

"It took me a while, but finally I understood God wanted me to believe his words of love and accept them into my heart.

"He helped me realize I need to embrace the kind words of others too. You know how I've often felt unworthy and pushed people's encouragement away."

Sherry interrupted. "Yes, I know you do. You are hard to compliment. I'm always trying to tell you how great you are, but you don't seem to hear me."

"I'm sorry. The Holy Spirit showed me that kind words from others are gifts meant to encourage me, to give me new strength and direction, and to create feelings of acceptance.[1]

"He taught me I was to take the life-giving words he sends through others, so my soul is fed. Then I'm to thank God for their praise and lay it as an offering at his feet. God wants us to know we are valuable to him and others."

Gayle took a deep breath. "So I went to the ladies and repented for not receiving their kindness and love freely. I promised them they would see a difference in the way I accept their affection, and I told them I value the importance of their kind words. And yours, too, I might add, my dear friend."

Sherry agreed with a nod.

"Wasn't it a strange teaching? And yet, I knew I probably wasn't the only one who needed the lesson."

"You're right. We think pushing praise away is a sign of humility, but it's not true. God can express his approval through others' voices. Thank you, for sharing what you taught. I need the lesson, too."

The ladies ate their lunch as they discussed the new thoughts. When Gayle finished, she pushed her plate back a little and straightened the knife beside it. "There's more."

Sherry looked up, stopped chewing and choked the food down. "More?" She laid her fork across the plate and leaned in to hear every word. "Tell me."

"I was driving home after the class, and in the quietness in my empty car I thanked God for the privilege of sharing what he taught me with the women. I stopped at the stop sign on the busy cross street at Randolph. You know. The older established neighborhood?"

"Yes. "Go on.""

"Suddenly, a deer stepped into the road and slowly walked across the street in front of me. I was so surprised. There are no woods or anything except houses around there. Where would a deer come from?"

Sherry asked. "Wasn't the traffic heavy? That's a busy street."

"No, I looked in my rearview mirror and no one was behind me. No cars were anywhere around. As soon as the first deer exited the street, something moved on my left. A second deer stepped forward and paraded in front of me not more than a foot from my bumper. The beautiful deer walked as slowly across as the first, so I was able to really enjoy one of my favorite animals."

Excited, Sherry burst in. "I know. You love deer. Amazing. If anyone else told me this story I would probably think they were making it up." She laughed so loud other diners looked over.

Gayle giggled, "That's exactly what I thought. How could it be that I was able to see two of my favorite animals step out, as if on cue, onto the stage of my life so I could watch them? It was unbelievable that no other traffic was on the road at that time of day, so the deer wouldn't be frightened. I didn't block the street for other cars, or need to move out of the way. What a magical moment.

"I checked my rearview mirror again to make sure no one was behind me. When I looked back in the direction the deer were moving, they were gone. The whole scene seemed like an illusion. As I started to drive forward, cars began to come and go in their usual manner."

"That is a beautiful story." Sherry picked up the pot and refilled their cups.

After Gayle took a sip, she said, "There's more."

Sherry smacked her hands over her mouth before saying, "Oh, my goodness. What else?"

Smiling, Gayle leaned forward. "I could not contain the joy I was feeling. While driving away, and thanking God for my special gift, the Voice inside me interrupted saying, 'That was my gift to you. Thank you for teaching the women the importance of receiving praise. Too many people don't believe they're worthy. You have shown them it's not about making themselves worthy. I have made them worthy'."

"That's beautiful. I think I'm going to cry."

The teacher nodded and held up her finger. "Behind his voice I could hear people cheering and applauding. I even caught a glimpse of a crowd in a grandstand.

"I said, 'Thank you, Lord. No one on earth could give me such a special gift. You are the only one with the ability to direct deer to walk in front of me so I could enjoy their beauty. Only you were able to keep all the cars away for my special reward. Thank you. Thank you.'"

Pleased she was able to share her excitement with her friend, Gayle said, "Then I asked, "What was all the cheering in the background?

"He answered in a matter-of-fact voice saying, 'Oh that was the Great Cloud of Witnesses.'"[2]

Sherry's eyes grew larger. "The Great Cloud of Witnesses?"

"I thought the same thing. 'The Great Cloud of Witnesses? Oh, my goodness.' I began to laugh. My outburst filled the car. Actually, it was more like hysteria. I'm so glad no one noticed me.

"Sherry, I saw the other realm. There really are people cheering for us. Heaven isn't as far away as we thought. It's as if we can push through a veil and be there."

"Wow! Who are the ones mentioned in the Bible who are urging us on? I don't remember."

"Right. Through all the laughter I knew I had to get home and find those scriptures. Some of the people are the ones mentioned in Hebrews chapter eleven. Abraham, Moses, David, all the ones who lived out their faith in God's plan for their lives. Sherry, they are cheering for us."

The two ladies smiled at each other as they thought about the revelation they were sure God wanted everyone to know. Without another word, Gayle picked up her teacup, and leaned back as they contemplated the wonder of it all.

(1) Ephesians 4:29, (2) Hebrews 12:1

Chapter 42

Micah sat quietly fishing along the brook's bank. He reflected on how good the peace inside him felt now that he was free from the desire for alcohol and pot.

The sixteen year old was questioning what he wanted to do in the future, and this was his favorite place to be alone and think about such things.

His thoughts turned to before, when the man he met said he was Jesus. *That had to be a miracle when I caught those fish so fast. Everyone says Mom's healing was a miracle. I believe it.* "God, you are the only one who could bring Kevin and David back to life. Thanks for letting me be part of that."

How does someone know God? Does he really have a plan for our lives? If so, how can we know what it is?

At the same moment he felt the first tug on his line, a group of angels revealed themselves. They beckoned him with their hands. He couldn't resist the draw of their excitement. "What's going on?" He nodded, having no idea what he just agreed to.

He yielded to the pull of something unknown, and enjoyed the thrill of a surge of power as he lifted into the heavens. Looking down, he watched himself by the water where a fish struggled to be released.

The zoom of speed soon felt natural, and was more like floating as he watched earth from a satellite's view. Filled with excitement to see what would happen, he relaxed to enjoy something out of this world. After some time, one of the angels suggested he experiment with his newfound agility. Feeling free to explore, the adventurer dived down, then shot straight up. The others encouraged him with their laughter as they swooped around him, so he whirled, and turned summersaults and flips to show off his new skills.

Suddenly, he shuddered as a powerful shadow surrounded him. "Where am I? This doesn't feel like heaven."

He heard one of the angels, now invisible, speak. "This is the second heaven of Mighty God's creation where the spiritual hosts of wickedness in heavenly places reside.[1] His enemy continually tries to keep people from moving through here so they won't reach the third heaven[2] where God lives. The demons' goal is to keep God's people from reaching him. You are now pure. Just go straight through. Don't fall for their wargames, we will protect you."

Micah drew back. "I'm not pure. You've got the wrong guy. I mess up all the time. Sure, I'm trying to make better choices, but I think being "pure" is impossible for me."

"Father God thinks you're pure. You repented and asked your Savior to take over your life. Father sees you through his son's perfect blood sacrifice which covers all your sins and makes you pure.[3] This is truth. Faith lives it out."

Doubtful, he responded, "Okay ..." There was no time to disagree further. Agitated voices screeched in protest as he continued forward. Micah covered his ears. "Oh, that noise is so awful. It would make fingernails on a chalkboard sound like music."

His guide advised, "Don't worry about them. Their anger is announcing we've broken through the boundaries of their territory. Father said it's time to take some of his young warriors into this realm to penetrate the dark power structures holding earth's nations captive. You are slicing through the resistance in the second heaven. As each of you fight your way through here, the evil one will weaken."

Micah heard another angel's voice. "They invade earth

without being detected, but they don't like holy traffic traveling through their domain. Holiness is most upsetting to them. It causes their deceptive defenses to lose power."

They proceeded into more darkness. Soon he couldn't see anything. The screams were truly horrid. Quick flickers of light revealed vileness beyond human description. Tormented souls begged, longing to be free.

I'll never watch a horror movie again. Feeling the "reality" of evil is more than enough for me.

"You are not fearful," one of the angels whispered. "That makes you far too powerful for them to come close. How did you, as a human, win over fear? Fear is a strong spirit.[4] Very few men accomplish that victory."

"I don't know," he said hoping for the experience to end soon. "But I don't want to forget what I'm seeing here. My world could become like this if we choose to ignore God's love and reality."

"Very Good," an angel responded. "Father is so proud of you."

Suddenly, he broke into the light. After a few blinks to adjust his eyes, he stared at a most brilliantly blue sky he ever saw. There was total silence. However, the awful sounds from before were still ringing in his ears.

Micah's spirit became more excited. "We must be in heaven now."

"Yes, you have the honor of meeting with the King."

With a look of surprise he asked, "Do you mean King Jesus?"

"Yes, of course. There is no other."

Micah gasped.

As they continued, mountains and valleys came into view. A very large mountain was on his left. He spotted two people moving. The angels gave a nod and they all swooped down for a better view. A man and woman were holding hands while running up the mountain. They were both dressed in white. He wore a crown on his head, and the woman was radiant in a wedding gown with a veil that flowed behind her.

Micah looked at his escort. "They're going straight up the side of that mountain with no effort at all."

The angel agreed. "Jesus is welcoming another bride home.

"Come, the Master is waiting for you." They flew to the top of the high mountain. As they circled the peak, he saw the most spectacular... *It must be a castle but it looks like it's made of crystal.* The sight was mesmerizing. As the visitor moved closer, the crystal-looking walls seemed to be a prism where brilliant light created more colors than a rainbow that danced as if alive.

"Wow! I've never seen so many colors before. They pulsate like they're alive when they hit the structure. I didn't know all those unusual shapes and angles existed."

"The King will see you now."

Just that quickly, Micah stood before a throne. He looked all around and knew his physical eyes would never be able to adjust to such a spectacular light show.

"Welcome, son. I've been waiting for you."

Surprised, Micah turned forward. "Oh, I didn't know anyone was ... Jesus." He dropped to his knees.

Jesus reached down. "Come, my boy. Give me your hand."

When the King's divine hand touched Micah, a surge of power went through him that would probably kill him in his human flesh. As the young man looked at him, he saw the fire in his eyes burned with a love so strong Micah could only take a quick glance before looking away. But, the draw of those eyes was also so irresistible he knew he would give everything for one more look. With all the boldness he could muster, he stared into Jesus's face. Waves of Love's purity surged through every part of him.

Too soon, the Savior blinked and said "Let's walk. This throne can feel a little crowded with all the activity. We'll walk along the river. I know you enjoy the water."

Micah didn't see any activity around the throne. The King laid aside the same crown Micah saw on him as he ran up the mountain with a bride.

Instantly, they were walking beside flowing water that seems alive. *Could this be the river of living water the Bible mentions?*[6]

The Master's robe was similar to the ones Micah recognized from pictures. Jesus settled himself on a small boulder. Micah sat at his feet and looked into his face. *I'll never forget his eyes.*

"I'm happy you are here with me, Micah. I have much to share."

Micah starred, trying to grasp the wonder of what was happening. All he could do was nod.

Jesus continued. "I want you to know you honor me when you honor your parents.[5] You honor me when you seek to know my plans for your life.[6]"

He realized he was hearing Jesus's words in his heart, not with his ears. They were communicating heart to heart.

"Remember when you were younger and you and your friends pretended to be soldiers? Your spirits knew the call on your lives before your souls could understand. You are a mighty warrior, like a military combat soldier. But, your weapon of warfare is the Word of God, which will do far more damage to the enemy than any war weapon has power to accomplish. Father said, 'It is time.' I have already reversed the curses in the second heaven so my kingdom can be fully established on earth. There will be no end to the increase of my government or of peace.[7]

"As you search the Word and gain deeper understanding on how to fight in the enemy's territory, chain reactions will take place on earth in response. Governments will become righteous. People's hearts will be set free.

"I promised I would remove the guilt of the land in a single day.[8]

"Micah, Zachariah wrote my promises to you in his book when he penned, *The Lord will be king over all the earth; in that day the Lord will be the only one, and his name the only one.*[9]

"Help Andrew prepare others. Learn, fight for, and live the

truth. Stand strong. I won the war on the cross. I want you to help me finish the work of preparing others for my kingdom to come fully."

Micah could almost feel his muscles bulge with power and strength in Jesus' presence.

"Here is your scripture to stand on my son. *I can do all things through Christ who strengthens me.*"

Micah responded with a thought. *I know that one. It's Philippians 4:13.*

"Very good. I fulfill my promises. I am coming and I will live among you."[10]

Jesus vanished.

Micah looked around to see where he went, but found himself beside the brook with his rod in his hand and a fish struggling on the end of the line. As he reeled in his catch, he talked to himself. *I have been with King Jesus. He was also the guy here fishing who said he was Jesus. I know what I'm to do. These are going to be the most important and exciting days in human history. My generation will prepare the way for his return."* He looked at the sky in wonder, then grabbed up his gear and fish. "I've got to go find my Bible"

(1) Ephesians 6:12, (2) II Corinthians 12:2-3, (3) I John 1:7, (4) II Timothy 1:7, (5) Ephesians 6:2, (6) Jeremiah 29:12, (7) Isaiah 9:7, (8) Zachariah 3:9, (9) Zachariah 14:9, (10) Zachariah 2:10

Chapter 43

Randy sat quietly with Cassius. He reflected on how his feelings had changed for this unusual friend. *I like the way his laughter splashes joy everywhere.* He remembered how annoying the intruder was at first. Now he treasures the angel's opinions as a voice of reason who untangles his confusion with a few wise words. He smiled. *Perhaps, I'm the one who changed. I wonder why my mentor is quiet. He seems so serious this morning.*

Cassius cleared his throat and said, "I have completed my assignment. Father says you are prepared."

"No!" Randy gasped as his heart felt like it dropped to his stomach.

The mentor looked thoughtful. "I've been trying to decide what my last words should be before I leave you. Remember, I told you things are changing?"

"Yes. I'm trying to keep up with all of them."

"This is different. You know how the air feels on a hot summer day when a cool breeze passes?"

"Sure. It's refreshing," Randy responded.

"Yes, well, that's what's happening in the Spirit realm now. Like a shift in the weather, fresh winds from heaven have begun to blow. God's glorious reign is on the horizon. He is ready to transform this world with his glory and fulfill his promise recorded in Numbers 14:21."

Randy flipped his Bible's pages and read, "All the earth will be filled with the glory of the Lord." He paused, trying to imagine what that would be like.

Cassius continued. "Right now, there is a great harvest of souls ready to come in. God's plan is to use his people to accomplish this.

"It is good they've learned their negative words magnify the evil one's power. Now they're declaring the truth of what God's Word says. *'Death and life are in the power of the tongue.'*[1] You might want to continue to remind them that the enemy finds power through negative words that are spoken, and heaven's host moves into action with life-giving words."

Randy grabbed his notepad. "Let me make some notes. Okay?"

"Yes, of course. Tell the people."

"Randal, please understand what I'm saying. Heaven's glory is about to burst across the earth. God wants you to prepare people to live a supernatural life in their natural world. Your spirits can freely be with him in heaven, even while your flesh is here on earth to fulfill his plans. Remember, even now you are seated with him in heavenly places."

Randy knew the angel was quoting Ephesians 2:6.

Cassius said, "Do you understand that it is because God's people have found their voices and prayed that we are here? I confess even I find it a wonder that the power of heaven moves when human's declare God's truth. Randal, if they could only see what happens in the kingdom realm when his people pray. It's like alarms go off and everyone becomes active."

The angel searched his face, so Randy responded. "Yes, I understand. Prayer really does make a difference."

His instructor nodded. "Tell the people.

"I've watched humanity while I've been privileged to be here. Some seem to have no idea who they really are as a child of God. If only they could see the Father's face as he watches each of you. He says you are shining lights reflecting his image. His pride is even more passionate than a human father's joy in his children. Too many people don't seem to know this, so they wander as if lost or in a daze.

"You see, when God created all of you, he deposited his very nature, power, and wisdom in you. These things rest in the spirit of every person, and they come in tune with heaven when they recognize God's reality, and his provision for their lives. Once awakened, the Holy Spirit will lead them into all truth.[2]"

Randy knew this was a defining moment of teaching so he tried to listen carefully.

Cassius shook his head, showing sympathy for his student. "I know this is hard for you to understand. The enemy's chatter confuses the true call of a man's destiny. What I am trying to say is, rise above the chatter. Push it away. Recognize the source.

"I guess this happens when they know the truth of God's love for them."

He looked at Randy. "I didn't know how hard it is for people to understand God's kingdom until I started trying to share what's coming with you. We don't have the pollution of another realm attacking continually. Your 'good versus bad', 'right versus wrong' world is very distressing."

Randy laughed. "You're just beginning to get that?"

Cassius didn't slow down. "I know the enemy's power. Oh, yes, I know. But, God's children have all authority to squelch anything he throws at them.[3]

"There is mighty power waiting to explode in every life. Dreams and hopes are planted in their spirits waiting to come forth. This causes them to long for something unknown. Tell them those feelings come because their Father in heaven is drawing them to himself.

"I'm trying to say, tell the people." As if a lightbulb turned on, Cassius smiled. "Tell them they are fearfully and wonderfully made.[4] The people need to know they cause fear in the enemy, and bring joy and wonder to heaven."

"Okay." Randy wrote down everything and looked up waiting for the next words.

Cassius said, "God is about to do something that has never been seen or experienced before. Don't let thoughts of limitations or impossibilities hold you captive. Impossible is *not* permanent. Your nation's history proved this to be true."

The angel looked toward heaven. "Father's plan is to use people to accomplish his great exploits.[3] He wants all of you to display his power through signs and wonders."

Suddenly, Cassius got excited. He jumped up like a preacher who sat on a tack as he pointed toward heaven. "Look." He shouted at the ceiling. The walls sent his words back. "People are parading into God's kingdom. As they march back, they are manifesting his glory on earth."

Randy was shocked by the sudden outburst, but he knew Cassius was seeing something awe-filled.

The angel declared. "Those who God calls friends will help set the captives free. They will walk in such power they will surprise everyone as they change the course of history. Yes, they will move into the spirit realm to get God's plans and return to earth to see them come to life. I just saw it."

Dumbfounded, Randy struggled to find his voice. "Wow."

"Yes." Cassius' eyes pierced his like burning fire. "Many others will join you in the days ahead. Do you understand?"

"I'm trying to."

He didn't have time to comment more before Cassius sighed and said, "I must go. Goodbye, my friend." He bowed and vanished.

Panic grabbed the pastor. His thoughts raced. Maybe this was one of Cassius' tests. He looked around the room and smiled. "Hey, Cassius, do you mean I've graduated? You know you just gave me a lot of information? I don't know what to do with it. I could really use your help. Please don't tell me I won't see you again."

Nothing seemed to tempt the angel to reappear.

"Well, do I get a diploma?"

The teasing had no power to bring his mentor back. All was silent.

Chapter 44

Weeks later, as Pastor Randy headed for his motorcycle to ride home after work, the unusual sky caught his attention. Golden color peeked around moving clouds while spears of light shot down. The erratic motion of the clouds created a kaleidoscope of colors that filled the sky. *What's making the sky look so unusual? Is a storm coming?*

He walked away from the building to see more clearly. At the top of the hill, he watched the clouds part and form what looked like a path. No, it was more a stairway. As the scene broadened, steps came from heaven until they appeared to touch the grassy slopes of the field behind the church.

Through what seemed to be haze, he could see a flurry of activity as beautiful beings descended on the left side of the stairs. Loud music filled his ears while he watched thousands of blissful people travel up the right side. Their response to each other filled Randy with longing. Surely, they were having the best time ever.

Randy rubbed his eyes, hoping to see more clearly. In the same way his binoculars worked when he got the setting just right, the sight came into focus. Now, he could see further up the stairway. Jesus was welcoming people.

Though silent, Randy's spirit yelled, *What am I looking at Jesus?*

The One who stood greeting others turned to him. God's love flowed through Randy's surrendered heart, and for the first time he was able to stand as living love owned him. The sight of the King standing in the brilliance of heaven's glory held him captive as

Jesus spoke.

"Why son, it's your way home. Heaven and earth have kissed. My Word is being fulfilled. I will leave nothing that I promised undone.[1]

"You have done well, good and faithful one. Come up here. Enter into my joy.[2]"

The pastor's spirit followed the Voice, and he began to ascend with the others. Awed by the beauty he did his best to absorb it all. "I need to draw a picture of all these colors for the girls.

"Oh, I wish I were a musician so I could bring some of this music back to earth. I guess it must be so loud because God wants us to hear the new sounds he created. They're so energizing and alive."

In hopes of being allowed to stay a while, he moved along with the others who were as fascinated as him.

The Voice in his spirit spoke. "As you experience heaven, the distractions of earth's enticements will vanish. The reality of the invisible kingdom of God's realm is all around you. The saints have filled the prayer bowls in heaven with their prayers until they've overflowed. You are seeing the fulfillment of the promises Isaiah wrote about when he declared that, '*My house would be established above all, and nations will stream to it.*'[3] Remember?"

Jesus continued, "Randal, this is the future. The house of God is established. Get that understanding deep in your heart, then nothing will deter you from fulfilling your purposes on earth."

Randy was overcome by the King's words and the splendor of everything else as far as he could see.

Jesus beckoned him to 'come up here and I will show you things which must take place after this,'[4] so he continued to climb. When he reached half-way his eyes were drawn from the King to those coming down. Cassius was waiting for him. The mighty angel looked so splendid that Randy gasped. His ancient garb was gone and Cassius stood beside him as a majestic warrior. The brilliance of fire flashed all around him. His shield and sword were radiant. The power that surged from the mighty weapons made Randy tremble.

The angel looked at him affectionately and reached out his hand. Never before had they touched. Randy responded. The natural man and supernatural man shook hands.

"I'm proud of you, Pastor. You have found your way. I told you religion can never put God's kingdom in a box and make it logical. God's kingdom is far beyond human logic.

"Do you remember what Father said? 'If you walk in obedience to him, he will give you a place among those standing here.'"[5]

Humility held Randy, but knowing the reality of love's power in this place, also gave him the boldness and the courage of a super-hero.

Cassius reminded him. "This is only the beginning."

Randy laughed. "Of course, I understand. With God, we are always beginning to know him. Thank you, Cassius, for helping me find my way. I'm so grateful you were allowed to come to me."

Cassius made a fist with his right hand and placed it on his chest. "It was my honor to serve you, sir."

Still fascinated by Cassius's appearance, Randy asked, "Did you get a promotion? You are a warrior now?"

"Not a promotion. To mentor man is a great honor. But I am also a warrior, and this is a time for battle. God's kingdom coming, in answer to your prayers, is causing upheaval in the nations. As righteousness is established the kingdom of darkness will fight hard. But it cannot win. The King already said, 'It is finished.'[6]Teach the people to stand strong as God's human kingdom warriors. We will be there to assist you.

"As things change, remember what you saw here today. This is reality. Everything else is just adjustments to put things in alignment with the King's will.

"Remember, Jesus has a place waiting for you beside him on his throne.[6]"

As suddenly as the vision came, it vanished.

Looking around, the sky was normal and he was alone, but inside he trembled with excitement. He could feel his spirit was alive and knew his soul was truly given over to the control of the Holy Spirit's leadership.

***

When Randy entered the kitchen, Sherry was coloring pictures with the girls. She looked up. "What's happened? You look like there's an orb of light surrounding you.

He kissed each of them on the forehead and commented on the girl's art.

"Sherry, go ahead and have dinner. I'll be back as soon as I can. Leave the crayons out. I want to make a picture for the girls."

"Okay." She responded. No longer surprised by anything that happened. "They'll be here on the table."

***

Settled in his man cave he picked up his Bible and let it drop open. He looked down and saw the pages parted at Isaiah 60:1. This time the words seemed to glow like neon signs. **"Shine. The glory of the Lord is on you. Lift up your eyes. See. They all gather together. Your heart will thrill and rejoice."**

He studied each word intently, realizing they described the truth of what he saw earlier.

***

At midnight, Sherry entered the kitchen and found Randy engrossed in coloring. The back side of a piece of wrapping paper covered the table. He held four crayons in his left hand while working feverishly with his right.

Sherry moved closer to see a scene emerging that looked like she imagined heaven to be. "Wow."

286

Without moving his head, Randy continued to scribble colors on the paper. "I've seen, Sherry. It's real. Here. All around us. Oh, the wonder of it all. I've got to get this while it's fresh in my mind."

She studied his work. "I didn't know you are an artist."

He shook his head. "I'm not. I don't know anything about this stuff, but I've got to try to capture the colors. Sherry, they're amazing." He layered one color on top the other. "We have no real idea how spectacular heaven is. Surely someone with painting talent could create it better than me." He didn't slow down or let her presence distract him. "The artists we call masters, didn't even get it right. The colors, I don't know ..." He grabbed three more crayons and used both hands, trying to blend color and texture around the places where white clouds burst through. "It's like the colors are alive. And Jesus," he tapped the white oval at the top of the stairs, "His beauty is beyond comprehension. Holy Spirit, help me get it down. My girls will love it."

Sherry gently rubbed his shoulders as she watched him work. Softly, she suggested, "Randy, maybe each of us have to find the colors for ourselves. Honestly, I wouldn't be surprised if the girls could draw your picture for you. They are seeing some amazing things."

His manic actions slowed. After a bit he reached around and took one of Sherry's hands from his shoulder and kissed it. Then he turned and pulled her into his arms. "You are exactly right. Jesus calls each one of us to our own experience. Try as we will, no one can ever completely share what God does for us individually. Just to know it's real and waiting for us is all we need right now."

Sherry nodded. "Exactly. Are you ready to get some rest now?"

"I guess." He took a last look and dropped the crayons on the paper. When she turned to leave he reached out and put his arm around her waist with one hand and lifted her hair with the other so he could kiss her neck. "You are the best wife in the world."

***

Olivia and Amanda wiggled into the chairs at the kitchen table to see what their daddy left for them. "Oh, look at those colors." Olivia picked up three of the crayons lying in one section. "He took these colors and made that dark blue-green-purple color behind the clouds."

Amanda filled her little hand with four yellow and orange crayons. "He made the light parts brighter with these. He's really a good artist. This looks almost like what we saw, except the colors we saw kinda danced."

She pointed at the empty oval at the top of the stairs. Look, there's Jesus."

In awe, Oliva responded, "Oh, yes. Come on, let's hang this beautiful picture in the dining room."

Amanda began to put the crayons back in the box, while Olivia rolled the paper so they could carry it. "Look, he used wrapping paper. That's how he made it so big."

Amanda asked, "Do you think Mommy would care if we took some of her gift paper?"

Olivia helped put the last few crayons in the box. "We better ask. But next time somebody gets a present we can save the paper and color on the back."

Amanda jumped off her chair. "Then we can make big, big pictures." She paused looking concerned. "We might need more crayons."

The girls giggled as they searched through Mommy's kitchen junk drawer for the tape. Amanda was so excited she held her tiny hands to her mouth and whispered, "Daddy's going to love this surprise."

(1) Ezekiel 12:28, (2) Matthew 25:23, (3) Isaiah 2:2, (4) Revelation 4:1, and 11:12, (5) Zechariah 3:7, (6) John 19:30, (7) Revelation 3:21

Chapter 45

Randy, Sherry, Olivia, and Amanda stared at the picture hanging on the wall in their dining room. Amanda was the first to speak. "Daddy, we love your picture. Let's never take it down."

"I can't believe I did that. It turned out so much better than I thought. God must have used me to draw and color it."

Olivia leaned against his leg and spoke softly, "It looks just like it's supposed to. I love how you showed us what Jesus looks like.

The couple looked at each other knowing the oval space was blank.

He and Sherry embraced, "I guess we all see Jesus the way he wants us too."

Sherry announced, "We'll get it framed."

"Yes!" the girls shouted. "Then everyone can see how pretty heaven is."

***

Randy and Sherry stood together greeting the people as they entered church. When finished, they walked in together, and he escorted her to a seat before he moved to the platform. Tony began to play one of his new pieces of music to announce it was time to start.

The Pastor looked across the room at his people. This time love filled his heart for each one. *Thank You, Father for freeing me to love with your love.* He noticed Barbara was among the smiling faces of Josh and Miranda's group. *They must all be happy knowing they finally have a church family who allows them freedom to follow God's plans for them.* He saw the ladies from the prayer group. Hillary had Sam and Amy at her side. They too had become a family. Mrs. Anderson and her husband, Gerald welcomed James and his wife and children. They regularly sit beside them now.

The teenagers were right up front ready to hang onto every word spoken. Among them were Glen and his family. Glen's brother, Lenard, who finally got tired of beating people up, sat next to Micah. On his other side were beautiful Anna, and Latisha and her friends. Andrew was in the row behind the group with his arm around Glenda.

God, this is beyond anything I ever imagined.

"Well done, good and faithful servant, enter into the joys of the Lord.[1]"

Seeing what you've done here does give me joy. He continued to scan the room. Once gang members, five young men were now part of Jethro's street ministry. Everett sat with his aunt, Ms. Brown, who he helped find a place to live. She loved coming to church with him.

Gene sat in the same seat he always chose. Now, Mr. Lewis was next to him. They smiled back at Randy. He was pleased the two renewed their friendship, and found fresh purpose for their lives by helping his dad with God's plans for the property that was given to the church.

Randy sighed and closed his eyes while he listened to the beautiful music Tony played. *How could life get any better?*

When he opened his eyes, angels were moving around the people. He was pleased to see they revealed themselves so clearly. *Heaven and earth really are becoming one.*

The door in the back opened, and his Mom and Dad greeted Mayor Bruner and his family, who they invited to sit beside them.

Randy smiled and continued to worship. Suddenly, he heard.

"Behold, I will do a new thing, now it shall spring forth, shall you not know it?[2]"

At those words the angels became excited. They swept through the crowd. He watched them toss gold dust on the worshipers. The people were so busy praising God they didn't notice the sparkly adornment.

"Lord, what's that? Did I miss a scripture about gold dust?[3] I don't remember ever reading about anything like this."

"Remember Hebrews 2:4? I testify of my truths by signs, wonders and various miracles... This is a WONDER, my son. A WONDER."

---

(1) Matthew 25:21, (2) Isaiah 43:19, (3) YouTube-Gold dust manifestation

www.ingramcontent.com/pod-product-compliance
Lightning Source LLC
Chambersburg PA
CBHW070314260626
47160CB00003B/842